0	1	2	3	4	5	6	7	8	9

In Australia write to:
THE ULVERSCROFT FOUNDATION,
c/o The Royal Australian College of
Ophthalmologists,
27, Commonwealth Street, Sydney,
N.S.W. 20

Love is
a time of enchantment:
in it all days are fair and all fields
green. Youth is blest by it,
old age made benign:
the eyes of love see
roses blooming in December,
and sunshine through rain. Verily
is the time of true-love
a time of enchantment — and
Oh! how eager is woman
to be bewitched!

MOONSHADOW

Sophy Franklin had loved her husband, despite his dubious lifestyle and irresponsibility which resulted in her being left a penniless widow with a tiny daughter. She was at the point of desperation when the letter arrived from Captain Ellard, offering her a cottage on the Essex marshes. But things at Silver Creek were not as they seemed — for slipping in and out of the marshes was the infamous and audacious Moonshadow — and amidst a whirlwind of intrigue and romance, Sophy found her life more exciting that it had ever been before . . .

Books by Patricia Burns
in the Ulverscroft Large Print Series:

THE MARRIAGE MART

PATRICIA BURNS

---◆---

MOONSHADOW

Complete and Unabridged

ULVERSCROFT
Leicester

First published in Great Britain in 1981

First Large Print Edition
published 1996

British Library CIP Data

Burns, Patricia
    Moonshadow.—Large print ed.—
    Ulverscroft large print series: romance
    1. English fiction—20th century
    2. Large type books
    I. Title
    823.9′14 [F]

    ISBN 0–7089–3625–3

Published by
F. A. Thorpe (Publishing) Ltd.
Anstey, Leicestershire
Set by Words & Graphics Ltd.
Anstey, Leicestershire
Printed and bound in Great Britain by
T. J. Press (Padstow) Ltd., Padstow, Cornwall

This book is printed on acid-free paper

1

JUST as the new passengers had settled into their seats and the stagecoach was about to depart, a small boy darted up to the door, thrust a clutch of handbills inside and melted back into the crowd. Curious, Sophy Franklin picked one up.

'Fifty Guineas Reward' it stated, in large type and underneath in smaller print, 'The Magistrates and Revenue Officers of the town of Maldon offer a reward of fifty guineas to any person giving information leading to the apprehension of the smuggler known as the Shadow.'

It made no sense at all to Sophy, and as the coach set off and rumbled out of the yard of the Blue Boar and down the winding street towards the river, she handed it to her small daughter.

"What is it, Mama?" the child demanded. "A letter?"

"No, pet. Just a notice about a smuggler. Nothing of importance."

But the other travellers seemed to

disagree with her. A red-faced, jovial man who had just boarded the coach chuckled derisively.

"They'll never catch him that way!" he remarked to his fellow passengers in general.

The sharp-featured lawyer opposite him, who had been silent all the way from Chelmsford, was moved to sniff disapprovingly and reply,

"More's the pity. The sooner they hang the rogue, the better."

Sophy listened with growing interest. As a young widow journeying alone, she was wary of striking up conversations with chance-met travellers, but the red-faced man and his stout wife seemed respectable enough.

"Who is this man?" she asked. "Fifty guineas is a high price to put on his head."

The other occupants of the coach looked amazed.

"You must be a stranger to these parts if you ain't heard of the Shadow," the stout woman declared. "Why, there's been nothing else talked about these twelve months past. Would you be from London?"

Sophy nodded. "That is so," she said. There was no need, after all, to go into the many places she had lived in the past five years, but they had all been fashionable towns and cities. There was something reassuring in coming to an area that buzzed with excitement over the exploits of one wrongdoer.

"There you are then, stands to reason, folks in London don't know aught of what goes on around our marshes," the stout woman replied. "It was the same during the Wars. In London they hardly knew there was a war on, but down here in Essex we was all ready for invasion. But what was I saying? Oh yes — you'll not find a soul hereabouts that ain't heard of the Shadow."

"The Shadow, indeed!" the lawyer snorted. "Damned foolish name — begging your pardon ma'am — the fellow's nothing but a common smuggler, puffed up out of all proportion by a few foolish and unsubstantiated stories. Just because he's slipped through their fingers once or twice, the revenue men seem to think he's invincible."

The stout woman was unconvinced.

She thrived on gossip and the young lady in the corner, who looked like a shadow herself in her black veil and deep mourning, was an ideal audience for all the local information. She leaned forward, ready for a long and satisfying chat.

"They do say," she confided, "that he's a gentleman born. They say he dresses fine and can quote you a line of poetry as easy as wink your eye."

The lawyer poured scorn on that theory.

"Any blackguard can wear a well-fitting coat, especially when he's ill-gotten gold to buy it with. And as for poetry, any fool can memorise a few lines to chalk upon the doors of his betters. There's some will tell you he's not even English, let alone a gentleman. They say he's a damned Frog, a one-time prisoner of war. But if you ask me, there's a deal too much arrant nonsense spoken about this fellow. The common people are beginning to think of him as some sort of hero, and when that happens there's no knowing where it will end. There was enough trouble in these parts with corn riots and rick-burnings in 'sixteen without some jumped-up Froggy smuggler raising the countryside."

Behind her veil, Sophy found herself smiling.

"Smugglers and riots!" she exclaimed in mock alarm. "Is Essex really so dangerous a place? I thought to come to the country for quiet and tranquillity."

The stout woman mistook her meaning and hastened to reassure her. "Oh, 'tis very peaceful hereabouts. Nothing happens from one year's end to the next. 'Tis just the place for a lady to live quiet and retired. Ain't that so, Mr Shaw?" she appealed to her husband. She hesitated, then, overcome by the desire to know about another person's business, and especially one who had evidently been recently involved in tragedy, she asked, "You're visiting a relation, maybe? Or a friend?"

"No," Sophy replied, "I intend settling here."

The coach rattled across the bridge over the river Blackwater and Sophy's little daughter Lucy came suddenly to life and tugged at her mother's arm, pointing out the tan-sailed barges unloading at the quayside. A flotilla of swans sailed majestically amongst the assortment of boats, and overhead wheeled the screaming seagulls. It was a cheerful and animated scene, even on a grey January day, far removed from tales of sinister smugglers. Sophy answered her questioner at greater length.

"I'm bound for a place called Silver Creek, near Tracey Nugent. Perhaps you know of it? I've taken a cottage there, the property of a Captain Ellard."

"Silver Creek? I've heard of it, to be sure, but I've never been there. A very out-of-the-way place, is it not, Mr Shaw? But quite pretty, I've heard tell." Unable to impart much information on the village, Mrs Shaw returned with greater confidence to personalities. "Captain Ellard! Now there's a fine gentleman, real quality. A connection of yours is he?"

"No — an acquaintance of my late husband."

It was not strictly true, but Sophy felt no need to explain that to Mrs Shaw. In his letter to her, Philip Ellard had claimed to have met a mutual acquaintance who was concerned about her fate. Who that

6

person might be, Sophy was at a loss to know, for all Jeremy's fairweather friends, though they had been helpful enough after the first shock of his demise, had long since melted away. The unexpected offer of help from a total stranger made a pleasant contrast to the neglect of all those cronies with whom Jeremy had so often shared his last guinea. Dear Jeremy! she sighed. Generous, thoughtless and impulsive to the end. The eternal optimist, he had bounded through life with all the enthusiasm of a half-grown puppy, and was just about as reliable. Many a time he would leave for an evening's pleasure and totally forget that Sophy was waiting for him at home. The only news she would receive of his whereabouts would be a hastily-scribbled note from Bath or Cheltenham or Brighton. He had turned Sophy's quiet, restricted life upside-down from the moment he arrived in her home village, leading a lame horse. Eligible young men were few and far between in her part of the world, particularly ones who could afford to think seriously of the daughter of a parson's widow, however pretty she might be. And none of the gentlemen she had met bore the slightest comparison with Jeremy Franklin, who appeared to have stepped out of a fashion print and had the air of one who moved in the dazzling ranks of top society. Sophy was amazed that he should even look twice at her, a country nobody. But look he did, and more than that, he put up at the local inn, and courted Sophy assiduously despite the loudly-voiced disapproval of her mother and cousins and aunts. Jeremy cared not a whit that all Sophy had by way of a dowry was an income of four hundred a year that would be hers on the death of her mother, and the capital so securely tied up in trust that he would never be able to get his hands on it. To be sure, he had always hoped to marry an heiress, but he had plenty of other schemes for making his fortune and one of them would inevitably come up trumps soon.

In the end, it took a threat of elopement to force Sophy's mother to consent to the match. She knew an adventurer when she saw one, even if her daughter did not. Sophy was borne off to Brighton for a protracted honeymoon and for a long while was too happy to care that the reality of Jeremy's life did not quite coincide with the impression he gave. They skirmished around the fringes of society, living from one run of luck to the next, moving frequently to escape creditors. But when Jeremy's rose-coloured dreams began to wear thin, Sophy would not admit even to herself that she had made a mistake in marrying him. He needed her to keep his life on something approaching an even keel, and there was no withstanding his charm and natural buoyancy.

It had been difficult to believe that he would never again come bursting through the door crying, 'Sophy, we're rich!' and drag her off to buy extravagant presents and celebrate his turn of fortune.

The inquisitive Mrs Shaw sighed gustily.

"Ah, 'tis sad to lose your husband, especially when you've a little one to bring up." She smiled sentimentally at Lucy, who hid her face in Sophy's pelisse. "Ah, the dear little lamb! How old is she? Four? Five? Such a pretty little pet, I'll warrant she's the image of her Mama. But she looks peaked, the darling, has she been ill?"

Sophy held the child more tightly and stroked the soft dark curls off her forehead. Lucy was indeed an immature version of herself, with large black-fringed eyes in an oval face, a short straight nose and serious set to the mouth. Both of them were thin and pale, Sophy from grief and worry, Lucy from illness.

"She's just recovering from the scarlet fever," Sophy explained. "It's because of her that I'm removing to the country."

Lucy snuggled up to her, and Sophy thought back over the past four nightmare months. As if the shock of Jeremy's death had not been enough to contend with, there had been the hopeless tangle of his financial affairs to straighten out. Even during his brief periods of prosperity, Jeremy Franklin had always been chronically in debt. At first, his boon companion, Perry Allington, had offered to take on the task of executor, and even went so far as to organise a subscription fund to pay off the creditors. But he soon lost interest, and when Sophy proved impervious to his insinuating charm he decamped and left her to cope as best she could. And then as the fogs of November shrouded the streets of London, Lucy went down with the scarlet fever. For an interminable week, the days and nights rolled into one long vigil, and the passing of time was marked by the visits of the physician. At the height of the fever, Sophy feared for her daughter's life, as Lucy tossed in her bed, bathed in sweat and muttering deliriously. Lucy survived, but her recovery was slow. The physician shook his head over her.

"What the child needs is country air and plenty of fresh food. If she is given a diet of milk and good fresh eggs and vegetables and allowed to run about and play, she may well grow strong again, but keep her here in this unwholesome London fog, and I cannot answer for the consequences."

This was easier said than done. The only people Sophy knew who lived permanently in the country were her relations in her home village, and they had refused to recognise her since her marriage. She had not even written to

11

tell them of Jeremy's death. Only in the very last resort would she turn to them for assistance in finding a new home. And yet there was Lucy, thin, pale and still dangerously weak. For Lucy, she might have to swallow her pride, for she could not possibly leave the child while she went searching for a place to live. She racked her brains for an alternative solution, and it was at this point that she received the letter from Philip Ellard, offering her the lease of Thyme Cottage on very reasonable terms.

Still she hesitated. After five years of living with Jeremy Franklin, she was a firm believer in Fate, the hand of which was clearly behind this new turn of events, but to move into the property of an unknown gentleman on the strength of one letter seemed foolhardy in the extreme. She wrote a cautious reply, asking for further details and expressing surprise that she had never heard her late husband mention a Captain Ellard. He evidently guessed just what suspicions she was harbouring, and enclosed with his own lengthy communication a letter from the rector of Silver Creek, vouching for his character and motives. The worst of her fears allayed, Sophy sought fuller information on the cottage itself. A further exchange of letters brought a detailed description, together with an account of the general neighbourhood, until Sophy felt reasonably sure that here was just the place for Lucy to get better. She finally accepted Captain Ellard's offer, though not without some qualms. Lucy must be moved, and it was Thyme Cottage and the unknown landlord, or the humiliation of having to apply to her relations to help.

Through the tedious weeks of convalescence, whenever Lucy was bored or fractious, Sophy talked to her about their new home, drawing mostly on her own childhood. She elaborated on all the animals they would keep, hens and pigs and a fat tabby cat, and talked about the big garden they would have for Lucy to play in, and how they would go for walks and pick wild flowers, until she was as excited as her daughter at the prospect of moving to the country. London held no charm for her now that Jeremy was no longer there to share it with. By Christmas, Lucy was up for most of the day, so directly the festival was over, Sophy packed up their scanty belongings and sent them on by barge, which Captain Ellard had assured her was the best and safest way, and followed three days later by stage.

Looking out now at the flat and uninspiring landscape, the heavy clay ploughland and stark black elms outlined against the wide, steel-grey sky, she wondered if she had acted wisely, taking the first cottage she heard of, sight unseen. Perhaps she should have made enquiries about other places before coming to a decision. She had only Captain Ellard's word as to the situation of Thyme Cottage, and of Captain Ellard himself she knew precisely nothing. Here, though, she was aided by the garrulous Mrs Shaw. Having treated the occupants of the coach to an exhaustive account of all her childrens' illnesses, she returned to the subject of Sophy's future landlord.

"Captain Ellard, now there's a fine-looking gentleman, and very generous to the poor. His coming was a blessing to Silver Creek, they say. No end of unemployed sailors turned off after the war have found work at Creek End House, no matter whether they may be missing an arm or a leg. Men who might otherwise be a charge on the parish for the rest of their days."

"Creek End was a wilderness when he took it over," her husband joined in. "It had been running down for years under the old gentleman, and when his grandson inherited it, it was let to go to rack and ruin. A shocking waste, it was, of a good estate and that was in wartime, too, when anyone with twenty acres to his name and a grain of enterprise was making his fortune. Not like now," he went on gloomily, "with trade going from bad to worse and the fund-holders eating up our taxes."

The lawyer, who had been ignoring the conversation, gave a grunt of agreement, and Sophy could foresee the talk turning from trade to politics, which did not interest her at all.

"Captain Ellard has not lived at Creek End for long, then?" she asked, in an effort to steer back into subjects she understood.

Mrs Shaw took her up with enthusiasm. "Oh no, only these two years past. Captain Ellard ain't a local man, he comes from somewhere down in the Rochford Hundred." She lowered her voice, and with a significant look, hissed, "Witch country, you know."

The lawyer pounced on her words with superior scorn.

"Superstitious nonsense!" he sneered. "Put about by people who should know better. It's all of a piece with this gossip-mongering about that cursed smuggler, Some people have nothing better to do than put about sensational stories."

Mrs Shaw ignored this pointed remark and addressed herself to Sophy again.

"I'd have thought you would have known him already, seeing as he was an acquaintance of your late husband."

"I never met him myself," Sophy explained.

She could see the next question hovering on Mrs Shaw's lips. She was quite obviously consumed with curiosity as to how Jeremy Franklin had died. Sophy had a set answer to impertinent enquiries of that nature: "He met with an accident." It was true in a way, Jeremy had never meant to get involved in a dispute, any more than he planned the rest of his life. Sophy had felt that something was amiss when he came home early that evening, subdued and relatively sober. Innocently, she had thought he was sickening for something, and was relieved to think that at least they could afford to call in a physician. But when she awoke just after dawn the next morning to find him creeping out of the room fully dressed she suspected the truth. Only a matter of the greatest urgency would get Jeremy out of bed before midday.

"Got an appointment," he explained sheepishly when she questioned him. "Nothing to worry about, sweetheart. Be back before noon."

"Jeremy! You're not involved in a duel?"

"Couldn't avoid it. Matter of honour, you wouldn't understand. Now, you go back to sleep, my darling, and don't bother your head about it. There's nothing to it, you know, fellows are doing this sort of thing all the time. Ten to one I shan't have to fire a shot,

I'm the wronged party and I'm perfectly willing to take an apology.

"But Jeremy . . . "

"Don't fuss, chicken! Can't stay now. Perry's waiting for me. Never do to be late. Give Lucy a kiss from me. We'll have a good laugh about it this evening."

And with a careless wave of the hand, he ran down the stairs, cramming his hat on as he went. Sophy hurried to the front window and watched as he jumped into a hackney coach with Perry Allington and drove off at a smart trot. She had a premonition then that she would never see him alive again, and she was proved right.

Fighting against the wave of desolation that threatened to swamp her, Sophy told herself that it was useless to dwell on the past. She was starting a new life now and must look to the future. But it was hard to work up much enthusiasm for a place she had never seen and people she had never met. The countryside looked bleak and dreary in the grip of midwinter and Thyme Cottage, however attractive its name, might prove to be tumbledown and damp. If her new neighbours turned out to be cold and unfriendly, she and Lucy could well be marooned until the spring.

She was roused from her gloomy train of thought as the coach rolled into a large, prosperous-looking village of weatherboarded cottages and solid brick-built houses and turned into the yard of the Crown Inn.

"Here we are: Tracey Nugent," Mr Shaw announced. "From here you've only a mile and a half to Silver Creek. Do you step down, ma'am, and I'll hand the little maid to you."

His wife pressed Sophy's hand, patted Lucy's cheek and wished them both a safe journey's end. Sophy thanked her, bade farewell to her fellow travellers and climbed down into the inn yard. The guard got her trunk out for her, and with Lucy clinging to her hand, she looked about, debating as to what to do next. The yard was alive with the bustle of the stage's arrival. A small crowd of sightseers had gathered to gape at the main event of the day, a new passenger was arguing with the coachman over the fare, the ostlers were checking the harness and running a professional eye over the horses, and waiters handed warming tankards of mulled ale up to the outside passengers shivering on the roof of the stage. Spying Mine Host approaching with a hopeful air, Sophy tried to decide whether to hire a chaise to take her on the last part of her journey, though it did seem an unnecessary expense for a distance of only a mile and a half. Just then a figure detached itself from the group of spectators, his brown coat, yellow waistcoat, cord breeches and top boots proclaiming his profession to be that of a groom. He doffed his hat respectfully and addressed Sophy.

"Begging your pardon, ma'am, but would you be Mrs Franklin?"

Sophy replied that she was.

"Mrs Vye's compliments, ma'am, and she'd be pleased if you would make use of the gig to take you to Silver Creek."

"Mrs Vye?" Sophy was at a loss. "I'm sorry, but I know nobody of that name. You must be mistaken."

"Oh no, ma'am, it was definitely a

Mrs Franklin," the man insisted, then added by way of explanation, "Mrs Vye is Captain Ellard's sister, ma'am."

"Oh, I see!" Sophy thought wryly that here was a piece of information that the inquisitive Mrs Shaw had missed. She hesitated to accept the offer, though, not wanting to be indebted to a woman she had not even met. But it seemed churlish to refuse, and it certainly was the heaven-sent answer to her present problem. "Thank you," she said. "Perhaps you would take up my trunk as well. It's not very heavy."

Walking with a decided limp, the man led the way to a smart blue-painted gig standing to one side of the inn yard. As the stagecoach set off again for Colchester with a clatter of hooves and a cheer from the bystanders, he set about strapping the trunk onto the back of the gig. Then he handed Sophy up onto the seat, swung Lucy up beside her, hopped nimbly into his place and set the bay horse going at a smart trot. They bowled out of the yard and down the main street of the village past the pudding-stone church and the

21

neat rectory, the craftsmen's shops and the general chandler's store. Sophy felt reassured. Tracey Nugent was every bit as pleasant as Captain Ellard had led her to believe, and it followed, therefore, that Silver Creek and Thyme Cottage would live up to his description as well. She was going to throw herself into her new life, and make the best of the fact that at least she now had some security. Certainly there would be no more 'Sophy, we're rich!' but then neither would there be any 'Sophy, we're ruined.' No more bailiffs camped in her parlour, no anxious days spent tramping the streets looking for lodgings that were cheap and yet retained a claim to respectability, no more long nights wondering where Jeremy might be, and when he was coming home, if at all. Housekeeping in a cottage would keep her busy during the day, and she was used to amusing herself in the evenings. She had, she told herself firmly, a great deal to be thankful for.

To prove to herself that she meant to take a real interest in her new surroundings, she started by asking the groom what his name was and whether he was a native of Silver Creek.

"John Jennings, Ma'am," he replied. "Born and bred in Silver Creek, I was, and if I'd had the sense to stay there, I might have been a coachman by now, and two sound legs into the bargain."

They passed the outskirts of the village and turned off the turnpike into a muddy land.

"You were a volunteer, I suppose?" Sophy asked.

"Oh no, ma'am, I was never such a fool as to take the King's Bounty. Pressed, I was, back in the year nine, when I was nobbut a lad. Went into Maldon for a bit of a spree and ended up the next morning with a sore head on board His Majesty's ship the *Sprite*. And all I have to show for six years of keeping Boney at bay is a lame leg. Still," he shrugged philosophically, "leastways I do have a good position, thanks to the Captain, which is more than a lot of my shipmates have got after spending their best years fighting for their country."

"Is Captain Ellard a good master?" Sophy enquired.

"The best, ma'am," was John's warm

reply. "Not that he ain't particular, mind, because he is. Kicks up a fine dust if something ain't done right, but then again he gives praise when it's due. You knows where you are, if you take my meaning."

The gig slowed to a laborious walk as the narrow lane between its high, thick hedges and stately elm trees became little better than a quagmire. It was the heavy clay soil, John explained, that made the roads so bad in the winter. Often they became impassable for heavy waggons and farm carts, which was why produce from the riverside farms and estates was taken by barge to be sold. Sophy enquired anxiously after her belongings, and was assured that they had arrived safely by that morning's tide and been carried up to Thyme Cottage. The mention of barges reminded her of Maldon and the town crier's announcement.

"Has the notorious Shadow ever been active in Silver Creek?" she asked.

"Not that I know of, ma'am. When the revenue cutters have sighted him it's been further down-river off Bradwell or Brightlingsea, but there's no knowing if he might have landed cargoes here without anyone finding out. Revenue men've been round poking their long noses where they're not wanted and asking a lot of foolish questions."

"In Maldon they were offering a reward of fifty guineas in gold for information."

John Jennings's reaction was much the same as Mr Shaw's.

"That's no use. They'll never catch him that way."

"Fifty guineas is a vast amount of money. It would be very tempting to anyone who did know something incriminating."

"But nobody does, you see, ma'am. They say not even the members of his crew know who he really is. He wears a mask. And besides, who is going to betray a man who stands between them and the poor relief? If the Shadow's transported, I warrant there will be families somewhere round the coast the worse off for it."

"You make him sound like a public benefactor," Sophy observed. She felt she ought to sound more disapproving, but the subject fascinated her.

"Smuggling's not like stealing, is it?" John objected.

"I doubt whether the local magistrate would agree with you."

"Sir Harry? He's itching to get his hands on the Shadow. A great stickler for law and order is Sir Harry, and especially when it comes to preserving his own game. There's a whole army of keepers in those woods and coverts over there." John stopped, conscious of having said too much that might be reported back to the most influential man in the neighbourhood. In a strictly neutral tone, he said, "We're passing the parkland of Tracey Manor now, ma'am. You can see the lodge gates ahead of you."

They passed a pair of fine wrought-iron gates, flanked by neat red-brick Jacobean cottages. A gravelled drive curved away between an avenue of limes towards the chimneys that could be seen smoking in the middle distance. Sophy wondered briefly what sort of people the Nugents would prove to be, but decided against questioning John Jennings on the subject. There would be time enough to find out and make up her own mind.

The lane, following the boundary of Tracey Manor park, rounded a steep bend and the landscape opened up before them. The hedges gave way to fences and wide pastures ran unbroken down to the sea-wall that separated them from the olive-grey of the marshes and the steely glinting river beyond. A gleam of weak light from the sinking sun escaped from under the dark blanket of cloud and lit the scene with a finger of pale gold.

Lucy tugged at Sophy's arm.

"It's the sea, Mama! You said it was a river, but it's the sea."

"Nearly the sea," Sophy explained. "The sea really starts a few miles further down. It's a very wide river mouth, not a little tumbling stream. Do you like it?"

"Oh yes! It's much better than London. Where's our new home?"

"Not much further now, Miss Lucy," John Jennings told her. "Once we get round this piece of woodland, you'll see the village. If you look over there, ma'am," he pointed with his whip to the left, down-river, "you'll see Creek End."

Sophy looked as he directed, and

saw about half a mile away across the fields an ancient, rambling house set amongst walled gardens. It appeared to have been built at several different periods and of various materials, the main part being of timber frame and plaster, with a wing of red-brick and a smaller extension of weatherboarding. Ornate twisting chimneys clustered on a roof that dipped in places and showed signs of recent extensive repairs.

"What a fascinating old place," Sophy exclaimed. "It must have a very long history."

"Finest house in the district," John Jennings declared, with unashamed partiality. "Older than Tracey Manor, Creek End is. Two years ago it was just about ready for the hulks, but the Captain's got it all caulked up and weatherproof now. You'll not find aught better this side of Colchester."

The lane turned up-river and Silver Creek came into view, a straggle of weatherboarded cottages, some painted white and others tarred, set haphazardly along a single street. A little church of grey pudding-stone with a short white

28

weatherboard spire stood in its midst, with a pretty modern stuccoed parsonage beside it, and beyond the last buildings could be seen the masts and spars of the fishing boats, moored at the mouth of the creek.

John pointed to the nearest cottage, on the edge of the village, a neat place with a tiled roof and casement windows on each side of a projecting porch.

"There you are, ma'am," he said. "That's Thyme Cottage."

2

AS Sophy and Lucy looked eagerly at their new home, one of the upstairs windows was thrown open and a head poked out and stared up the lane towards them. This, Sophy realised, must be the maid she had asked the rector's wife to engage for her. She felt a sudden twinge of superstitious apprehension. Everything had gone so well so far, the swift and uneventful journey, the gig waiting for her at Tracey Nugent, her belongings arriving safely, and now the cottage looking every bit as sound and picturesque as she had hoped, that she was afraid her luck was on the verge of running out.

The gig pulled up in front of Thyme Cottage, and faces peeped out from behind curtains and shutters of the neighbouring homes. A crowd of muddy urchins ran out to see the new arrivals, stopping at first in the lane, then edging forward slowly to stare openly, nudging each other and giggling. A small boy, bolder than the rest, scampered forward to hold the horse, and John Jennings unstrapped the trunk and followed Sophy and Lucy up the front path to where the maid, a round-faced sturdy girl, stood in the open doorway bobbing curtseys.

Her name, she told Sophy, was Susannah Greenways, and she showed her round the cottage with an air of anxious pride, pleased with her own efforts in preparing the place but unsure of her new mistress's reaction. She need not have worried, for Sophy was delighted. Thyme Cottage had its minor inconveniences, but it was just what she had hoped for. A dark, wainscotted central passage led straight through the house, with a front and back parlour on one side of it, and a dining-room, kitchen and pantry on the other. At the top of the narrow, twisting stairs, there were two large and two smaller bedrooms and further up still in the attics, two garret rooms, one of which Susannah had already claimed. The wallpaper was all rather faded, and the furniture an odd assortment of various styles, but every room had been scrubbed and scoured, the wood polished and the hangings washed, so that they looked immaculate and smelt fresh, though as yet they had the impersonal look of a house that was not yet a home. Two of Sophy's packing cases stood unopened in the back parlour.

"I put away all the clothes and china and such-like," Susannah explained, "but I didn't know where you would want the pictures and books, so I left them in the boxes till you came."

"You have done very well, Susannah," Sophy approved. "The whole cottage is shining like a new pin. If this is the way you work, I am sure we shall get along splendidly. Did you do it all yourself?"

Susannah beamed at the praise, fidgeted with her apron and launched into an involved speech.

"Well, no, ma'am, not all myself ma'am. My sister Polly came in to help. She's got three little 'uns to feed you see, ma'am, and the extra comes in awful useful seeing as her man's been transported to New South Wales. Terrible hard it is, ma'am, being left to fend for yourself like that, not that he hadn't been warned, Abel hadn't, because Sir Harry said to him last two times he was up for poaching, he said, 'Abel Harris, I'm giving you a chance to reform your ways and learn to be an honest man, but you know what the penalty is for poaching, and I'll not let you off so light if I find you setting snares on my land again.' But Abel, he didn't take no heed, and now he's on t'other side of the world though he could've turned King's evidence and split on the man what was with him and got away, but he didn't. So anyway, Polly was hoping you'd put a bit of work her way, so as to help make ends meet . . . " Susannah paused to catch her breath and added as an afterthought, "Oh, and Lady Isobel looked in too to see as we hadn't missed aught."

"Lady Isobel?" Sophy was struck by the growing number of people who had concerned themselves in her arrival: Captain Ellard and Mrs Vye, the parson and his wife, Susannah and Polly, and now even Lady Isobel Nugent. And none of them had ever met her before. After living so long in cities amongst a constantly changing crowd of acquaintances, she had forgotten how important just one addition could be to the limited society of a country village. Of Polly's situation she had not quite grasped all the details from Susannah's hasty and breathless explanation, but it was evident that she stood in need of assistance, and that was within her power. "If your sister comes in tomorrow morning, I am sure we shall come to some arrangement that will suit us all."

Susannah was effusively grateful, repeating her thanks until Sophy dispatched her to prepare supper for Lucy, who was almost dropping from the excitement of the long day's travelling.

In spite of her violent protests, Lucy was packed off to bed directly she had eaten, and fell asleep in her new nursery almost immediately, clutching her well-worn rag doll. Sophy closed the shutters against the rising wind, and went downstairs to examine the packing cases. She was achingly tired herself, but could not rest until she had put her mark on Thyme Cottage. Long experience of moving had taught that wherever the place might be, from cheap backstreet lodgings to elegant houses in Mayfair, once she had hung her small collection of pictures, it would begin to feel like home. Accordingly, she found the hammer and nails she had packed with the pictures, and set to work. And as she put up each familiar print and watercolour, she made mental notes of the small improvements she could make to the cottage, and caught herself actually enjoying the prospect of being able to plan ahead with confidence for the first time in five years.

She had just unpacked the twin miniatures of herself and Jeremy, purchased during one of their prosperous period, when a sound from outside caught her attention. She stood still, one small painting in each hand, listening. Perhaps it was the wind banging one of the outhouse doors, or Susannah paying a visit to the privy. But Susannah was in the kitchen preparing the dough for tomorrow's bread, and the sound was not the persistent slam of an open door. It was a furtive scrabbling noise. Quietly, Sophy set down the miniatures and grasped the hammer, then drew aside the long faded curtains a fraction and tried the handle of the French windows. Susannah and Polly had done their job well — the door opened smoothly and Sophy slipped outside.

Shivering in the penetrating midwinter wind, she waited a moment, letting her eyes get used to the dark. The garden was full of indistinguishable lumps and blotches, and there was nothing to be heard now except the trees moaning in the rising gale. Sophy told herself that she had been living too long in the artificial urban world. She had forgotten what the small sounds of the countryside were like. If she suspected every noise she heard outside her window, she would never have five minutes peace. It was probably an animal looking for a safe lair on such a foul night. But then the moon showed its ghostly silver light. Sophy stiffened, her fingers tightening round the slim handle of the hammer, every sense alert. There was something moving, something bigger than any wild creature, and it was backing out of the woodshed. Sophy was filled with sudden anger. How dare anyone threaten the security of her new-found home? How dare they? She marched forward, her arm raised.

"Come out of there!" she demanded, her voice sharp with indignation. "Come out at once and don't try to run away, or I'll — I'll shoot!"

The figure whipped round and straightened up.

"Ye gods!" he exclaimed softly. "Would I be right in assuming that you are Mrs Franklin? A thousand apologies, I had no intention of disturbing you. Allow . . . "

"I'm sure you did not. What were you doing in my woodshed?" Sophy snapped, interrupting him. The uncertain light of the moon showed the outline of a man in a black riding cloak and beaver hat, and his accent was that of a gentleman. This, then, was no common felon or vagabond.

"I was just making sure there was no contraband hidden there," came the glib reply.

"Contraband? In *my* woodshed?" Sophy exclaimed incredulously. "And do you not have to seek permission before searching private property? I presume you are a — a revenue officer?"

The man laughed.

"Great heavens, no! The very idea! I . . ."

"Then I suppose you are this Shadow person I've heard so much about," Sophy retorted, and even as she did so the heat in which she had first sprung to the defence of her domain began to cool, and it occurred to her that what she had meant as a sarcasm might actually be true. Her hand shook slightly, but she held her ground.

"Nothing so extraordinary, I regret to say," the stranger assured her, much to her relief. "Look — ah — there's no need to threaten me with that thing, whatever it is. Odd though appearances might be, I am acting with the best of intentions. Allow me to introduce myself: Philip Ellard, entirely at your service."

Sophy let her arm drop abruptly.

"Oh!" she said, feeling distinctly foolish. "Oh I see — Captain Ellard." She paused, frowning in the darkness. "But — I still do *not* see why you should be searching around out here."

"Do you not think," the other suggested, "that it might be warmer indoors? I was going to call and make sure you were comfortable. Perhaps if you were to go inside, whilst I went round to the front door, we could start all over again?"

"Don't be ridiculous," Sophy said briskly. "There is no need for an elaborate charade. If you would care to step this way, the French windows are open."

Once safely inside the cottage, Sophy turned to study her unexpected visitor. She found a man of medium height and slender, wiry build, with sharp intelligent grey eyes in a face tanned and lined from half a lifetime spent at sea. From his letters and the reports she had heard of him, Sophy had imagined him to be middle-aged, but now she was surprised to find that he was only a few years older than herself, certainly no more than thirty. He seemed not in the least put out by the unconventional way in which they had met.

"Ah, so it was a hammer," he remarked, shedding his cloak at Sophy's invitation. "Do you know, I don't think I have ever before had my life threatened by a lady wielding such an object."

"I was hanging pictures," Sophy

explained briefly. Although she was willing to accept that he was who he purported to be, she still did not understand the reason for his odd behaviour.

"Then perhaps I can be of some assistance? I'm quite a useful knocker-in of nails," Captain Ellard offered.

Sophy could believe that. He had strong, capable-looking hands. He also had a charming smile, but she was not yet ready to be charmed.

"Thank you, but I can manage quite well by myself," she said coolly. "Won't you come through to the front parlour? It's more comfortable there. Would you care for some tea? I don't believe I have anything stronger in the house at the moment, unless, of course, you did find some contraband in my woodshed."

"Tea would be splendid," Captain Ellard replied, watching as she rang the bell and gave orders to the astonished Susannah.

Sophy indicated a chair by the fire and sat down opposite him.

"Well, Captain Ellard?" she said.

"Well, Mrs Franklin, I did not find

any contraband, much to my relief. The cottage has been empty for over three months, and it would not surprise me in the least if it had been used as a hiding-place. It would have been very embarrassing if the revenue men had decided to make one of their raids on the village and discovered a hoard of brandy kegs in your outhouses."

"Yes, I suppose it would," Sophy replied slowly. It sounded plausible enough. "I had no idea this was such a lawless corner of the world," she said.

"I rather thought you might not. That was why I was trying to look round without your knowledge. It occurred to me that if you arrived here after a long and trying journey to find a small cottage at the end of a muddy track, infested with smugglers, you might well turn round and move out again the next day."

"Oh, it takes more than that to discourage me," Sophy said. A fleeting smile lit her features, and she went on, "It was most considerate of you, Captain Ellard, and I thank you. Not many people would have come out on such a wild night."

Captain Ellard disclaimed any great effort. "It's not far to ride," he said, "and I wanted to see if everything was to your satisfaction. Thyme Cottage is probably rather small compared with what you are used to, and it certainly cannot be described as elegant. I hope it hasn't been too much of a disappointment?"

"No, it's a charming place," Sophy hastened to assure him. "I feel as if I am returning home, for I was brought up in just such a cottage as this. In size, it's just right for my daughter and myself, and as for elegance, I shall gladly exchange that for warmth and comfort."

She was about to ask him how he had come to hear of her, when Susannah came in with the tea tray, and she had to attend to the ceremonies of pouring out.

"I'm glad to have found a suitable tenant for the place," Captain Ellard said. "I wanted to get somebody who would look after it. It is not easy to convince people that they would like to live out here by the side of a tidal estuary. Mention the word 'marsh' and it conjures up images of flood and ague in most people's minds, not to speak of the sheer monotony of the landscape. Our marshlands and rivers are a far cry from the popular ideal of a picturesque countryside, but after you have been here a while you may come to appreciate them. I am prejudiced, of course, but I find they have a strange subtle fascination of their own."

Sophy, finding herself diverted from her question, replied that she would reserve judgement on her surroundings until she had seen more of them. "In any event," she said, "it should be a healthy place to live, with fresh breezes coming in from the sea. I left London smothered in a pall of fog, which does no good at all to a child in Lucy's delicate state of health."

"I hope you still feel the same when the sea breezes become winter storms," Captain Ellard smiled, "and the wind rattles the shutters and blows smoke down the chimney. We had a bad one just before Christmas. My sister was convinced that the roof was about to blow off Creek End, and spent all night by the fire in the old hall, as she thought the great chimney would protect her if the worst happened."

Sophy found herself smiling back at him, and thought how favourably he compared with Jerermy's cronies. Philip Ellard did not seek to impress her with stories of his dazzling genius or flatter her with unwanted compliments. His friendly, pleasant manner and the easy way in which he entered a conversation was very different from the half-condescending, half-insinuating air of the likes of Perry Allington. In looks he might be considered inferior to her late husband, for Jeremy had been strikingly handsome, and like all his friends had cared for his smooth complexion as anxiously as any woman. But the lines on Philip Ellard's face were those of good humour, and there was besides an air of purpose about him, an inner driving force that stirred the feminine atmosphere of Thyme Cottage. Sophy felt instinctively that here was a man who let nothing stand in his way. She had been fortunate, she decided, in finding such a neighbour and landlord so unexpectedly.

"It was most kind of Mrs Vye to send

the gig for me. It was a pleasant surprise to be met at the end of my journey and taken to the door," she said, picking up his reference to his sister. "I was somewhat confused at first, though, as I had no idea who Mrs Vye might be. You made no mention of your sister's living with you in your letters."

"Charlotte is only visiting Creek End, though I suspect it might be a stay of some length. Her husband is a Greek scholar, quite an eminent one, and he has taken a sabbatical year and gone off to see the birthplace of civilisation for himself. And in the meantime, Charlotte has decided to keep a sisterly eye on me." He smiled rather ruefully, and Sophy got the impression that Mrs Vye's presence was not entirely welcomed. However, he went on, "Which enables me to entertain mixed company, something I have not been able to do up till now. I hope you will often come and dine with us at Creek End — unless, of course, you mean to live a very secluded life here?"

"I do not intend to cut myself off from society," Sophy replied. Would Jeremy have expected that of her? Probably not, she decided. He had lived for pleasure, and would not begrudge her the occasional quiet dinner. She was just about to revert to her enquiry as to who had told him about her, when Captain Ellard asked if she found Susannah suitable.

"She seems a good, hardworking girl. She and her sister have made a capital job of preparing the cottage."

"And has she told you of her sister's plight?"

"Yes, indeed. I am sure I shall be able to employ her as well, for there is too much here for one girl to do, even if I attend to some of the cooking myself. But what a terrible punishment, to be transported to New South Wales for poaching! I doubt not that the man was only taking a rabbit or two to feed his family, and now Polly is left to cope on her own."

Sophy spoke with feeling, as she too had been left alone in the world. How much easier it was for her to manage, with only one child to provide for and an income on which to do so. Polly's only hope was to apply for Poor Relief.

Leaning forward, Captain Ellard said, "Can it be that I have found an ally in you, Mrs Franklin? We would make a formidable team against Sir Harry. I have the greatest respect for him in many ways, but when it comes to politics we don't see eye to eye at all. Dyed-in-the-wool reactionary that he is, I think he considers me to be but one step removed from a rick-burner. 'Recruiting sergeant for General Ludd' he once called me — he has a priceless line in rhetoric, you must hear him when he gets into full flight. Mostly we argue over matters of principle and contrive to stay the best of friends, but over the question of Abel Harris we were scarcely on speaking terms for over a week, which makes life difficult when you live in a small community. It took all of our harassed parsons's tact and diplomacy to restore peace to the dining-tables of the neighbourhood."

"I know very little about politics," Sophy demurred, "but I do know that transportation is almost as terrible as hanging, at least for the family of the offender."

Captain Ellard looked at her thoughtfully. "Do you know, you're not the least how I imagined you to be," he said.

He had expected a weak, easily-led woman, helplessly adrift without the support of her husband, and instead here was a creature who, though she looked fragile, possessed the courage to threaten to shoot him with a hammer and, what was more, held radical views on the sentencing of poachers.

"You're not quite my idea of the parish philanthropist, either," Sophy replied, with equally devastating candour.

"Philanthropist? Me?" Captain Ellard laughed. "That's not what you'll hear me called in the village. Slave-driver is one of the milder terms used. I don't even let the poor devils on the estate spend a couple of hours in the Plough and Sail at midday. Shameful, is it not?"

"Cruel," Sophy agreed.

"I have an idea we might think alike on quite a few issues," Captain Ellard predicted. "Sir Harry will have to beware if you start taking my side. But you must be wishing me away, I have trespassed on your time and patience too long already.

48

I meant merely to call by and see if there was anything you needed."

"No, indeed, everything is just as it should be," Sophy assured him. "In fact it has all gone so smoothly that I am beginning to wonder if there is some terrible flaw I have so far overlooked. It all seems to have fallen so neatly into place that something is bound to go wrong. There is just one point I am curious about: you said in your first letter that you heard of me through a mutual acquaintance, and I am at a loss as to who that might me."

To her surprise, Captain Ellard looked distinctly uneasy at this, and did not reply immediately. "Is it of great importance?" he asked evasively, pushing one of the logs further into the fire and watching the flames begin to lick around it.

Sophy looked at him curiously, her interest heightened by his evident reluctance.

"It seems that it is," she said. "I did wonder if it was some member of my own or my late husband's family working indirectly, which seemed rather odd. Why not come straight out with an offer of assistance?"

"No, it is nothing to do with your family, but rather with mine — " he paused, fixing his grey eyes thoughtfully on her face, as if trying to determine her reaction to what he was about to disclose. Finally, he said, "I was in Calais a couple of months ago, the resort, as you probably know, of numerous Englishmen on the run from creditors or the law. And I was surprised to meet one of my cousins — we're not a particularly close family and I was not aware that he had left the country. Naturally, we fell to talking, and when I asked why he was living in exile he explained that he was lying low for a while because — " he glanced briefly at Sophy and then looked away " — he had been involved in a duel and had killed his opponent. I have to confess that he did not seem unduly worried about it, although he admitted that it was he who had provoked the quarrel. But he did suffer from some qualms of conscience over the fate of the man's family, so I undertook to trace them and offer such assistance as seemed appropriate. I made some enquires and found out your address, and the rest you know."

Sophy jumped up and paced over to the window. Leaning her forehead against the cold glass she stared unseeing into the darkness of the winter's evening, battling with a number of emotions, predominantly disappointment. So this was the awful flaw she had been afraid of! She had not expected it to appear in this form. How could she possibly stay here now with the shadow of Jeremy's murderer haunting her? Turning to face her visitor, she exclaimed hotly, "I consider it extremely underhand dealing not to have told me of this at the outset."

"Possibly it was," Captain Ellard admitted. "But I think the end justifies the means, for had I done so, you might well have turned down Thyme Cottage."

"Certainly I would have!" Nothing would have induced me to come here."

"And yet you did want to move to the country."

"This is not the only cottage in the world! I am perfectly well able to shift for myself," Sophy declared. "I have already heard of your efforts at helping the rag, tag and bobtail of humanity, you seem to have acquired quite a reputation for it, but I am not in need of your patronage, Captain Ellard, and I certainly do not want to be classed as one of your — your lame ducks!"

"Not for one moment would I dream of regarding you as such," Captain Ellard assured her, the faintest smile tugging at the corners of his mouth. "I should imagine you are an extremely resourceful lady, and hardly likely to be in danger of being thrown upon the parish and becoming a charge on the Poor Rate. You recall that I said I needed a reliable tenant for this house. It occurred to me that you might be just the right person. Will you allow that it might be of advantage to us both if you were to stay?"

Feeling suddenly rather ashamed at her outburst, Sophy allowed herself to be mollified. She was in general of a calm and practical nature, and had long since learnt that it was no use railing against the twists of fate. Here was just one more that had to be considered.

"I will think it over," she replied with

dignity, adding with an apologetic smile, "it is far too late to make any hasty decisions, and I am too tired to look at the situation rationally. I will see what the morning brings."

And think about it she did, long after Captain Ellard had taken his leave. Lying awake in her unfamiliar bed, listening to the rain on the windowpanes and the myriad knockings and creakings of an old house complaining of the rigours of the winter's night, she tried to weigh the advantages of living at Silver Creek against the pain of being reminded of Jeremy's death every time she saw Captain Ellard. Finally, she took her own advice and decided to wait until the morning and calculate whether the village and its surroundings were really what Lucy needed to recover her strength. It was for Lucy, after all, that she had come here in the first place.

She awoke the next morning to find Susannah creeping into her room with a cup of chocolate.

"Good morning, ma'am," she said cheerfully. "Rained something awful in the night, didn't it? But 'tis all cleared now, 'tis going to be a nice day."

She drew back the yellow-flowered curtains and let in the weak winter sunshine. Sophy, sipping her chocolate, looked round appreciatively. The room was painted white and the walls covered with a pretty sprigged paper, which, though faded in places, gave it a cheerful air. The uneven oak floor was dark with polish, as were the plain wash-stand and the two stick-back chairs. Sophy reached out to finger the bed hangings and found that the faded fabric was worn almost threadbare along the folds. She would have to buy some new ones, she decided. Yellow would look well, as the room faced east. Yellow with a white fringe. Would one have to go into Maldon to buy fabric, or did the chandler's in Tracey Nugent stock a good selection? Then she reminded herself that she might not be staying, and felt something like regret.

There was a patter of bare feet on the landing. The door burst open and Lucy ran in chattering with excitement.

"Mama, I can see the garden from my window, and there's ducks in it! Brown ones and patchy ones. Are they ours, Mama? Are we going to have ducks *and* hens?"

"Lucy, you have nothing on your feet! You'll catch your death of cold!" Sophy cried. She slipped out of bed and wrapped a shawl round the child, her heart wrung as always by the painful slenderness of the wrists and ankles that protruded from her linen nightdress. She hugged the little girl and stroked the short, dark hair that was just beginning to grow again after having been shorn at the height of her fever, but Lucy slid out of her arms and scampered over to the window.

"You can see the fields this way, and a bit of the river, and some houses. Come and see, Mama! Mama, there are no cobbles, the road is just mud, it's ever so dirty, all puddles."

Sophy sat beside her on the window seat, and agreed that the lane was indeed a quagmire. But above it the sky was showing blue between scudding clouds and on the river the rising tide was crowned with tossing white-crested waves. Seagulls wheeled and soared on the blustery wind and a solitary barge was working her way upriver under short sail. In the middle distance, the red-tiled roof of Creek End House could be seen rising above the trees that surrounded it, and Sophy found herself wondering if Mrs Vye had considered last night's storm bad enough to take refuge by the great chimney.

"Do you like it here?" she asked, though she had little doubt of what the answer would be. Lucy's wan little face was alight with enthusiasm.

"Oh yes, it's lovely! London's horrid and smelly and there's no animals. Mama, are we going to have ducks?"

"Hens are better," Sophy answered. "There is more meat on them and they fatten quicker." And as she said it she realised she was repeating her own mother's words and wondered what she would say if she had survived to see Sophy here, living in just such a cottage as the one in which she had been brought up. 'I told you so,' probably. Well, Mama may have been wrong about her marriage to Jeremy, but at least her good training would be very useful here at Thyme Cottage. And it was only as an afterthought that Sophy added, If I stay.

When Sophy and Lucy came downstairs, they found the fire freshly banked up and drawing well in the dining-room and the table neatly laid. Susannah, clearly out to make a good impression, hurried in with pots of tea and coffee, jugs of milk and cream and dishes of butter, eggs, ham, kidneys and porridge. As the array of food was placed on the table beneath her startled gaze, Sophy realised that she had neglected to give any precise orders about breakfast the night before, and Susannah was using her initiative. She decided to wait until after the meal was over before pointing out that such a feast was unnecessary for just two people, and turned her attention to persuading Lucy to eat. To her delight, she found that instead of having to coax the child to a mouthful of this and a spoonful of that, as had been the case ever since she had fallen ill, Lucy not only ate up all that was given her, but actually asked for another glass of milk. The salt air, Sophy had to admit, was already doing her good.

Susannah, on being told that the repast was excellent but too lavish, looked abashed and muttered apologies.

"Pray don't be downcast, Susannah, I am not scolding you," Sophy assured her. "I expect you are used to a larger household than this. Where was your last position?"

"Armsley Hall, ma'am, over t'other side of Chelmsford. I was housemaid there, ma'am, but I was turned off when the family moved to London and the place was let."

"And you don't object to being a maid-of-all work after serving in a big house?"

"Oh no, ma'am! You see, I wanted to be nearer home, so as to help my ma. My pa's not able to work regular, on account of he gets the ague so often. Terrible it is, ma'am, and leaves him weak as a babe. So when my ma heard Thyme Cottage was to be let, she went and asked parson's wife about me getting a place here. And besides, not meaning aught impertinent, ma'am, but now as I've met you and Miss Lucy, I think as it'll be much nicer working here than at the Hall." She ended in a rush, her already rosy cheeks glowing scarlet.

"Thank you Susannah that was nicely said," Sophy replied, touched by the girl's sincerity. "Now, is your sister here? I would like to see her as well."

Polly Harris was similar in appearance to her sister; both having sturdy figures and round faces with appealing snub noses, but the older girl lacked Susannah's bright cheerfulness, and the careworn look about her eyes made her seem more than her nineteen years. She had, she told Sophy, been in good service before marrying Abel Harris, working as a kitchenmaid at Tracey Manor, but she was willing to do any task, however humble. Sophy was in something of a quandary. She had not meant to set up as a fine lady, doing nothing but stitch at her embroidery frame and teach Lucy her letters. Before coming to Thyme Cottage, she planned to do most of the cooking herself as well as caring for the poultry and doing some of the household tasks. But having seen the place, she realised, as she had told Captain Ellard, that there was more than enough for one maid to do. And besides that, there was Polly to consider. To employ the girl would not make a vast difference to Sophy's budget, but it would transform Polly's prospects. In the end, she decided that Polly should come in six days a week, going home to her children once dinner was on the table. Both sisters were profusely grateful, making Sophy feel rather ashamed she had even considered not taking Polly on. She cut short their thanks, and swiftly outlined how the work should be divided between them, making a mental note to start overhauling her linen store as soon as they were settled in. Patching, darning and turning sides-to-middle would keep both girls purposefully occupied should they find time on their hands in the afternoons. Then, when Susannah had gone upstairs to see to the bedrooms, and Polly to the scullery to deal with the washing-up, Sophy and Lucy started on the pleasant task of unpacking the books and ornaments that still remained in the cases.

* * *

At Tracey Manor, there was rebellion in the air, and as usual, George was the cause of it. He saw no reason why he should be included in a visit of ceremony on the new tenant of Thyme Cottage.

"I can think of few things more boring," he said slouched in a chair by the morning-room window while his mother and sister, in their outdoor clothes, waited for him to get ready.

And as usual, his sister supported him.

"There's no need for George to come, surely? I should not think that this Mrs Franklin will expect it. After all, you and I can represent the family quite well enough by ourselves," Anna-Maria pointed out reasonably.

Lady Isobel Nugent looked from one golden head to the other in exasperation. A plain, square-built, forthright woman, she had never quite recovered from her astonishment at producing two such beautiful children, and now they were becoming difficult as well. George, of course, had always been a problem, but not Anna-Maria, at least, not until recently. And determined not to be thwarted, she spoke with more than her usual blunt authority.

"George will come because *I* expect it," she insisted. "Now come along, George, the carriage is waiting."

For half a minute more, her son glared back at her defiantly, then heaved a sigh and said, "Oh, very well then, if it means so much to you." It had occurred to him that he might as well go, for there was nothing to do at home, and the warning tightening of his chest told him that it was no good attempting anything the least bit strenuous today. But he was not going to let his mother know that.

In the roomy, old-fashioned family coach, lurching down the lane to Silver Creek, George continued to make plain his opposition to the visit.

"If this Mrs Franklin is anything like the crabby old hags that lived at Thyme Cottage before, you'll not find it much of a pleasure making her acquaintance, Mother," he said. "She'll talk of nothing but the transgressions of her maid and the place will stink of cats."

"There is no odour of cats about Thyme Cottage. I have seen to *that*," his mother replied, adding as an afterthought, "not that I'm saying there ever was, mind you."

"I don't believe she is so very old," Anna-Maria ventured. "Captain Ellard mentioned a child, a small child."

"Did he?" Lady Isobel pounced on this piece of news with alacrity. "Then he has said more to you than he has to me. I found him singularly uninformative about his new tenant."

Anna-Maria merely smiled and looked conscious.

It did nothing to change her brother's view of their new neighbour, however. Even if she was under thirty, a widow with a child was hardly likely to be of any interest. For though he had led a rather restricted life, George had, at seventeen, already learnt just what a powerful effect his extraordinary good looks had amongst the girls of his acquaintance, and any female not willing to join the ranks of his admirers was hardly worth bothering about.

"I hope it's better trained than the Hanson spawn," he commented sourly.

"Whatever Mrs Franklin or her child

may be like, you will at least be civil," Lady Isobel snapped. "I have some doubts myself as to whether she will be entirely suitable to be admitted to our circle. There's no knowing what sort of person Ellard might choose to let the cottage to, he has some very odd ideas on these matters, as we all very well know, but until we meet her, we must at least keep an open mind on the matter."

George muttered, "Oh yes, do let's keep our minds open," and stared gloomily out of the window. Mrs Franklin was beginning to bore him even before they got to Thyme Cottage. No doubt by the time the set fifteen minutes of the visit had dragged by, he would be utterly suffocated by the woman.

Following his smother and sister through the cramped entrance hall of the cottage, George noticed first that the smell of cats had indeed been banished, and second that Susannah Greenways was a good deal more attractive than the housemaids at the Manor. In the interval afforded by his mother's lengthy introductions of herself and Anna-Maria, he managed to catch her eye and raise a startled flush that changed swiftly into a look of flattered complaisance that he was beginning to expect from the fortunate females on whom he bestowed his attention. Small wonder, then, that when called on to make his bow to Mrs Franklin, he did so in the most perfunctory manner, and noticed little more about her than that she was under thirty, but still a good few years older than himself.

He took a seat by the window, and fell to speculating about Susannah, a pleasant train of thought that was, to his exasperation, constantly interrupted by Lady Isobel's obtrusive voice as she questioned Mrs Franklin on where she had lived in the past, how long she had been married, when she had been widowed and what had been the cause of the late Franklin's demise. His mother, he observed, was pursuing her usual course of bludgeoning information out of people. There was no subtlety about Mama, and very little tact. The only thing that could, grudgingly, be admired about her was that she was straightforward. She left you in no doubt as to where you stood in her estimation. And with a glimmering of interest, he realised that Mrs Franklin was not allowing herself to be bludgeoned. Politely, coolly, she deflected the questions, imparting just as much about herself as she chose.

Lady Isobel learnt only that she had resided in London, Bath and several other fashionable cities, and was connected to the Lincolnshire Franklins, but did not care to ask them or her own family for a place to live, had been married five years and widowed nearly five months, and that her husband had 'met with an accident'. When pressed on that point, she emulated Lady Isobel's frankness and replied that she did not care to talk about it. George started to take a greater interest in the exchange, and tried to catch his sister's eye to see what her reaction was, but Anna-Maria was engaged in playing quietly with the Franklin child. It was, after all, no use trying to slip the least word into the conversation whilst Mama was holding court.

In the meantime, Lady Isobel had heard and seen enough of their new neighbour to make a judgement. She found Mrs Franklin evasive, but there was no denying that she was quiet, respectable and well-bred. She also had a certain presence that Anna-Maria, observing covertly from her corner, defined as elegance. In spite of the widow's cap and the ill-fitting black dress, Mrs Franklin brought with her an exciting air of sophistication, coming as she did from the fashionable world that Anna-Maria longed to be part of.

Lady Isobel, having made her mind up, leaned forward and patted Sophy's hand. "You'll become used to my blunt ways, Mrs Franklin," she said. "I always say what I think. You are most unfortunate to have suffered such a blow," her voice softened several degrees, "but you are lucky in having your daughter. One child gives a reason for going on, several would have been a burden."

And having delivered her wisdom on this point, she moved on to domestic matters.

"How do you find Thyme Cottage?" she asked, and before Sophy could reply, continued, "I have always thought it a prettyish sort of place, and not too large for a family of your size. If I were you, I would have the dining-room door hung the other way round, it would be far more convenient. And some more shelves in the closets upstairs are essential. Speak to Wat Styles, he will make a good job of it. Of if he does not, tell me and I shall send our carpenter over from the Manor."

George's attention began to drift. He had heard his mother handing out advice of this sort countless times in the past and was inured to her persistent enquiries into the smallest details of other people's domestic arrangements. When she moved on to the question of servants, however, George was all ears once more.

"I hope you find that Susannah Greenways suitable. She's a flighty little baggage." George looked out of the window with an expression of studied boredom and listened all the closer. "I had to come in here and make sure she was getting on with preparing the cottage for you, or there's no knowing what sort of a muddle she might have got into. However, you make her bustle about, and she'll turn out well enough, I'll warrant.

But be firm, Mrs Franklin, or she will be eating you out of house and home and not doing a hand's turn. And as for that Polly Harris! I trust Mrs Franklin, that you were not prevailed upon to employ that worthless hussy?"

And, quietly firm, Sophy replied, "As a matter of fact, Polly has already proved her worth. She is to come in each day to help out."

"Humph! No good will come of that, you mark my words," Lady Isobel prophesied. "If you want a second maid, I can recommend a good hard-working girl. It's a pity I did not know of your coming sooner, or I could have engaged her instead of Susannah. But Ellard did not tell me until it was too late." Her voice sharpened with suspicion. "I suppose Ellard has not been filling your head with his crack-brained ideas, has he?"

"He has told me why Abel Harris was transported," Sophy relied, "though he did not need to prompt me to employ Polly — I already had half a mind to do so."

Abandoning all pretence of not listening,

George looked across the room at Anna-Maria, who signalled back her interest with a quickly-suppressed smile. And, addressing nobody in particular, he remarked, "Another lame duck provided for." He could never resist an opportunity to stir up a promising dispute, particularly where Captain Ellard was concerned. He was torn between admiration and envy of him. Philip Ellard was everything George would like to be: tough, outspoken and resourceful, entirely the master of his own destiny. By the time Philip was seventeen, George's present age, he had already been at sea on active service for four years, and he had gone on to carve a career for himself in the Navy without any patronage in the upper echelons of the Admiralty. George's prospects seemed hopelessly limited in comparison, and he resented it.

His mother exclaimed, "Really, it's too bad! Just because he chooses to take on every bit of riff-raff with a tale of hard times, there is no need for him to expect you to support a convict's family."

"Whatever the rights and wrongs of

Abel Harris's case, I fail to see why his wife and three children should be penalised," Sophy retorted "Polly is only too willing to do any task to feed her family, and if I am able to be of assistance in giving her a place, then I am glad to be of use."

For the first time, George looked her full in the face, and observed the fine bone structure, the dark eyes, the faint flush of annoyance across the cheeks.

"Capital," he approved, with malicious glee. "Someone else who is prepared to stand upon their principles. And my father will not be able to storm and bluster at you, ma'am, as he does at Captain Ellard. It will be enough to give him an apoplexy."

Mrs Franklin looked back at him with just the same expression of contained tolerance that Captain Ellard was wont to do. And she was not, George realised to his chagrin, the least bit struck by his looks.

"George, you will not speak of your father in that fashion," Lady Isobel commanded. Her son grinned back and held his counsel. To Sophy, she said,

"Well now, Mrs Franklin, I like a person who can stand up for herself, even if we might not agree. If there is one thing I cannot abide, it is a mousey dab of a creature who does not know what she is about."

There was little doubt that Mrs Franklin knew what she was about. George had seldom seen someone assess his mother so quickly nor deal with her so effectively. Mrs Hanson, the rector's wife, was an archetypal 'mousey dab' and constantly on the receiving end of an endless stream of good advice, and Captain Ellard's sister, Mrs Vye, had managed to put Lady Isobel's back up within ten minutes by being excessively obsequious whilst running down practically every aspect of the neighbourhood. But Mrs Franklin, in answer to Lady Isobel's commendation, smiled and said,

"I hope there will not be too many points on which we do not agree, ma'am. Life is so much more pleasant when one is on good terms with one's neighbours, don't you think? And I was hoping you might advise me on quite a few matters.

Who, for instance, is the best butcher in these parts . . . ?"

It would not be long, George could see, before Mrs Franklin had his mother eating out of her hand, which was no mean feat. He might even be able to turn this to his advantage, if he went about it in the right way. Quite how, he could not immediately see, but any ally in his bid to escape from the gilded cage he lived in was bound to be useful. In the meantime, his interest in a conversation centring round tradesmen and poultry rapidly waned. To fill up the gaping stretch of time until his mother saw fit to leave, he ran an eye along the rows of books ranged upon the shelves in the alcove. Most of it was pretty predictable stuff — the Bible, of course, Shakespeare, a selection of modern novels — but of improving works such as Fordyce's Sermons there were no examples at all. George contemplated the bliss of a Sunday evening free of Fordyce's sermons.

And what did Mrs Franklin read instead? Mostly poetry, it seemed, for there were examples of the works of practically all the better modern poets, and a complete set of Lord Byron's. He was distracted from his occupation by voices and footsteps outside, and looking out of the window saw that deliverance was at hand, in the unlikely form of the rector of Silver Creek and part of his numerous family.

"Heaven help us," he commented ungraciously. "We are about to be invaded by the Hansons. All attempts at rational conversation, however appallingly mundane, will hereby cease."

His prophecy was all too true. In the space of a few minutes, the front parlour of Thyme Cottage became uncomfortably crowded. The Hanson children — only three of them today, George noted, but it sounded like more erupted into the room, followed by their harassed parents. Mrs Hanson made a feeble attempt to stop them from running about and climbing on the chairs, and when they took no notice of her, sent a look of silent entreaty to her husband, who quelled them by ordering them to "Sit!" as if they were a litter of puppies. Mrs Franklin sent Susannah hurrying to the kitchen for biscuits.

As George had forseen, the advent of the Hansons was too much for his mother. Lady Isobel did not relish competing with the Hanson boys for attention, and in any case, she had achieved the object of her visit, which was to inspect Mrs Franklin. Satisfied that the new tenant of Thyme Cottage was not only genteel but likely to be a positive asset to her social circle, she rose to take her leave.

"I am glad to have you settled here," she said to Sophy, with a quick approving nod. "You must come and dine with us at the Manor. Just a family dinner, very quiet, no ceremony. Will Thursday suit you?"

Sophy accepted gracefully, and Lady Isobel, glaring balefully at the Hanson child who was fingering her gown, hastened to go.

"The pleasure is ours, Mrs Franklin. I will send the coach for you at half-past four. Come, George, Anna-Maria."

She could not, however, resist the opportunity of handing out a timely piece of advice to Mrs Hanson, and while she was engaged in pointing out the deficiencies of the parsonage cook, Anna-Maria seized the chance to speak to Sophy.

"I wish you will come and visit us, I do so long to hear about the London fashions and parties and everything. It's so dull here you cannot imagine! And do bring your little girl," she added, with a smile at Lucy. "I have a very pretty doll that has been sitting neglected in the nursery for years, and I am sure she would like it."

Very few people ever refused a request from Anna-Maria. Strangers were generally overcome by her fair, English-rose beauty and those who knew her were pleased to treat her with the same generous friendliness that she always showed. Sophy was no exception.

"That is very kind of you, I shall be pleased to come," she said. "And if you would not find it terribly dull, you are very welcome to call at Thyme Cottage any time you please."

And George, counting himself as included in the invitation, determined to talk his sister into taking it up as soon as possible. Not that he admitted as much on the way home. In the coach, Anna-Maria spoke warmly of Mrs Franklin's knowledge of the world, Lady Isobel of her good sense, but George, when appealed to for his opinion, merely shrugged and said he supposed she was better than the last tenants of Thyme Cottage, and when pressed on the point admitted that she might have been handsome once.

Sophy, meanwhile, had no time to think over her impressions of the Nugents, for her new set of visitors were claiming all her attention. James Hanson, a quiet-spoken and courteous man of about thirty-five years, wore a slightly harassed expression. Looking at his wife and children, it was not difficult to discover the reason for it. Mary Hanson was short and slight with wisps of mouse-brown hair escaping from the cap that sat awry above her anxious face. She had discovered, when he was but a few hours old, that her first-born had a stronger will then she, and he and the brothers that followed him into the world in rapid succession had been profiting from it ever since.

Mary was continually on the verge of being overwhelmed by the difficulties of getting from one day's beginning to the next. A busy and conscientious shepherd to his flock, James Hanson stayed only ten minutes to enquire after Sophy's well-being, before hurrying off to attend to his sick and needy parishioners. He glanced enquiringly at his wife, to see if she was ready to leave, but Mary was quite unequal to the effort of dragging her children away from a house that supplied them with a plateful of fresh-baked biscuits and seemed likely to contain a store of toys somewhere. Sophy, seeing her dilemma, pressed her to stay longer.

"Oh, Mrs Franklin, you cannot think what a comfort it is to have someone like you at Thyme Cottage," Mary Hanson enthused in her breathless, distracted manner. "The last tenants were two old spinsters who had been here since the Ark, and they could not abide children. I had to leave the boys behind when I visited them, and they always contrived to get away from their nursemaid and hang about the gate teasing the cats until

I came out. It was terribly embarrassing. And, of course, there are not many houses within walking distance and I do so like a little chat, do not you? There is only Creek End and Tracey Manor this side of Tracey Nugent, and although I would not say a word against Lady Isobel — she really is the kindest woman and so full of good advice but she is rather — rather — "

"Overpowering?" suggested Sophy, with a smile.

"Yes, that is it exactly. Overpowering. And Sir Harry . . . ! You have not met Sir Harry, of course. He is absolutely terrifying! He has such a loud voice and always a pack of ferocious dogs at his heels. He renders me quite speechless. And then Anna-Maria is a nice girl, but she is only a girl and doesn't understand the problems we mothers have."

"But so beautiful," said Sophy, refusing to take up the subject of children. "Such striking colouring and perfect features. She and her brother together are quite stunning. They appear to be very close in age — which of them is the elder?"

"They are twins," Mary explained. "I

often wonder how Sir Harry and Lady Isobel came to have two such beautiful offspring, but I suppose they must be throwbacks to a previous generation. Of course," and here a note of superiority crept into her voice, "they are the only ones. There are no other young Nugents in the nursery. I suppose that is why Lady Isobel does not understand what a handful a family of young children can be."

Here they were interrupted by a crash, screams of delight and howls of rage, as the tower the youngest Hanson had been building with Lucy's alphabet bricks was smashed by his big brother. Mary squeaked at them to stop fighting, but they took no notice and continued to hurl bricks and abuse at each other, aided by the middle child, who stamped on their fingers each time they reached for a fresh weapon. Lucy, appalled, retreated into a corner with her rag doll. Sophy, fearing that one of them might be laid out by a flying brick, fixed all three with a quelling stare.

"Stop it at once," she said, in a voice that brooked no disobedience. "I only have well-behaved little boys in my house."

The children gaped at her, momentarily silenced, and three pairs of hazel eyes watched her warily as she swiftly divided the bricks into three equal piles.

"Now," she said firmly, "you can play here, and you here, and you over there, and in a minute I will see who has made the best building."

The boys waited a few moments to see if she was going to waver, and finding that she expected to be obeyed, did as they were bid.

Mary Hanson lookd at Sophy with unfeigned admiration.

"I wish I could manage them like that," she sighed. "They never pay the least heed to me. Lady Isobel thinks me such a poor thing not to be able to control my own children."

"I have often observed that children obey a stranger better than their own mother," Sophy said lightly. And returning to the previous subject, asked, "Should not George Nugent be at school, or university?"

"He has been ill," Mary explained,

delighted to have a new audience for all the local gossip. "He has a naturally weak constitution, poor boy, and was sent to a private school rather than one of the great public ones. But last autumn he was laid up with a fever and had to be sent home to recover. He wants to go up to Cambridge, but he may not be strong enough. After all," she lowered her voice dramatically, "You know what excesses young men are inclined to indulge in at University. Sir Harry declares it will be the making of him, but Lady Isobel worries about his health. But in any case, James is to start coaching him next week, right up until the summer, which is a great comfort, you know, for it will mean a little extra income. But I shall have to keep the children quiet, which is a worry. James says one cannot study with noise about the place. I do see what he means, but it will be very difficult . . . "

Sophy made sympathetic noises and refilled her visitor's teacup, thinking as she did so that it was a good thing she had taken on Polly as well as Susannah. If many of her days were going to be occupied with paying and receiving calls, she was going to have less time than she expected for attending to household duties.

Mary had just started recounting some of her maternal worries when Susannah entered, bearing a basket.

"If you please, ma'am," she said, "this has just come from Creek End."

Sophy's suspicions were immediately aroused, and on looking in her basket she found them confirmed, for it contained a pair of mallard. She frowned, annoyed to be on the receiving end of Captain Ellard's munificence.

"Please'm, there's a note as well," Susannah said, holding it out.

Sophy was in half a mind to send the gift back, but realised in time that to do so would be both rude and childish. Instead, she told Susannah to hang the birds in the pantry and offer some refreshment to the man who brought them. The maid bustled off to the kitchen, and as Mary prattled on about Captain Ellard's kindness, Sophy opened the note. She had expected a carefully-worded missive claiming prodigious good sport that morning and begging her to be so obliging as to take the birds as they had more than they could eat at Creek End. But instead of a thinly-disguised excuse for charity, she read: —

Dear Madam,
Dispatched herewith, two more lame ducks in need of attention. Can you do anything for them?
Yrs. etc., P.Ellard. (Philanthropist)

Sophy smothered a chuckle. Lame ducks, indeed! A dreadful joke, and impudent as well, throwing her words back at her. And yet she could not help but see the funny side of it. She pushed the note under the tea-tray, not wanting to have to explain the significance of it to Mary Hanson. She suspected that Mary had a rather limited sense of humour, and would chew it over with her husband and Lady Isobel. She was tempted to write back something in a similar vein, but remembered in time that she was now living in a small community where everyone's business was of concern to everyone else. It would not do for it to be known that she and Captain Ellard

84

were sending notes to each other within a day of her arrival. Tongues would soon begin to wag. She would have to postpone her thanks until next she happened to see him.

Mary, meanwhile, had thought of something concerning Captain Ellard of more interest than his well-known tendency to look after his less fortunate neighbours. Lowering her voice to an eager whisper, Mary asked if Sophy had heard of the notorious smuggler they had about the coast, the one known as 'the Shadow'? Sophy replied that she had.

"Well, Captain Ellard had a brother, and very like him, so they say. And this brother, Richard, was also a Navy man, and his ship was sunk somewhere off the coast of France — I forget quite where, someone did tell me once but I cannot recall the name — anyway, not all of the sailors were drowned. Some of them were picked up by the enemy ship, and one or two swam ashore. And nobody knew what happened to Richard Ellard. He was presumed dead, but it is possible that he got ashore, for he was a strong swimmer. That was, oh, several years ago, back in 'thirteen or early 'fourteen, just before the end of the war. But then this smuggler started operating around our rivers. Of course, there have always been smugglers, small ones, but this man has built up a network that the revenue men know about but cannot break.

"Anyway people started to say — you know how these things get about — that the Shadow was no common sailor or fisherman but a gentleman. And then one night he left an impudent quotation — I forget what, something of Lord Byron's I think — pinned right on the front door of a magistrate who had boasted that he would send the ruffian to the Assizes by Michaelmas. That was when the rumour started that he might be Richard Ellard, for the gentleman in question is a first-rate seaman and knows the creeks like the back of his hand, and the Ellards were brought up near the Crouch or the Roach or thereabouts and used to sail all round the rivers in a skiff. Of course, our Captain Ellard has always denied it, but you never know, do you?"

"I was told that the Shadow was supposed to be a Frenchman, a one-time prisoner of war," Sophy said.

"Oh yes, I heard that as well," Mary gave a nervous little laugh. "Silly me! In that case, he couldn't be Richard Ellard, could he?"

"I suppose we shall have to wait until the Shadow is caught before we find out," Sophy said thoughtfully. It was an intriguing story. She had not thought, when she first heard of Silver Creek, that the place could be connected with mysterious criminals.

"James says he cannot evade capture much longer," Mary said, a mite sadly. "He's beginning to take risks, and now there's this reward. James says, however loyal his gang might be, they will find the prospect of fifty guineas difficult to resist. After all, there's no honour amongst thieves." She then glanced up at the clock and gave a squeak of horror. "Heavens, is that the time? Have I really been here that long? Baby will be crying for his feed."

"You have another child at home, then?"

"Two more," said Mary, with an odd mixture of pride and despair. "All boys!

I would so like a dear little daughter like your Lucy."

When the boys learnt that they had to go home, they raised a storm of protest and declared that they wanted to stay for ever. Their mother, unable to take the easy way out this time and give in to their superior willpower, stood making ineffectual promises of coming another day. In the end, Sophy stepped in.

"You must go home now with your mama," she told them, "because Lucy is going to have a rest. She has been very ill and has to sleep in the day as well as at night. But if you are good, you may come back later and play. Would you like that?"

The boys hurled themselves enthusiastically at her, shouting their delight, then struggled into their coats and hats, trying to prove just how good they could be when they tried. Sophy buttoned up the youngest and smiled at Mary.

"I hope you don't mind," she said. "It will be nice for Lucy to have some children of her own age to play with. She's led rather a lonely life these last few months."

Mary could scarcely believe her luck in finding someone actually volunteering to take her rumbustious offspring off her hands.

"Mind? of course note! It's very kind of you," she said, with unfeigned gratitude. "I wonder if you would care to come and drink tea with us tomorrow evening? It's only a step along the village and I'm sure James would be glad to see you. He's fond of company, but somehow I always find dinners such a worry, and Cook makes such a fuss already about nursery meals that a dinner party might drive her to give notice and then it would be so difficult to get someone to work out here . . . "

Sophy smiled, sympathised, thanked her and ushered her out, with the boys running ahead of her like puppies let off the lead. And turning away from the door, she shook her head. Five babies in six years! Small wonder Mary Hanson found dinner parties a worry.

And that evening as she went over the day's events, Sophy realised that she had found more real friends in this one small village than in the whole of London.

Lady Isobel might be domineering and Mary Hanson helpless, but they were both good-hearted in their own way and seemed genuinely pleased to have her settle amongst them. James Hanson appeared to be a sensible and pleasant man and the little Hansons, when tamed, would help draw out the shy and over-quiet Lucy. It would be interesting to watch the young Nugents as they started out in the world, particularly as they reminded Sophy of herself at the same age, restless and impatient with the dull restraints of home, thinking that life was passing them by because they were not part of the high society of London or Cambridge.

Only Sir Harry and Mrs Vye remained unknown factors. Sir Harry, she imagined, was not nearly so terrifying as Mary Hanson made out. Mrs Vye she had formed no clear picture of. Which brought her to Captain Ellard. There was no longer any question of her leaving Thyme Cottage. It was ridiculous to hold him responsible for the actions of a cousin he had not even seen for several months, and impossible to remain affronted by a man who could turn her own hasty words back on her so neatly. What was it he said Sir Harry had called him? 'Recruiting sergeant for General Ludd'. She smiled to herself as she repaired a curtain one of the Hanson boys had inadvertently torn. It was just about as likely that Captain Ellard was a Luddite leader as it was that his dead brother was the mysterious Shadow.

3

SOPHY looked forward to the dinner at Tracey Manor with some misgivings. It was to be the first party she had been to in nearly five months, and though she was becoming accustomed to going about without Jeremy, she had not yet ventured out in the evening alone. Peering at herself critically in the glass whilst getting ready, she was not at all satisfied with the reflection that gazed back at her.

"I look like a scarecrow," she declared, surveying her thin cheeks and pale complexion. "See how this dress hangs on me! It was not very well made in the first place, to be sure, but now it looks dreadful. If I lose much more weight I shall disappear altogether."

Susannah, hastily stitching in a couple of tucks at the back, loyally maintained that she looked 'a proper picture' but Sophy was unconvinced. The black silk gown in question had been very hurriedly made, like the rest of her mourning clothes, and she had taken no interest in its design at the time, simply accepting whatever the dressmaker turned out. Now she looked with dissatisfaction at the old-fashioned cut of the bodice and the limp hemline, so bare of the flouncing that was currently the mode. She consoled herself with the thought that the Nugents, though undeniably well-bred, were hardly in the first flight of fashion. What she did not stop to consider was the fact that in actually taking an interest in her personal appearance, she was making a great step forwards.

When she arrived at Tracey Manor, Sophy found that the 'small family dinner' to which she had been invited also included Captain Ellard and Mrs Vye, and Sir Harry's brother, Colonel William Nugent, a retired Peninsular veteran, together with his wife, his five grown-up children and a visiting friend of his sons. Sir Harry, on first sight, seemed quite as terrifying as Mary Hanson had predicted. He was short and barrel-chested, with bristling eyebrows and a voice that would have carried with ease across a parade-ground. Sophy soon discovered, however, that the blustering manner only thinly covered a friendly, hospitable character who was fond of his wife and immoderately proud of his two beautiful children. Sir Harry's passion was hunting, and the greatest worry of his life the rising cost of maintaining his pack of hounds.

"Well, Mrs Franklin, how d'ye like that cottage of yours?" he asked. "Pretty little place, but no stables. Can't keep so much as a donkey there. D'ye hunt, Mrs Franklin?"

As her experience of horses was limited to ambling around Hyde Park on a hired hack, Sophy had to admit that she did not. Sir Harry looked relieved.

"Very sensible!" he beamed. "Hunting field's no place for a lady. Can't abide a flock of females screeching their heads off and spoiling the sport. Glad to meet a woman who knows her place. Young girls these days have far too many opinions of their own, laying down the law about what they want to do! They should leave that to the gentlemen."

Sophy remembered George's remarks and decided not to take issue with her host so early in their acquaintance. Perhaps later on she would surprise him with the warmth of her opinions on some subjects. They were joined by Philip Ellard, fashionably elegant in his black evening dress.

"Now here's a fellow with a head full of crack-brained ideas!" Sir Harry exclaimed, clapping a friendly hand on his guest's shoulder. "Mad as a hatter! Who else would have taken on that estate in 'sixteen when those of us who have been at it all our lives were struggling to keep our heads above water?"

"My fatal predilection for lost causes, Sir Harry," Philip explained, and with a significant look at Sophy added, "it's forever getting me into scrapes."

Sophy said, "I think even your not-so-lost causes might have reason to thank you at times."

Philip smiled his acknowledgement of peace between them, and Sir Harry, unaware of the double meaning to the exchange, boomed cheerfully,

"He'll be thanking himself before

five years are out, you mark my words. Hardly knew wheat from barley when he first came here, and already Creek End is showing a return for his efforts. Determination! That's the stuff the defenders of England are made of!"

"Sheer pig-headedness is a more accurate description," Philip laughed.

"There you are," said Sir Harry, "that's the spirit that kept Boney away from our shores. Ain't that so, Mrs Franklin?"

It was obvious to Sophy that the impression George Nugent had given of his father and Captain Ellard being at each other's throats was vastly exaggerated. However different their views might be, they did not allow it to spoil their friendship. It struck her that George was looking for allies in his rebellion against parental authority, and enjoyed stirring up trouble where none existed, and she made a mental note to keep out of that particular battle. She might well side with Philip Ellard on the question of poachers and other minor wrongdoers, but George Nugent could look elsewhere for help.

The meal was a cheerful affair of

three courses and a vast variety of dishes. The Nugents still kept to the old-fashioned custom of carving and serving at the table, hosts and guests helping each other to roasts and pies, flans and fricassees, rather than waiting for footmen to serve from a side-table, as was the mode amongst people of fashion. Sophy decided that whatever they lacked in elegance, the Nugents made up for in friendliness. Everyone went out of their way to put her at her ease. Somewhat to her surprise, she found she was enjoying herself.

It was later on in the evening that she discovered a way to repay some of the kindness shown to her. As they waited in the drawing-room for the gentlemen to join them, the female contingent divided into two distinct groups, Lady Isobel, her sister-in-law, Mrs Nugent, and Mrs Vye comprising one, and Anna-Maria and her young cousins the other. Sophy found she was claimed by the married ladies, but could not help overhearing the girls sighing over the dullness of the gathering. Lady Isobel too heard the rumblings of discontent, and tackled it in her usual forthright manner.

"Now then, miss, you've no right to be questioning the way your elders order the evening. A nice cheerful round game was good enough entertainment when we were young, and it is good enough for you. Perhaps if you practised at your music more often, you might be able to oblige us with a song or two."

Anna-Maria looked mutinous, but dared not oppose her mother. Sophy, taking pity on her, ran over the list of younger people in her head. There were the four girls, and five young men, George and the two Nugent cousins, their friend and Captain Ellard. She moved over to the pianoforte and sorted through the heap of music sheets piled on top of it.

"Could we not have some dancing?" she asked, pulling out a copy of one of her favourite quadrilles. "There are just enough of us, I think and those who wish to play cards might still do so without being disturbed.

Anna-Maria bounded up to her, eyes shining with delight.

"Oh yes! That would be lovely! Do you play, Mrs Franklin?"

"I'm sadly out of practice, I fear, but if you do not mind a few wrong notes, I think I can still remember enough to play some guadrilles and country dances."

"Delicious! Oh Mama, do say we can!" Anna-Maria begged, and her request was echoed by her cousins until Lady Isobel graciously gave her consent. "Darling Mama, thank you so much! And Mrs Franklin, you are an angel, sent to cheer us all up!" Anna-Maria gave Sophy an ecstatic hug and flew to an old carved cabinet at the side of the room. "There's music enough here, though some of it is rather old-fashioned. Look — here's 'Lambskinnet' and 'Yellow Stockings' oh, and 'The Sow in the Sack'."

"'The Sow in the Sack'. I remember that one, that was all the rage in my dancing days," Lady Isobel reminisced. "That quite takes me back. Would you be so kind as to play it, Mrs Franklin?"

Happy to oblige, Sophy sat down and tried over the music, whilst the girls chattered about the ball they had been to at Christmas and Lady Isobel laid down the law about the only way to organise a private dance. The only dissident voice was Mrs Vye's.

"I'm surprised to find a lady in your circumstances suggesting dancing," she said, and Sophy wondered briefly whether she was supposed to go about in sackcloth and ashes for the rest of her days. But Lady Isobel came to her rescue.

"It's not as if Mrs Franklin is going to dance herself," she pointed out. "I think it most kind of her to offer to amuse the girls."

The tedious wait for the gentlemen to tear themselves away from their port and brandy and what sounded like a heated argument passed away with remarkable speed. Sir Harry finally rolled in in high good humour and accepted the cup of coffee that his daughter handed to him.

"D'ye know what this addle-pated radical has been advocating?" he asked the company in general, gesturing in Philip Ellard's direction with his cup. "Universal Suffrage! Can you imagine it? There are enough bedlamites in Parliament at the moment, just think what it would be like if every Tom, Dick and Harry was entitled to vote.

Universal Suffrage! By thunder, he'll be suggesting we give the vote to women next!" Overcome with his own wit, he let out a veritable gale of laughter.

Philip Ellard, catching Sophy's eye, gave her a conspiratorial smile.

"Why not?" he asked, in a tone of innocent enquiry.

Sir Harry practically choked on his coffee.

"Why not?" he spluttered. "Why not? If you cannot . . . ah, but you'll not get me to rise to that one, you impudent young dog. You just wait, I'll play you for every guinea you've got this evening. I've been waiting for a chance to get my revenge for that trouncing you gave me last week."

"I think not, Sir Harry. Tonight my luck is in, I can feel it at my fingers' ends."

He flexed his hands to underline his words, and Sophy, staring at him, went deathly cold. So many times she had seen Jeremy make just the same gesture, scoffing at her doubts as he made ready to go out, always supremely confident that a miraculous run of luck was about to begin, as if the cards or dice would, of their own accord, fall in his favour. She could almost hear him laugh as he took up his hat and marched jauntily out, jingling his last guineas in his pockets. And many times, of course, he had been justified in his confidence, like the night he came home with a diamond necklace for Lucy, then four months old, or the time they had danced on Brighton beach at three in the morning after a party celebrating his unprecedented win on an outsider at the races . . . deaf to the talk going on around her, she wandered back through the path of memory.

It was only when Anna-Maria came to ask her if she was ready to play for them, that Sophy was brought abruptly back to the present.

"Is she not an angel to think of letting us dance?" Anna-Maria appealed to Philip Ellard, who had already secured her as a partner. "Mrs Franklin is the answer to my prayers."

"A veritable angel indeed," Philip agreed, turning to smile at Sophy. But she looked away, not trusting herself to speak.

When the floor was cleared, Sir Harry and his brother sat down to a game of backgammon, and the older ladies settled themselves to watch the dancing. George Nugent made no attempt to find a partner, but prowled moodily about the room before finally leaning on the piano and scowling over Sophy's head at the dancers.

"Deuced stupid scheme of yours, this is," he muttered, just loud enough to be heard.

"Do you not like to dance?" Sophy asked, ignoring his bad manners.

"I can't, it would bring on one of my attacks. And anyway, it would be no pleasure to stand up with one of my cousins. A plainer trio of girls one could not find in a day's journey."

"That is neither kind nor true," Sophy reproved, frowning as she hit the wrong keys. She glanced up at his handsome profile, set in lines of sulky discontent, and thought that it must indeed be galling for him, having to sit by and watch whilst the others enjoyed themselves. "You look just like Lord Byron," she said. "He used to stand and glare at every fashionable

103

ball in London. He even forbade Lady Caroline Lamb to waltz because he could not bear to see her in another man's arms."

"Do I?" George brightened visibly, his vanity touched by even the slightest resemblance to the greatest and most notorious poet of the day. "Did you ever see him? You must have done, surely, if you were living in town for the last few years?"

"Yes, I did, as a matter of fact."

"Where? What was he like? Did he really look capable of all that they said he did?"

Sophy was glad of a chance to keep her mind occupied. Forcing a smile, she said, "If you will make yourself useful and turn the pages for me, I'll tell you what my impressions were, though if you ask my opinion, I think it was all a pack of lies put about by his wife."

She was rewarded with George's undivided attention, much to the chagrin of his young cousins. And between answering his persistent questions and wrestling with the problems of sight-reading music after not having touched an instrument for a couple of years, Sophy found she had little opportunity for further brooding.

The evening was voted a success by all concerned, so much so that in the course of the next month Sophy found her services as an accompanist regularly in demand, both at Tracey Manor and at 'Farthings', Colonel Nugent's house. Running a matchmaker's eye over the shifting pattern of couples, Sophy soon realised that a good deal of manoeuvring went on amongst the girls to secure Philip as a partner. As for his preference, it seemed inevitable that Anna-Maria's blonde beauty should outshine the pleasant but ordinary trio from Farthings. Anna-Maria was still rather shy of him, Sophy thought, but that only added to the attraction. It was easy to see which way the wind was blowing.

In the meantime, Sophy found that rarely did a day pass without someone calling into Thyme Cottage with the intention of staying ten minutes and remaining for half the morning, eating Polly's Madeira cake and talking over the sparse news of the countryside. Mrs Vye regarded her brother's new tenant with sharp, disapproving eyes. A small, thin woman, several years older than Captain Ellard, she wore an injured air and was quick to respond to supposed slights. Within ten minutes of meeting Sophy, she gave her the benefit of her opinion of men in general and her husband in particular. Dr Vye, she claimed, has used her barbarously in deserting her to go off to Greece. She saw no need for it — he could just as easily obtain all the information he required from the well-stocked library of his Cambridge college. It was a theme she was to return to on each successive visit.

Mary Hanson fluttered into Thyme Cottage almost daily, accompanied by varying numbers of her boys and invariably left some or all of them behind to play with Lucy. Sophy, who had resumed Lucy's reading and writing lessons as the child grew stronger, included the Hanson boys in her instructions as she found their education was sketchy in the extreme. Mary was breathlessly grateful, but begged that her husband should not hear of it, as he was likely to be annoyed at her shuffling off her maternal duties.

"I keep meaning to give them regular lessons," she explained, "and most days I do get the books and slates out, but they never seem to want to attend. And then there are so many other things to do! James had some notion a while ago of starting a Sunday school. He said it was shameful that the village children should grow up not able to read their Bibles. But I could no more teach them of a Sunday than fly! The very idea makes me go quite weak."

For both young Nugents, chafing at the boring round of country life, Sophy was a messenger from the outside world. Through the wet cold days of January, when the quagmire of mud outside made it impossible for Sophy to venture far on foot, they rode regularly over to Thyme Cottage and stayed to talk about London and Bath, Cheltenham and Brighton, balls and fashions and scandals. George, changeable as the winds, was by turns gloomy and silent or truculently resentful, as Lady Isobel continued to treat him as an invalid and fuss about his going out in the slightest shower. Occasionally he would appear in oppressively high spirits and boast about what he was going to do once he got away from home. And when he went off to the parsonage for his daily studies, his sister would sigh and envy him.

"Does your mother not intend to take you up to town at all?" Sophy enquired at last. It seemed to her that the Nugents could well afford at least a month or so, if not a proper season, and they must surely want to see their daughter make a good match.

"Oh, she has some idea that I might get carried off by some wicked fortune-hunter. She and my father both have a very low opinion of people who desert their estates to go junketing up to town in the winter and round the watering-places all summer. They seem to think that once I came into contact with that sort of fast set, I'd run off with a handsome rake or something. Chance would be a fine thing!" She made a comical face, and, recovering her usual cheerful humour, said, "Heigh ho! Perhaps I shall be held up by a highwayman one day on the road to Maldon and be rescued by a nobleman of untold wealth."

"Who will, of course, instantly fall madly in love with you," Sophy laughed.

"Of course. And we shall be married by special licence and live happily ever after," Anna-Maria elaborated, and added with a self-conscious smile, "but until then, the neighbourhood is not entirely empty of beaux . . . "

Then, one day in February, the Nugent twins came bursting into Thyme Cottage rather later than usual and full of the latest news.

"It's the Shadow — you'll never believe this — it's the best story I've heard yet," Anna-Maria began.

"And it's true, it's all true," her brother interrupted. "Mr Marshall, one of the Justices from Maldon, you know, rode over first thing this morning to tell my father. It will be all over the county by tomorrow, the revenue men won't be able to go out for being laughed at!"

"Even my father had to see the funny side of it!"

They wrangled over who should tell the tale, and finally George began.

"Well, last night being moonless and high tide at eleven, Lieutenant Forster, the revenue officer, thought there might be some illicit cargoes run in, and they had the *Queen* lying in wait off Osea Island. They waylaid a fishing-smack and seized a quantity of brandy, and then just before midnight they spied a cutter running in, and came alongside before she had a chance to get away or jettison her cargo. And who did they find but the Shadow himself . . . !"

"A great tall fellow in a long black cloak and a mask," Anna-Maria elaborated, "just like they always said! Undoubtedly a gentleman, but a foreigner, a Dutchman. The officer said he definitely spoke with a marked Dutch accent."

"Hush, I'm telling this! Now, before the revenue men could board the cutter, the Shadow offered to parley with Lieutenant Forster, pointing out that he would not give in without a fight, and the law men might well come off the worse, as he had a tough and desperate crew, but he was willing to hand over part of the cargo if he was allowed to go free. Forster claims he *pretended* to go along with this, thinking that he would be able to capture the Shadow without endangering his men, but I have my doubts. Anyway, the Shadow's crew started to transfer some of the brandy kegs onto the *Queen* and the Shadow suggested that they should breach one of them and seal the bargain with a drink. Forster agreed, and several toasts were drunk in contraband, and the Shadow's crew filled up tankards of the stuff and passed it round the revenue men, and before they knew where they were, they were all as drunk as lords. According to Mr Marshall, Lieutenant Forster prides himself on being able to drink any man in Essex under the table, and he thought he could get the Shadow helpless, bring him back to face justice and claim the reward. But the boot was on the other foot, for the Shadow and his crew left them all totally inebriated on board the *Queen* and sailed off not only with their own cargo intact, but with the brandy that had been seized from the fishing-smack as well!"

Sophy, caught up in the Nugents' hilarity, agreed with George that it was a famous tale.

"There'll be some red faces in Maldon this morning!" she laughed. "And some sore heads. But the authorities must be infuriated, the Shadow seems to be able to run rings around them. What was Sir Harry's reactions?"

"Oh, you know my father," George said. "He went seven shades of scarlet and started cursing the preventive men for incompetent idiots and the Shadow for an audacious scoundrel, until my mother had to remind him that there were ladies in the room. But you could see that he had a sneaking admiration for the Shadow, and that made him speak even more violently, as he didn't want Mr Marshall to think he was on the side of the smuggler." George swaggered round the room, in a creditable imitation of his father. "'Those revenue fellows will have to wake their ideas up! What are the riding officers doing? The contraband must be brought ashore somewhere. They ought to work together, catch the rogue in a pincer movement. If the populace sees the law being flouted in this way and nobody able to stop it, we'll find ourselves with a revolution on our hands!" And so on — it was famous sport, I haven't see my father in such a taking since the hounds got loose."

George dissolved into helpless laughter at his father's expense, and Anna-Maria, though protesting dutifully, was seized with a fit of the giggles. Sophy could not help but join in, and the Nugents, seeing they had a receptive audience, regaled her with tales of their father's comic blustering and the Shadow's previous exploits, all very much exaggerated, until Sophy, tears streaming down her face, had to beg them to stop. At length, George reluctantly went off to the parsonage and his sister rode back to the manor, leaving Sophy feeling decidedly flat after so much merriment.

She determined to go out in search of company. The day was fine and inviting, with a false promise of spring in the air, and she decided that as Lucy was getting so much stronger, it would be a good opportunity to take her over to Creek End for the first time. To be sure, Mrs Vye was not the liveliest of hostesses, but even she might be diverted by the day's news, and Lucy would like to see the old house and its tangled jungle of gardens. So after Lucy had had her mid-morning rest, they set out, collecting the two eldest Hanson boys, Jamie and Johnny, on the way.

The lane from Silver Creek to Creek End was still so muddy as to be impassable on foot, so they took a short-cut across the fields which was rather better, though the boys still managed to fall in the wettest places and cover themselves with dirt, much to their own and Lucy's amusement. Lucy had so far recovered from her shyness as to find their antics hilariously funny, and from the safety of Sophy's side egged them on to worse and worse crimes. Sophy calmed them all down when they reached Creek End, made them promise to behave and supervised their taking off muddy boots and coats before being escorted to the kitchens by the kindly housekeeper in search of milk and hot cakes.

Sophy paused in the screens passage to peep into the old hall, the oak-panelled, stone-flagged core of the house. She had been all over Creek End on a previous visit and had been infected with Philip

Ellards's enthusiasm for his home, and his plans to restore it in time to its former glory. The old hall was fifteenth-century, and all that remained of the original house. Attached to it was the west wing, a suite of rooms now in everyday use that had been built in the prosperous days of Elizabeth and altered after the Restoration. Added to the south, looking over the river was a large and beautifully proportioned drawing-room with handsome bedchambers above it, that had been built by the previous owner's grandfather but were at present empty and forlorn. Philip had a host of ingenious ideas for redecorating and improving the place, but needed time and money to carry them out.

Mrs Vye's greeting was not exactly warm.

"Oh, 'tis you, Mrs Franklin," she said, looking up from the length of fringe she was making, "I did not think I should see you today."

She was in a more than usually querulous mood, and the reason soon became clear: her brother had been thoughtless and unfeeling enough to go away for a few days and leave her alone in his draughty and ramshackle house. In vain did Sophy try to distract her with the tale of the Shadow's deeds. Mrs Vye could see nothing remotely amusing in it.

"It's disgusting," she commented with a sniff of distaste. "Officers of the King drinking contraband brandy with a low smuggler. Drunkenness is the scandal of our times. If I had my way, all intoxicating liquor would be entirely done away with. It is quite sickening the way men of all degrees drink away their health and fortune. That is one point on which I cannot criticise Mr Vye: at least he does not indulge himself in that way. The same cannot be said of my brother, I fear. He *said* he was going to a sale of household effects in Hertfordshire, but I suspect that it is just an excuse for meeting with some of his old naval acquaintances and spending his time in drunken revelry at some house of ill-repute in Chelmsford or Colchester. Just like a man! He has no respect for my feelings at all . . ."

Sophy felt a dead weight of depression creeping over her. She had every sympathy with both Captain Ellard and the absent Mr Vye. It was no wonder that they needed to escape at times from such a sour and puritanical companion. And as Mrs Vye reverted to her oft-repeated complaints about Creek End — that it was uncomfortable, old-fashioned, half-empty and cold, that the servants were too few and the roads deplorable — Sophy wondered why she bothered to stay, when she had a perfectly good home of her own in Cambridge. She suspected that Mrs Vye rather enjoyed, in her own peculiar way, being part of the 'big house' and therefore a person of consequence, whatever its disadvantages.

"I think you are altogether too particular about Creek End," she said sharply. "It's a beautiful old place, and what it lacks in modern conveniences, it makes up for in character. As for being cold, this room is delightfully cosy, and so are the other west wing rooms, which are all you need with only two of you staying here. The old hall and the long drawing-room might well be draughty at present, but what need have you of them? And as for being half-empty, your brother told me himself that he was waiting until he could find furnishings that would fit the character of the place, which must be why he went to this sale in Hertfordshire."

"You know nothing of the matter," Mrs Vye snapped. "He had no right to go gallivanting off like that, when he knows I dislike being alone. He should have more consideration for me."

Sophy's patience was beginning to wear thin. She considered Mrs Vye fortunate in having both a husband and a home of her own and a brother with whom she could stay for as long as she pleased.

"In my experience," she said, "no good ever comes of trying to chain a man to your side. It only breeds resentment. My late husband often went off for days at a time without even telling me where he was going, but I knew he would always come back, always," her words came out disjointedly as she thought of how he returned from his last fateful journey, "because however thoughtless he may have seemed at times, he really loved me."

Captain Philip Ellard, R.N., unwillingly retired, was in the very best of spirits that morning, in spite of the fact that the top of his head felt as if it had been blown off, and his mouth tasted of bilgewater. He rode into the stableyard at Creek End, noting as he did so that everything was in order: the yard swept, the stables tidy, the gig newly polished. John Jennings was a reliable man, not given to slacking when there was nobody directly supervising him. If fortune was kind and things kept going as well as they had been lately, John might well attain his ambition by next year and find himself in charge of a neat carriage and pair, with a couple of grooms to do the dirty work. Philip handed over his horse, made one or two enquiries about what had been happening during his absence, and went across to the house, meaning to go in by the garden room. His attention was caught, however, by the sound of childish laughter coming from the direction of the kitchens, and he decided instead to find out its source.

An unusual sight met his eyes as he pushed open the door. The cook and the kitchenmaid were both standing precariously on chairs, the one gasping, "Where? Where?" and the other squeaking in alarm, whilst Jamie Hanson was pointing to something on the floor and shouting, "There it is! I saw it!" and his brother was cackling with uncontrollable glee. The noise reverberated round his aching head.

"What the devil's going on here?" he demanded, noticing as he did so the fifth member of the scene. Lucy Franklin was quietly taking it all in with a kind of horrified delight. He thought, that child has Spanish eyes, just like her mother.

Jamie and Johnny Hanson clapped hands over their mouths and exchanged fearful glances. The women, looking distinctly sheepish at having been caught in such a ridiculous position, climbed hastily down and stood smoothing their skirts and looking round apprehensively. For a moment nobody spoke. Philip restrained an impulse to laugh. Laughing was to painful.

"Is this some new kind of game,

Cook?" he enquired blandly.

"Oh no, sir, certainly not, sir. It was a mouse, sir, ran right across the floor, it did," the cook assured him, her three chins wobbling in corroboration. The kitchenmaid nodded vigorously, but from the Hanson boys there came a sound of strangled snorting.

"You two saw it as well, did you? And what colour was it? Green?"

The Hansons shook their heads, unwilling to admit that the mouse was sheer fabrication, but afraid of the awful consequences of telling lies.

"Do you know what happens to little boys who play nasty tricks on kind people?" Philip asked them.

The boys nodded. They knew well enough, their father was for ever telling them.

"Well?"

"They make Jesus very, very sad," said Jamie solemnly.

"And they get sent to bed wiv not any supper," added the more practically-minded Johnny.

"Exactly," agreed Philip, trying hard not to laugh. He recalled the many times he and his brother had been hauled up before authority to answer for some misdeed. Then they had been threatened with hellfire, or Bonaparte, or worst of all, the Headless Horseman. They lived in mortal fear of the Headless Horseman. "And if they do it again after they've been warned, the pirates come and take them away," he added, for good measure.

Jamie and Johnny looked suitably impressed. Philip turned to Lucy, asking her if she liked Creek End, and whether it was her mama, or Mrs Hanson, or both who had brought the children here. He was pleased to learn that Mrs Franklin alone had come.

There was still the cook's ruffled dignity to soothe. She was quite clearly put out by her master witnessing her foolish behaviour.

"Would you send me up some of your excellent coffee?" he asked. "I haven't tasted anything remotely drinkable whilst I was away. You're the only person who understands how I like it."

The woman beamed and sent the kitchenmaid scurrying for water, and leaving the kitchen in a somewhat calmer state than that in which he had found it, Philip walked through the labyrinth of pantries and stillrooms and storerooms towards the old hall. The place needed children running about to bring it to life. It was ridiculously uneconomic to run a large house just for himself, or at the most, Charlotte as well. And he might have had a whole string of them by now, if it were not for Louise the Unfaithful. But it was no use dwelling on that old tale — Louise would have hated it out here at Creek End.

Entering the corridor leading to the Elizabethan part of the house, he heard his sister's voice, peevish as usual, and Mrs Franklin's reply, slightly sharpened with exasperation, and wondered how it was that Charlotte managed to annoy the most even-tempered of people. As he approached the room in which they were sitting, he almost decided to retreat to the study and seek the undemanding company of his dogs, when Mrs Franklin's words stopped him in his tracks.

"In my experience, no good ever comes

of trying to chain a man to your side. It only breeds resentment. My late husband often used to go off for days at a time without even telling me where he was going, but I knew he would always come back — " her voice shook and she stopped, recovered herself and went on, " — because however thoughtless he might have seemed at times, he really loved me."

Philip walked into the awkward silence, deliberately cheerful.

"Behold, the wanderer returns! Good morning to you both, I trust I am not interrupting a private tête-à-tête?"

Charlotte jumped guiltily, and rushed to the attack to cover her embarrassment.

"Philip! How long have you been standing there? And what is the reason for your creeping in this way, unannounced?"

"I hope you are well, Charlotte?" he said smoothly. "And is everything all right here? Creek End has not fallen down since I left, I see." Receiving only an inarticulate mutter as a reply, he went on, "I hardly need to be announced in my own house, I think. But don't worry, I have not been eavesdropping on your conversation, I have only just arrived." He sat down on the chair next to Sophy's, wanting to repair in some way the damage done by his sister's unhappy knack of upsetting visitors. He launched out on the subject he thought might lie closest to her heart. "I see your little daughter has brought her admirers with her. Perhaps after a few more months of her good influence, the Hanson brats might grow to resemble human beings rather than wild animals."

"I rather think the influence is in the other direction," Sophy admitted, with a ghost of a smile.

"For your sake, I hope not," Philip said, and related the tale of the non-existent mouse.

His efforts were rewarded with an exclamation of mingled amusement and exasperation from Sophy.

"Oh, they are terrible! I particularly told them to behave themselves. Now I shall have to give them a scolding." And, pulling herself together and making an effort to keep the conversation on safe lines, she asked, "Did you have a successful journey, Captain Ellard?"

"Extremely successful, I thank you. I shall soon have Creek End as well fitted out as Tracey Manor. I have bought a magnificent carved oak table and thirty matching chairs for the old hall, and two beds, an inlaid cabinet and half a library of books. There was plenty more I would have liked, most especially a beautiful tapestry that would have set off the old hall to perfection, but the bidding was very keen . . ."

He broke off as three ecstatic dogs, two pointers and a retriever, came bounding into the room and flung themselves joyfully upon him, followed by the butler with the coffee and the day's post. He calmed the dogs, sorted swiftly through the letters, putting one in his pocket and leaving the rest on a table, and took up a cup with a sigh of satisfaction.

"'Black as hell, strong as death and sweet as love!' Thank God for a cook who can make decent coffee," he commented.

"'Coffee, which makes the politician wise, And see through all things with his half-shut eyes,'" Sophy returned, to his surprise.

"So, Mrs Franklin, the renown Shadow is not the only person hereabouts who can throw off an apt quotation," he said. "Who wrote that? I don't recognise it."

"Alexander Pope. His work is a very useful source of well-turned lines. I used to note them down, in the days when I had nothing better to do, and produce them to astound my elders and betters with my wit and learning. My mother disapproved, she said that gentlemen were not attracted to clever young ladies, and that in my case it was not even genuine intelligence, but a thin veneer of other people's wisdom, which was worse. I expect she was right, but at least it did lead me to enjoy reading, which has been very useful to me over the years."

"And what do you enjoy reading most?" Philip asked, "No, let me guess — I think it is the great Lord Bryon."

"How did you know?"

He could have said that it was a fairly safe hazard, since women who never normally cast their eyes over anything more taxing than a dressmaker's bill sighed over the tortured fates of Childe Harold and The Corsair and the Bride of Abydos. But this was not the case with Mrs Franklin. Instead, he replied,

"It does not require any extraordinary perception on my part, I'm afraid. I merely noticed that you had a full set of his works on your shelves at Thyme Cottage."

At this juncture, Charlotte broke in, her voice stiff with disapproval.

"I hardly think that person is a fit subject of conversation amongst ladies," she said repressively, and to make sure that she carried her point, asked her brother if the roads had been very bad, that he had been delayed on his return.

Philip reflected that the trouble with Charlotte was that she always expected the worst of one. Indeed, she would almost have been disappointed if he could have told her that a genuine accident had stopped him from coming back on the day he had specified.

"Not at all bad, Charlotte, for I travelled almost entirely by turnpike," he said, confirming what she knew already. "The reason for my being a day later than expected is just the one that you suspect me of: namely, that I happened to run into some old friends, and naturally had to crack a few bottles whilst reminiscing over old times. If I have put you out at all, I apologise, but you need not scold me, for I have already been punished enough in having one devil of a thick head this morning."

His sister sniffed, her thin mouth pursed in indignation, but before she could speak, Mrs Franklin surprised him for the second time.

"What you need," she advised, "is the juice of two oranges and one lemon mixed with a tablespoonful of honey."

"That sound a degree or so less revolting than most other remedies I've tried," he said. "The question is, does it work?"

"My late husband used to call it the sixty-minute life-saver."

"In that case, I shall most certainly try it," Philip said, reaching for the bell-pull.

He listened with half an ear as his sister talked with gloomy relish of how dreadful the weather had been during his absence, managing to imply that the downpour had somehow been his fault, and wondered momentarily why he did not throw out a hint or two about other members of the family who might benefit from her staying with them for a month or so. But if Charlotte were to depart, Mrs Franklin would be unable to visit Creek End, and that would be a loss. A considerable loss. He studied her profile as she bent over the retriever, stroking its head, and was visited by sudden inspiration.

"Brandy has taken to you," he said, as soon as there was a pause in his sister's list of complaints.

"He's a lovely animal," Sophy replied, not looking up.

"Do you like dogs? I have a litter of spaniels I want to find good homes for and they make splendid pets. They are about eight weeks now, old enough to be weaned. Would you take one off my hands?"

"I had thought of getting a cat. I don't know much about keeping dogs."

Philip smiled to himself. It was just as he had hoped.

"A dog makes a much better companion," he said persuasively. "They keep you company when you wish to stay in and are a ready-made excuse for a walk if you feel like going out."

"Very well then, a spaniel it shall be, and thank you," Sophy said, raising her head to look back at him. "But you will have to advise me as to how I should train it properly."

"I shall be delighted to," he assured her, with complete honesty.

He listened with admiration as she speedily extracted herself from Charlotte without giving the appearance of haste, even eliciting a fairly pressing invitation to come again whenever she was able. Then they made their way out to the stables, where the puppies were housed, collecting the children on the way. Lucy was thrilled to learn that she could choose one to keep, and the boys were loud in their disappointment at not being allowed to take one home as well.

"There are going to be some almighty battles of will at the parsonage over this," Sophy predicted.

To distract their attention, Philip showed them his horses, letting them pat his raking black hunter, the sturdy bay used to pull the gig, and the only draught animal not out working on the farmland, a huge Suffolk punch mare due to foal in the spring. But though they admired the horses, nothing could keep them from playing with the puppies, and all three children rolled around in the straw, squealing with delight as the animals clambered over them and licked their hands and faces.

"We've not had any pets before," Sophy said, watching them play. "It was impossible, really, moving about from one set of lodgings to another all the time. The longest we ever stayed in one place was five months, one winter in Cheltenham. It was a terrible set of rooms, but at least I was able to make a few friends before we moved on again."

Philip's opinion of the late Jeremy Franklin, which had never been very high, sank several notches lower. Unsuccessful adventurers, he decided, had no business to get married, unless it was to heiresses, or to women of their own type, who could give as good as they got.

"It sounds as if it was an unsettled kind of existence," he commented. And, hazarding a cautious probe, continued, "I suppose it must be quite a pleasant change to be able to plan ahead now, and make a permanent home?"

The moment the words left his lips he knew he had said the wrong thing. Sophy turned away from the frolicking dogs and children and fell to stroking the mare's nose with apparent all-consuming interest. Philip followed, anxious to make amends but not at all sure, at that precise moment, how he was going to do it. And while he hesitated, Sophy spoke, her voice muffled against the horse's lowered head.

"You make the same mistake as everybody else. They were all against us, my mother, my aunts, all the busybodies. They all said he was a ne'er-do-well and sure to bring me sorrow, and they were all wrong!"

Philip was taken aback by this fierce loyalty, particularly as he knew it to be sadly misplaced. For though he had no especial affection for his cousin, neither had he any reason to doubt his word as to the cause of the ill-fated duel. Indeed, it was a wonder that Jeremy Franklin had not met with a similar end any earlier in his brief life. But shaking Sophy's faith in her late husband was not going to help her at all, even if she were to believe him, and it would almost certainly turn her against him.

"I'm sorry," he said "I was in no position to make any judgement . . . "

There was no reply from Sophy. And, guessing that he had very little to lose by now, he continued tentatively, "I believe it can be helpful, sometimes, to talk to a comparative stranger, so if I can be of any service to you . . . "

For a moment he thought she was going to tell him to go away, but instead she muttered disjointedly, "You're very kind, but — you wouldn't — couldn't understand."

"My pardon, but I do understand, far better than you realise."

Sophy looked at him at last, disbelief in her eyes, as her fingers compulsively twisted and retwisted a strand of chestnut-mane. For the briefest second, Philip wondered what possible good it would do to resurrect Louise now, but it was too late to change tack.

"I was married too, you know. She — died a couple of years ago, not long before I came here."

Sophy said, "Oh, I am sorry — I had no idea — "

"No, I don't generally talk about it." Now that he had started, however, he went on with the rest of the story. "It all ended a long time before that, though. It wasn't much of a life for her, I suppose, left to spend the winter in Deal whilst I was at sea for months on end. When I came back to collect her, with the prospect of a good spell of shore leave, she had gone — ran off with a militia ensign. Preferred a red coat to a blue, I suppose."

"But that's terrible!" Sophy was appalled. Her own troubles paled in the face of such infidelity. At least Jeremy had always come back. "Did — did you ever find them?" she asked.

"No. I tried, but they went to ground in London somewhere. It's easy enough to disappear without trace in the metropolis. I never heard of her again — until two years ago, that is, when I received a letter through the Admiralty from a clergyman in Harrogate telling me she had died. But — and this is the sum of my wisdom on the subject, for what it's worth — one does get over these things, however impossible it may seem at the time. It's past history now; I can think of her, when I remember her at all, with complete indifference." And that, at long last, was true. Louise was consigned to the nebulous realm of semi-oblivion.

It was too soon yet for Jeremy Franklin to travel the same way, but to know that amongst her new-found friends there was one at least who understood her feelings made Sophy feel lighter of heart than she had done for many a month. She was saved from having to explain this by an outbreak of squabbling in the end loose-box.

"Those children!" she exclaimed, with more relief than annoyance, and hurried to quell the riot.

She pulled the boys apart and propelled them into the stableyard, then returned to pick up the chosen puppy. It looked up at her, a round bundle of black and grey hair, with anxious brown eyes under a high domed forehead.

136

"I know," Sophy said, struck with inspiration, "I shall call him 'Shadow'."

And to prove that she was making an effort to forget, she related to Philip the latest tale of the smuggler's exploits.

4

SPRING crept across the face of the countryside, warming the cold clay soil and spreading a veil of fresh green over trees and fields and saltings. •In the woods and spinneys, celandine and wood anemones pushed their way up through the carpet of last year's leaves, followed by primroses and violets, a bright deceptive camouflage in the coverts of Tracey Manor for the vicious man-traps that the keepers set for the marauding poachers. The yearly tasks of ploughing and sowing occupied the lengthening daylight hours, and at Creek End, work was started on draining the waterlogged meadows nearest the sea-wall.

At Thyme Cottage, Sophy employed Susannah and Polly's father, Josh, in clearing and digging her garden, and sowing flower and vegetable seeds that she had, by charm and flattery, managed to obtain from the ancient and crabbed

138

head gardener at Tracey Manor. The hens that had been allowed to go broody fussed over families of chicks, another fowl-run was built to accommodate half a dozen young turkeys and two piglets occupied the sty. Sophy looked forward with some satisfaction to being able to supply the greater part of her own food by the autumn. Shadow the spaniel grew almost visibly, bursting with youthful energy and always anxious to please. Of his human namesake, however, nothing was heard.

"Which don't mean that the rogue ain't running in cargoes as often as ever, it's just that he ain't been caught," Sir Harry pointed out in disgust. "Those revenue men are about as much use as a hound with no nose."

As the evenings grew lighter, Sophy fell into the habit of taking Shadow out for an hour or two after Lucy was in bed, her favourite walk being down to the staithe and along the sea-wall, the high grass-grown bank between the saltings and the meadows, that protected the lower ground from flooding. And quite often she would meet Philip Ellard walking along from Creek End, and find herself pitched into a heated debate on anything from poetry to politics. Some of his views she found so extreme that she suspected him of exaggerating for the sake of argument, as she knew he did with Sir Harry, but when challenged on this point, he always insisted that his was the only stand an intelligent and right-thinking person would possible take. Sophy began to study the reports and editorials of the newspapers for verbal ammunition, instead of just glancing through the society columns, and when she returned home, she would sit down to her sewing with her mind still working out reasonable lines of argument, instead of merely brooding over the day's small domestic details or dwelling on the past.

It did not occur to her that this was exactly what Philip intended, nor that he turned down a good many invitations in order to walk out on the chance that he might meet her. He was a sought-after guest in many houses that ignored Sophy's existence: careful parents worked out the possible income from Creek End and pushed their daughters in his direction. And, besides that, he was acknowledged as being good company, able to enliven the dullest evening, whilst his lunatic ideas on reform were tolerated in view of the fact that he not only listened to but acted upon advice on practical matters.

One evening, as she prepared to go out, Sophy, mentioned to Susannah that she might be rather later than usual, as she planned to walk right along the sea-wall as far as the place called Dead Man's Point, which was beyond Creek End.

"I want to take a look at the place," she said. "I'm sure I saw lights there last night. I was looking out of my chamber window just before going to bed and there seemed to be a flashing red light, just as if someone were making a signal."

Susannah's eyes widened in horror at the suggestion.

"Oh ma'am!" she exclaimed. "I wouldn't go near it, not nearer than half a mile, I wouldn't, not if you was to give me a hundred pounds."

But Sophy was not to be so easily frightened.

141

"Why, what superstitious nonsense is this, Susannah?" she asked. "I'm sure I have nothing to fear. It's a lonely spot, but no different from any other part of the marshes."

"But it *is* different ma'am, begging your pardon," Susannah insisted. "'Tis haunted. If you see the lights again, ma'am, you must close the curtains quick and ask the good Lord to protect you. 'Tis the Ghost Ship, ma'am, that's what it is."

Sophy laughed out loud.

"The Ghost Ship? For shame, Susannah! You don't believe tales of the supernatural, do you? There is certain to be a perfectly simple explanation for the lights, and I intend to find out what it is."

"Oh really, ma'am, it ain't safe." Susannah's voice rose to an agitated squeak. In her anxiety to show just how serious she was, she even went so far as to lay hold of Sophy's arm. "There's a curse on the place, ma'am. They say there was a ship washed ashore there in a great storm one winter, years and years ago, and after it was over, people from Silver Creek went out to see what was left of the wreck. When they got there, they found a rich cargo, and just one man on board, all the rest had been washed overboard and drowned, and he was more dead than alive. Anyway, this man offered them a share in the goods if they would but take him in till he was recovered, but the men from the village were afraid that once the sailor was well he'd send to the ship's owner and they'd not get a penny of the cargo, so they knocked him down and started to carry the stuff away . . . " Susannah paused to see what reaction her tale was gaining, then continued in an awed whisper, " . . . and with his dying breath, the sailor cursed them and theirs. And inside of a twelve-month, all the men who stole the cargo were dead, and their families in want. And sometimes, when the night is stormy, the ship sails on to the Point again, glowing with an unearthly light . . . "

To Susannah's dismay, her mistress was not the least impressed with this dramatic story.

"Superstitious nonsense," Sophy said firmly, disengaging the maid's fingers from her arm. "I wonder at you,

Susannah, believing such far-fetched tales. I took you for a sensible girl. Now, mind you make up the fires while I'm out, and listen for Miss Lucy."

And with that, she whistled to Shadow and set out for the sea-wall.

Before she was even halfway to Dead Man's Point, however, she was intercepted by Philip Ellard, and as he was going into the village to speak to James Hanson, Sophy turned and walked back with him.

"Did you know that you have supernatural occurrences on your land?" she asked, and, treating the whole matter as a joke, told him of Susannah's fears for her safety.

To her surprise, Philip said, "She was right, it's not a place to go to alone, if at all. I should keep away, if I were you."

"You don't give credence to this superstitious vapouring, surely?" Sophy asked incredulously. "One might expect it of a maidservant, but not of you."

"It's easy enough to pour scorn," Philip replied, "but I've seen enough inexplicable events to keep an open mind on the subject, at the very least."

Into Sophy's thoughts a scrap of half-forgotten gossip floated — 'he comes from somewhere down in the Rochford Hundred, witch country, you know.'

Philip, looking at her sceptical expression, thought of the headless Horseman and old Mother Pettigrew and her cure for warts. She would never believe it, not sensible Mrs Franklin. Neither did he now, though as a child he would have endured any punishment rather than cross Mother Pettigrew's threshold. Superstition was a useful tool at times.

"There was a witch in my home village," he told her.

As he expected, Sophy scoffed at such a ridiculous assertion, and he produced a whole string of examples of Mother Pettigrew's powers for her to attempt to explain away. They were back at the gate of Thyme Cottage before he even had the opportunity to mention the Headless Horseman. As a parting shot, he told her,

"They used to say she kept a skull with living eyes in the corner of her kitchen."

"Ghoul!" laughed Sophy, unmoved.

"You ought to be ashamed of yourself, trying to frighten me with outlandish fables!"

But when, about a week later, she saw the lights flashing at Dead Man's Point, although she did not go so far as to say a prayer for protection, she was not quite confident enough to venture out looking for a rational cause the next day.

Easter brought a flurry of baking and brewing and roasting in preparation for the festival, and groups of children and young people went the rounds of the parish, knocking at doors and singing the 'pace-egging' song for rewards of eggs and ale and hot-cross-buns. Lucy listened with uncritical approval, and threw a tantrum when told that she could not join the singers, even when she was older. She no longer needed a mid-morning rest, and could hold her own with the Hansons in their rowdy games of hunting and tag and pirates. It was Lucy who invented their most popular game, Walking the Plank, which involved pirates, sharks and a victim, and appeared to outsiders to consist mainly of shrieking and pushing. Sophy, sorting through her daughter's summer clothes, found that she had outgrown nearly all of them. She gave an armful of frocks and boots and petticoats to Polly for her ragged brood, and thought about making an expedition into Maldon to buy a selection of cottons and cambrics.

When she mentioned this to the younger Nugents, she found herself co-opted into Anna-Maria's plans.

"You must come with us when we go to Colchester next week. I'm sure that if I mention it to Mama she would be pleased to take you up, and there's plenty of room in our coach, which is the only thing to be said in its favour, the lumbering old-fashioned thing! Mama is going to buy me some new gowns for the summer, but you know what her taste is like — she would have me wearing dreadful dowdy things twenty years out of date if she could! But she will listen to you, Mrs Franklin, she respects your opinion, she says you are a very sensible lady. So you will come, will you not? I shall be absolutely lost if you do not."

"Put like that," smiled Sophy, "how can I refuse? Indeed, I shall be very grateful for the opportunity."

"Darling Mrs Franklin! I knew I could rely on you! They do say that the Maceboroughs might be coming down this summer, and just think how dreadful it would be if I only had horrid old provincial-looking gowns to wear!"

And Sophy, recalling that the Earl and Countess of Maceborough had two sons of marriageable age, was not hard-put to guess why Anna-Maria would wish to look her best.

The trip to Colchester was a success for all concerned. Sophy and Anna-Maria evolved a method of getting round Lady Isobel's dislike of London modes, which she regarded as being decadent in the extreme. Anna-Maria chose several items that she liked, only to have them condemned by her mother, who turned to Sophy for support. Sophy agreed absolutely over one or two of the fabrics or bonnets or trimmings concerned, convincing Lady Isobel of her sense and good taste, then said that the remaining items of Anna-Maria's choice were, however, quite unexceptional and entirely suitable for a young girl. And

Lady Isobel found herself manoeuvred into buying things she would never otherwise have countenanced. She was not herself given to subtlety, invariably meeting any problems with a head-on attack, so it did not occur to her that her obedient daughter and the level-headed Mrs Franklin were leading her by the nose.

Sophy found the shops of Colchester a great temptation after three months of relying on the chandler's stores at Tracey Nugent. She had meant to buy only practical items, new curtains and fabric for Lucy's summer wear, but while helping with Anna-Maria's wardrobe, she found herself considering her own limited and unbecoming collection of clothes. Encouraged by Anna-Maria, she bought a very pretty bonnet, that only needed re-trimming with sober black ribands to make it suitable to go visiting in. And having made the first step, she boldly chose fabrics for two new gowns, and took them to the Nugents' dressmaker to be made up. As she paid for her purchases, she reflected that it was very pleasant to be able to spend out at the beginning of the quarter without worrying as to whether the money might be needed for repaying gaming debts. The income that she could never stretch far enough before now supported her with comfort.

"How soon can one of the evening gowns be finished?" Anna-Maria demanded of the dressmaker, as her measurements were taken and noted down. "Could you do it by next week? I would very much be obliged to you if you could."

"Next week?" her mother questioned. "Why so soon? That would mean coming here again for a fitting, and your father will not like to send the coach out twice in less than a sennight."

"Oh please, Mama!" Anna-Maria begged. "Surely you cannot have forgotten? We are to dine at Creek End on Wednesday of next week, and Captain Ellard promised to bring Zacchy the Fiddler so that we might dance in the old hall. I must have a new gown for then!"

"Dancing, dancing! That's all you think about, girl. Your mind runs too much upon frivolity. Do you never think of aught else?"

"Of course I do, Mama, but it's so dull in our neighbourhood, one has to make the best of every small entertainment." She turned to Sophy for support. "You understand, do you not, Mrs Franklin?"

"Oh yes, I understand," Sophy smiled. After all, she was but seven years older than Anna-Maria. Twenty-four, a young woman still, not a middle-aged matron. Sophy looked critically at herself in the dressmaker's pier-glass, and was well satisfied with the reflection that gazed back at her. Lucy was not the only one for whom three months of country air had worked wonders. Sophy, too, had lost the scarecrow look and regained the dark charm that used to draw admiring glances in the days when she and Jeremy gave large parties for the fringes of fashionable society. She smiled at the attractive figure in the glass and silently agreed with Anna-Maria that a little excitement to liven the predictable daily round of life at Silver Creek would indeed be welcome. And as she gave instructions to the dressmaker for a gown of the latest mode, she thought how fortunate it was that black suited her, and wondered why she had not gone to the trouble of buying some becoming clothes earlier.

Sophy was invited to dine at Tracey Manor on returning from Colchester, and found when they arrived that the excitement she had wished for was in the air, though not in the form she had anticipated.

"There's trouble brewing over at Kingschurch," Sir Harry informed them, after making a pretence of listening to his wife's and daughter's accounts of the day's expedition.

"Trouble? What sort of trouble?" Lady Isobel demanded. "Not riots again, I hope? The mob at Kingschurch were amongst the first to rise in 'sixteen, if I remember rightly."

"So they were, so they were," Sir Harry agreed, "and it looks like breaking out again. There's a dangerous unruly element in that place, always ready to stir up the law-abiding members of the community and make trouble for their masters. But their days are numbered now. The ringleaders have been accused of forming a combination, and if they're found guilty, that's the last we'll hear of them." He paused and looked round the table to lend emphasis to his pronouncement. "Transportation! That's the way to deal with these dangerous malcontents. Throw them out, like the rotten apples they are, before they contaminate the rest of the crop."

Lady Isobel agreed wholeheartedly, and Anna-Maria nodded dutifully and murmured, "Yes, indeed." George looked at Sophy with gleeful anticipation, but she failed to notice, being engaged in marshalling her thoughts. Philip Ellard had mentioned something about the situation at Kingschurch, but she was not entirely sure of her facts.

"Am I not right in thinking that there is a great deal of unemployment in the parish?" she asked. "Two of the largest farms failed in 'sixteen, did they not, putting many of the villagers out of work, and new tenants have not yet been found?"

"Quite so," Sir Harry agreed warily. "But attempting to combine against the masters won't make even half a day's work for a one-armed half-wit. It's just an excuse for fermenting trouble and discontent."

"But surely the trouble and discontent are caused by the starvation wages," Sophy ventured, unconsciously using Philip Ellard's rhetoric. "Because of the lack of jobs, the employers can pay as little as they choose, as anyone not willing to work for a pittance can easily be replaced by somebody a degree more desperate."

Sir Harry, far from regarding this as a point against his philosophy, took it as being in his favour.

"That is the way of the world, Mrs Franklin," he said. "Just as it should be. How else are we to keep the lower orders in their place? If this combination madness is allowed to get out of hand, we'll find the rabble dictating terms to us, and where will that lead us? Anarchy and revolution! The present system serves us very well, and the labourers don't suffer by it. If they can't feed themselves on their wages, they can always apply to the parish for relief. Nobody ever starves."

"But that is iniquitous!" Sophy cried. "It leaves them with no choice, and no pride . . . " she trailed off, losing the thread of her argument, and wishing that Philip Ellard were there to pick up the point and express it with more force. But Philip had gone away three days ago and was not expected back until the end of the week. As if reading her mind, George said,

"I'd like to hear our Captain Ellard's view. I warrant he'd have a thing or two to say."

And Sophy, seeing him seething with barely suppressed delight at the gathering dispute, felt decidedly annoyed. George had no fixed opinions at all on the matter. His loyalties were probably with the employers, but he was prepared to take any stand as long as it stirred up dissent against his father. She thought fleetingly that Sir Harry had better stop worrying about malcontents in parishes ten miles distant and take steps to deal with the one he himself had bred.

"Aye, and none of it containing a grain of sense," Sir Harry retorted. "Good thing the young hothead's not here, or he'd be over at Kingschurch inciting the men to riot, like as not. Where is it he's gone, anyhow? Bath, was it?"

"Not Bath, Sir Harry, Cheltenham," his wife corrected him. "He's gone to a friend's wedding."

Sir Harry chuckled. "Wedding, was it? That'll keep him out of mischief. By the time he gets back it will all be over, the ringleaders will be safe in Chelmsford gaol, waiting trial."

"That won't stop him instructing a lawyer for the defence. What do you think, Mrs Franklin? Should the sedition-members plead Not Guilty?" George persisted.

But Sophy was determined to let him know that she at least saw through him. "Where do you stand?" she asked him. "What would you do if you were magistrate at Kingschurch? Where do your sympathies lie?"

"With the underdog, naturally," George replied glibly.

"Really? So when you employ somebody, you discuss terms with them until you come to an agreement about wages and conditions that suits both of you?"

George fell straight into the trap.

"Of course not! I set the terms, take it

or leave it. I don't let myself be dictated to by my inferiors . . . " He stopped short, realising that he was repeating almost word for word his father's opinion. Lady Isobel, seeing that her chick was on the losing end, jumped in to change the subject, much to Sophy's chagrin. She thought it would do George a great deal of good to admit that he and father stood together against the forces of change, but was aware that she was in the Nugents' debt for her trip into Colchester and was now a guest in their house. With reluctance, therefore, she did not pursue her point, but took up Lady Isobel's remarks on the wedding.

"It's about time young Ellard found himself a wife," Sir Harry commented. "All very well preaching radical notions when you've only yourself to keep. Just you wait till he's a growing family to support, he'll soon see sense, you mark my words." And he added, significantly, "Very nice little property, Creek End, especially if he buys up a bit more land further east. We could tie up this corner of the county very nicely between us."

"Yes indeed. He's quite a good catch,"

Lady Isobel agreed, "not a great match, but very acceptable."

They both looked at Anna-Maria, who smiled self-consciously and blushed. And for some unaccountable reason, Sophy felt quite out of patience with all of them.

During the next two days, the news grew more alarming. Far from suppressing the unrest, the arrest of the Kingschurch leaders stirred those that remained into outright opposition. With nothing to lose, they gathered in an angry mob and marched on the magistrate's house, only to be turned back at the gates by a determined band of armed retainers. Foiled of their prey, they turned on the most hated farmer in the parish and fired one of his barns. In Tracey Nugent and Silver Creek, the law-abiding citizens trembled lest the trouble should spread through the countryside. Bars and bolts were strengthened and weapons cleaned and made ready. There was talk of the militia being brought in. And in the midst of the growing anxiety, the news that the Shadow had narrowly escaped capture after hand-to-hand fighting with the revenue men went almost unnoticed.

Sophy thought the whole situation had been exaggerated out of all proportion. To listen to Mary Hanson, one might think a revolution had started, instead of a small outbreak of violence ten miles distant! And she was conscious of a feeling almost of disappointment as she reassured Mary that they were not all about to be murdered in their beds. At least a rising would give an opportunity for action, for excitement. And annoyed at herself for harbouring such childish and irresponsible thoughts, she determined to take Shadow for a walk after Lucy was in bed, just to prove how quiet and peaceful the countryside was.

Under the covering shade of the trees at the edge of the Great Wood at Tracey Manor, Philip Ellard kept watch for patrolling gamekeepers. Tracey Manor was the very last place he would have picked for his present adventure, but he had no choice in the matter. The man who lay unconscious by his side was in no fit state to be moved by the longer route round the estate. The light was just beginning to fade now, so the worst of the long wait was over. Another three hours or so and a barge would be waiting for them in the river, ready to spirit the injured man away to safety. That was if his message had got through. There was just a chance that it might not have done, in which case a far more risky alternative plan would have to be put into effect, but with luck that would not be necessary. In the meantime, any poachers misguided enough to chance the well-guarded Tracey preserves might with the approaching evening be preparing to steal into the woods, which meant an increased danger of discovery. Philip lay still, reserving his strength for the arduous task of carrying a heavy man from one spot of cover to the next down to the shore, his senses alert to any sight or sound that might warn him of human presence.

A man marched purposefully along the footpath towards the village, whistling as he went. Probably, Philip guessed, a gardener from the Manor on his way to the Plough and Sail. His dry throat ached at the thought. He would have given a good deal for a drink of water, let alone a tankard of ale. A pair of lovers passed slowly along the path, arms entwined. Nothing to fear from them, they were totally absorbed in each other. Then a solitary female figure climbed over the stile. Philip caught his breath, for even from this distance he recognised her, simply by the way she moved. And sure enough, the dark shape of a dog come bounding after her, circled, and gambolled on ahead. Philip thought of all the occasions when he had walked out with the express view of 'happening' to meet her, only to be disappointed, and now here she was and it was imperative that she should pass by without seeing him. Sophy of all people must not suspect what he was about.

Philip was so engrossed in watching Sophy that he failed to notice that Shadow was questing along the edges of the wood. The dog emerged from the undergrowth with a yelp of recognition, paused to nose curiously at the other man, who stirred and moaned faintly, then greeted Philip with noisy enthusiasm.

"Get away, go on!" Philip hissed forcefully. "Off, you stupid brute!"

But Shadow obstinately refused, and in the middle of the field, Sophy stopped and called to him. The spaniel, used to his two favourite human beings sharing the pleasure of his company on his evening walks, ran a little way towards his mistress, then back again to the wood, looking over his shoulder at intervals to see if Sophy was following him. The injured man moaned again, more loudly this time as he began to regain consciousness, and Philip cursed the day he thought of giving Sophy a dog. Why had he not found a cat for her, as she had suggested? Still he lay without moving in the shadow of the trees. There was yet a good chance that she might continue on her way, and to try to retreat into the wood was an open invitation for the dog to come racing after him.

Sophy tried again to make Shadow come to her, then started towards the spot from which the dog had last emerged, uttering threats of punishment. Philip decided that it was time to make a move. Getting to his feet, he walked forward to met her with the air of one who was out for an evening stroll.

162

"Good evening, Mrs Franklin," he greeted her. "You're a long way off your usual path."

Sophy gasped and stared at him, the start of fear she had felt on first seeing a figure spring out from the shadows turning rapidly into amazement.

"Captain Ellard! What in heaven's name are you doing here?"

"Much the same as you, I should imagine. Were you about to turn for home? I'll walk along with you, if I may."

He began to move away from the wood, but Sophy stood still, taking in his raffish appearance. Under her critical scrutiny, he realised that he must look decidedly dishevelled, for his torn and muddied clothing had been slept in the night before, and on his face was a day's growth of beard and an ugly bruise.

"You look as if you have been to a prize fight, not a wedding." Sophy commented.

"There was a disagreement over the settlement, Philips informed her with the utmost gravity. "Fighting broke out amongst the guests. Terrible affair, I

163

doubt if my unfortunate friend and his bride will ever live it down."

"If you expect me to believe that, you must think me an utter fool," replied Sophy. "But if you had rather not tell me the truth . . . "

"As it so happens, I had much rather not. Shall we go? But as for thinking you a fool, nothing could be further from the truth. I have the greatest respect for your intelligence."

Sophy gave a sceptical smile and to his relief took the arm he offered and began to move towards home. Another minute, and he might have succeeded in getting her away, but just at that moment, the injured man uttered a groan.

"What on earth was that?" Sophy demanded, looking back and straining to hear.

"Nothing — an animal, perhaps," Philip offered hastily, but with little hope of convincing her, for the sound was unmistakably human.

"Nonsense," retorted Sophy, "that was no animal."

She marched resolutely to the spot from whence the noise had come, and found the man lying in the cover of the undergrowth, his head swathed in a makeshift bandage, soaked with congealed blood. She sucked the breath in through her teeth, shocked at the ugly sight. But she did not scream, Philip noted with admiration, or faint, or even demand what had happened. Instead she decided immediately what should be done.

"You must get him to a surgeon as soon as possible," she said sharply. "Whatever are you thinking of, keeping him here?"

"I cannot be certain that either of the local surgeons can be trusted to keep quiet," Philip explained.

"Not even if they were bribed?" Sophy asked.

Philip stared at her incredulously.

"Mrs Franklin, you amaze me! I took you to be a sober, law-abiding lady. But bribery is not the answer. Once you buy someone's silence, you put yourself in their power. I intend to get this fellow away by barge tonight, and he will be taken to a certain ex-ship's surgeon I know of whose own reputation is so shady that he won't dare go to the authorities."

Sophy nodded slowly, still looking at the half-conscious figure, and Philip, acting on the principle that in an emergency, everyone should be given a useful task, hit on an idea that would involve her in the affair without further endangering her position.

"Do you think you could get into Thyme Cottage and out again without being discovered?" he asked.

"Yes, I imagine I could, providing Susannah's still in the kitchen. Why?"

"If you could fetch some medical supplies, a fresh bandage, say, and some kind of ointment, I could patch him up before I take him out to the barge."

This gained Sophy's instant approval.

"Good idea," she said. "I'll go straight away. You had better keep Shadow here, though, for I don't think he can be trusted to wait quietly outside for me while I steal in."

Philip looked at her with alarm, for this was not at all what he had meant.

"There's no question of your coming back here," he said. "That would be far too risky. I shall come with you to the village and wait outside Thyme Cottage with Shadow for you to bring the things out, and then you are going straight back in."

"Nonsense!" retorted Sophy. "I shall be quite safe walking across the fields alone. Everybody knows me, they'll think nothing strange to see me out of an evening. And besides, what do you know about dressing a wound?"

"With respect, a good deal more than you do," Philip replied.

"That," said Sophy calmly, "is where you are wrong. I was in Brussels at the time of Waterloo, and I've seen far worse cases than this fellow."

Philip laughed softly, shaking his head. "You're a most remarkable lady, Mrs Franklin."

"I?" she said, in unfeigned disbelief. "There's nothing remarkable about me, I'm very ordinary. Half of London was in Brussels then, you know."

"Nevertheless — " Philip began, then stopped abruptly and pulled her down onto the ground. "Quiet!" he breathed, and edged cautiously forward to peer through the gathering gloom along the edge of the wood. About a hundred yards away a solid, uncompromising figure with a dog by his side and a long-barrelled shotgun over his arm was making his way towards them. Cursing under his breath, Philip retreated. "Keeper," he explained shortly.

Sophy bit her lip, thinking hard.

"Perhaps if I were to walk out with Shadow, as if nothing untoward was happening?" she whispered.

"No!" Philip was almost startled into raising his voice at this suggestion. "Absolutely not. You stay here, and keep these two from making the slightest sound. I'm going to create a diversion, lead him back into the wood."

And before Sophy could reply, he melted into the shadows under the trees and disappeared.

Left alone with a half-grown dog and a helpless man, Sophy felt the silent wood begin to close in on her. Up till now, events had moved too fast for her to feel any fear, but now the danger of the situation came home to her. The man with the head wound must be one of

168

the Kingschurch rioters and wanted by the law, so anyone caught giving him aid would be counted as an accessory to the crime. Sophy pictured courtrooms, bewigged judges, the stinking, brawling mob in Newgate gaol, Lucy left alone in the world . . . then pulled herself together, telling herself that this was no time to succumb to hysterical imaginings. She closed her hand over Shadow's nose as he started to yelp at a faint rustling he had heard, and shivered in the penetrating chill of the evening. It was growing rapidly darker now, as a bank of raincloud spread across the sky, and Sophy was just wondering if she dared creep forward to see if the keeper was still in the vicinity, when deep in the wood behind her a shot cracked out, tearing apart the veil of silence and reverberating amongst the trees.

Sophy jumped and caught her breath, but had the presence of mind not to cry out, and simultaneously there was a hoarse exclamation quite close to her and a trampling of boots as someone, presumably the keeper, made off in the direction of the shot. The injured man, roused by the sharp noise, began to mutter incoherently, and Sophy tried, with difficulty, to silence him. The seconds dragged by, measured out in heartbeats. From deep inside the wood there were more shouts, and the barking of an excited dog. The answering growl from Shadow was stifled to an ominous rumbling by Sophy's restraining hand.

And then there was a cracking of twigs behind her and Philip reappeared, spattered with fresh mud and breathing heavily.

"Good girl," he approved briefly, and stooping swiftly, raised the injured man and heaved him over his shoulder. "Come on," he whispered, "fast and silent."

They broke out of the cover of the wood, Sophy holding Shadow by the collar, Philip moving in the quick, gliding trot of the heavily-laden, making for the gate in the opposite edge. Sophy ran ahead, held it open for Philip to go through and caught up with him again as he laid his burden down under the protection of the thick, spreading hedgerow. The man groaned in protest, but Philip, laughing as he gasped for breath, was short on sympathy.

"Hold together," he said cheerfully, "we've seen worse on the old *Termagant*."

Comprehension dawned on Sophy.

"Was he one of your tars?" she asked, kneeling beside him on the dew-soaked grass.

"Yes — good old *Termagant*, my first and only command. Used to wallow like a cow in a following sea."

Sophy considered this piece of information.

"So you had to help him out of trouble," she said. "But all the same, it was very foolhardy to get yourself entangled with a wanted man."

"Extremely foolhardy, sensible Mrs Franklin," Philip agreed disarmingly. "But, you see, the chance of a little action was irresistible."

"I have wondered, occasionally, whether you find it dull here after life at sea, but obviously my concern was wasted," she said dryly.

"I keep myself amused," Philip smiled. "But the last thing I expected was an accomplice. Come, we must get you home at once."

He explained to the man that he would return shortly, then offered his arm to Sophy with exaggerated ceremony.

"Mrs Franklin," he said, in the mincing accents of high society, "might I have the honour of escorting you to your door?"

Sophy was forced to smile. The contrast between his manner and his appearance made it impossible to keep a straight face.

"Very well," she agreed, "but I refuse to become part of any more 'diversions'."

To her chagrin, Sophy could wring no further information about his activities during the past few days from Philip. Clever surmises and roundabout questions were firmly diverted, and when at last she resorted to outright interrogation, she was told that the less she knew, the better, for her own safety. And with this she had to be satisfied.

"Never mind about the bandages," Philip said, as they reached the back gate of Thyme Cottage. "You have done enough on my behalf for one evening."

But Sophy, when she undertook a task, believed in doing it properly.

"Nonsense," she said briskly. "That

man needs some attention if he is to survive the journey to this sawbones you are sending him to. Just hold Shadow for me, I shan't be more than five minutes."

With which she slipped through the gate and trod silently down the garden. A candle was burning in the uncurtained kitchen, revealing Susannah employed in stitching herself a new cap to show off at church next Sunday. Faintly through the closed window came the sound of a sentimental song. All was well there, Sophy noted. Susannah would be less likely to notice any unusual sound if she was singing. She unlatched the French windows leading into the back parlour and stepped indoors, conscious of a quickened heartbeat and a stirring of pleasurable excitement. She made her way cautiously across the room, avoiding with ease the familiar obstacles, and reached the narrow hall. Here she hesitated for a moment, for Susannah seemed to be moving around in the kitchen.

Realising that she might be about to make up the fires, Sophy hurried for the stairs, taking care not to tread on the steps that creaked. On the landing it was completely dark, and she had to feel her way into her chamber. Once there, she swiftly gathered together some linen strips that had been torn from an old sheet, the pot of ointment used for Lucy's frequent cuts and grazes and a cloth wrung out in the ewer on the washstand, and tied them up in an old scarf. She had just opened the door again to make her way back downstairs when footsteps in the hall froze her. To her horror, Susannah did not go into the parlour, as she expected, but began to mount the stairs. Quick as thought, Sophy darted into the nursery. Lucy was visible only as a darker hump against the shadows, and in the stillness of the room, Sophy's straining ears could just make out the soft rise and fall of her breathing. Sophy waited, statue-like, for Susannah to pass by on her way up to her attic room. But Susannah did no such thing. She softly opened the nursery door, and went over to the bed to study Lucy's sleeping form. Sophy, flattened against the wall behind the door, held her breath and realised that Susannah must have heard movements above and thought that Lucy was restless. For once, she fervently wished that Susannah was not quite so conscientious.

Lucy sighed and turned over as the candlelight touched her eyelids, and Susannah, satisfied that she was all right, muttered, "Funny" and crept back to the landing, passing within inches of where Sophy was standing as she shut the door behind her. Letting out a long sigh of relief, Sophy waited for her to go down again, and when she heard the unmistakable clink of tongs and poker, deemed it safe to slip out. In the hall, though, she changed her mind. There was just time, she decided, to get into the kitchen before Susannah finished making up the fire.

She took a knife out of the drawer, trod swiftly across to the pantry and groped inside its cool depths for the plum cake that she knew stood on one of the shelves. She hacked off a generous slice of that and added a large portion of pigeon pie for good measure. Next she snatched up a jug filled it hurriedly from the water keg, and, clutching her illicit haul, escaped through the back door and dashed triumphantly up the path. She knew now why Philip had been laughing when he returned from creating his diversion in the woods: a frisson of danger added an edge of excitement to life. For the first time in months she was really alive, using all her faculties to their fullest extent. Feeling absurdly pleased with herself, she presented her gifts to Philip.

"Food as well! And water! You think of everything. How can I thank you enough?" Philip asked. "I drag you into danger and you repay me thus."

"Pray, don't concern yourself," said sensible Mrs Franklin, respectable widow, indispensable prop to Mary Hanson, valued friend of Lady Isobel and Anna-Maria's good angel, "I enjoyed it. You can hide the jug under the hedge where you left your lame duck; I'll retrieve it in the morning."

Philip took her hand and kissed it.

"Mrs Franklin, you're a friend in a million," he said, and made off into the night.

5

IT was unusually quiet at the parsonage that morning. Jamie Hanson, hands in pockets, wandered round the house looking for something to do. Cook had already smacked his hands and chased him out of the kitchen when she found him dipping his fingers into the cake mixture, and Mama was upstairs in the nursery feeding Baby, so it was no use going up there. He paused outside the study door, listening to the murmur of voices from within. Papa was in there with Mr Nugent — George. Jamie grinned. "Yoo-hoo, George," he sang softly, "bet you can't do this!" In the middle of the corridor, he did his best trick, standing on his head for a count of twenty. But even if Mr Nugen could have seen him, he would not have been impressed. However hard Jamie tried to scrape a friendship, Mr Nugent just brushed him off. Not like Captain Ellard. Captain Ellard said, 'Bravo!' when he stood on his head, and told him stories about pirates. Jamie gave the door of the study a good kick, to give vent to his feelings, and dashed off into the garden.

Under the apple trees, Jemima the nursemaid was playing 'Pat-a-cake' with the little ones.

"Come on, Jamie," she called to him. "Come and play with us."

Jamie made a face.

"That's a baby game," he sneered.

Jemima tried to persuade him that it was not, but he trotted off without bothering to listen. She was silly, anyway. Beyond the kitchen garden, on the scruffy, unclaimed piece of ground leading to the sty and the hen-run, he found his remaining brother. Johnny was dragging logs from the woodpile and pieces of rubbish from behind the sty and laying them with infinite care in the middle of the dusty wasteland. His clothes and all visible bits of his body were covered with dirt and he was humming a monotonous tune to himself.

"What are you doing?" Jamie asked.

"Making a ship, stupid."

Jamie brightened up at once.

178

"Cor! That's good. Where's the sails?" He wrenched the piece of wood Johnny was carrying from his grasp and balanced it precariously on top of the heap. "There — that can be the mast, now we need sails."

"That isn't the mast, *that's* the mast! You've spoilt it now!" Johnny cried indignantly. "Go away! It's my ship, I don't want you in it, you always spoil things!"

"Anyway, it's a stupid ship," Jamie taunted. "I don't want to play in your silly old ship, so there!"

He went back up the garden again, kicking at things that got in his way, skirted round Jemima, and tried the side gate. To his delight, it opened. Without further thought, he slipped through, ran down the weed-grown pathway and into the village street. Here he hesitated again. He could go and see Lucy, but if he did, he would be made to do lessons, and he did not feel like that. Then, looking the other way, he caught sight of a top-mast between the cottages. Pirates! The pirates were there again! Capering with excitement, he scampered along the street to the staithe. There, sure enough, a pirate ship stood, half-laden with the hatch-covers still off. And apart from a couple of boys fishing for flounders and an old man asleep in the sunshine, there was nobody around. A natural opportunist, Jamie jumped aboard. He explored round the deck, pulling at ropes and fiddling with blocks, pretending to steer and peering up the mast. Then one of the boys scrambled up from his prone position and looked round. Lithe as an eel, Jamie disappeared into the open hold, and landed on a pile of grain sacks. Sliding down, he began to investigate.

* * *

Seething with impatience from the interview with his bailiff, Philip let Dauntless the black hunter have his head and galloped across the riverside meadows, jumping the post-and-rail fences at a pace that drew sounds of admiration from the labourers working on the new drainage ditches. By the time he reached the first cottages of Silver Creek, his irritation had evaporated and he was able to shrug off the bailiff's infuriating conservative attitude. He was a good man, after all, what he did not know about the estate was not worth knowing. But the habit he had of stroking his chin and sucking in his breath and saying that they never did such a thing when the old master was alive when ever Philip suggested the slightest innovation was enough to try the patience of a saint.

He rode along the street, exchanging comments about the weather with some of the villagers. They still, he knew, regarded him with a degree of suspicion. They did not understand his insistence on things being done immediately he asked it and at double speed, instead of with the slow deliberation that enabled them to work from dawn till dusk in all weathers. Behind his back, they grumbled to each other, and self-appointed jesters in the Plough and Sail raised gales of laughter by mimicking him saying, 'Jump to it, man, or it won't be done till Doomsday.' None of this bothered him in the least. They would see, sooner or later, that he produced results. By fair means or foul, he meant to get the estate on its feet again, which in turn would guarantee steady work to all his labourers and decent food and homes for their families. But it all took time, and time was running short. This summer was destined to see the making or breaking of his plans. By autumn he would either be settled here for the rest of his life or — God only knew where. But he would worry about that if the time came. An optimist by nature, he did not expect his luck to run out at such a crucial point.

Besides, there was an additional reason now for wanting the enterprise to succeed. Philip pulled up at the gate of Thyme Cottage and tossed a coin to the urchin who ran up to take Dauntless's reins. If he could but exorcise the unspeakable Franklin, prospects in that direction might be a little brighter.

He found Sophy listening to Lucy as she repeated her lessons. The child's face lit up as he came in, and after bobbing a curtsey, she extracted a promise of a ride on Dauntless. Sophy dispatched her to the kitchen with a message to Polly.

"If you continue to make a habit of interrupting Lucy's lessons, she'll grow up as ignorant as a savage," said Sophy, with mock severity. "You spoil her abominably."

"Nonsense, Lucy's a very clever little girl. I was quite out of charity with the world until it seemed that she at least was glad to see me."

"I suppose that is a bid to engage my sympathy over some problem," Sophy said. "No, don't tell, I think I can guess, you have been worrying the life out of your unfortunate bailiff again. The poor man cannot keep pace with you."

"But there is so much that needs to be done still. Every time I go out, I see something else that ought to be attended to. The trouble is, the place had been running down for so many years that most of the people here hardly know what a well-kept farm should look like. It never occurs to them, for instance, that a leaking roof should be properly repaired, not just bodged up with a bit of driftwood and a couple of rusty nails."

"There are times when I feel quite sorry for the people on your estate,"

Sophy smiled. "It never occurs to *you* that they cannot change their whole way of thinking overnight, or that not everyone is blessed with your ability to plan ahead, or even your energy."

Indeed, Sophy had found his seeming tirelessness surprising at first. Jeremy had been a nocturnal creature, rarely seeing the light of day before three in the afternoon. Sir Harry and James Hanson, on the other hand, were generally up with the lark but yawning by ten in the evening. Only Philip could drive into Maldon in the morning, spend the afternoon making sure his latest improvements were being properly carried out and still be found after midnight dancing or playing a hand of whist that Jeremy's gaming friends would have found hard to beat.

"If there were twice as many hours in the day, I might be able to achieve all I set out to do," Philip said. "But as it is, some things have to be neglected. Now, take my house. Over half of it is furnished now, but it still looks as if I'm camping in it. Whereas you had not been living here a week before Thyme Cottage was a proper home."

"Ah well, if you really want the solution to that particular problem, I can easily supply it," Sophy replied.

"And what might that be?"

"Why, you must marry, of course. Creek End is a prime example of a house in need of a mistress. I wonder you have not thought of it yourself."

He was tempted to say that once was enough and steer clear of the subject, seeing that she was treating it so lightly. But on the other hand it was an ideal chance to find out what her views were.

"Is there anyone you particularly recommend?" he asked.

Sophy laughed. "If you really need my guidance, there's no hope for you. Anna-Maria must be the obvious choice."

"Anna-Maria! I imagine Sir Harry would have something to say about that."

"Nonsense — Sir Harry has the greatest respect for you. He says you have achieved more at Creek End since you took over than has been done in the past twenty years."

"That's as maybe, but I couldn't stand

before Sir Harry and guarantee a secure future. Creek End may look reasonably seaworthy above the waterline now, but beneath it's leaking like a sieve. And besides," he paused on the excuse of patting Shadow who had just come bounding in from the garden, "I don't think she and I would suit."

"Why ever not, pray? She's a charming girl, good-natured and a beauty. What more could you ask?"

"Don't misunderstand me, I've nothing against Anna-Maria," Philip replied hastily. "She's a pretty girl, as you say, and charming company for a social evening, but — she has no depth of character." He did not add that she would not remain loyal through thick and thin to a gamester who neglected her shamefully, or set up house on her own instead of running back to the protection of her relatives, or calmly offer to draw off a keeper in order to aid a man on the run.

For her part, Sophy was finding that what had started off as a lighthearted discussion had unaccountably turned into something more serious.

"You must set a very high standard," she said.

"Perhaps so. Once bitten, as they say. What I want," he gave her a considering look, "is someone who is loyal and loving and tolerant and resourceful, who is neither cold nor subject to fits of jealousy. Do you think that is asking too much?"

"It sounds," said Sophy, "as if you are searching for a paragon."

"Possibly, and yet — " he looked down at Shadow, leaning against his knees, and stroked the dog's black head, " — I do believe I have found such a lady. The trouble is, I have to wait till she finds me. Perhaps she never will." And before Sophy could question him further, he forestalled her with a teasing smile and said, "Now it's my turn. What qualities will you be looking for when you marry again?"

Involuntarily, Sophy looked up at the portrait of Jeremy. What qualities indeed? If only it was as simple as that. But she knew enough now not to fall in love with another feckless gambler, if she could help it. On the other hand, neither would she be happy with a reliable but dull country squire, or even a quiet and mild-mannered man like James Hanson, pleasant though he might be. No, if she were to marry again, she realised, it would be to someone very like Philip Ellard. And to cover the confusion this revelation threw her into, she said,

"Oh, but I do not intend marrying again."

"Yes, that is the stock reply. Shall I embarrass you by asking what you really think, or shall we have a lively discussion on the prospects of good weather for the haymaking?"

Fortunately for Sophy, she was saved from having to reply to this by a frantic hammering on the front door. Then Mary Hanson came bursting into the parlour, breathless and hatless, in a state of panic.

"Oh Sophy! What am I to do? I can't think — it's so dreadful! And James — what will James say when he hears? Oh dear — it's too awful — what shall I do? Sophy, you must help me!"

"Yes, yes of course I shall," Sophy assured her, leading her to the settle and making her sit down. "Now just calm yourself and catch your breath and tell me what is the matter."

"It's Jamie — oh Sophy, what can have happened to him? I'm in such a taking! I shall never trust Jemima again, Lady Isobel always said she was not fit to be a nursemaid and she was quite right. Lady Isobel is always right. But Sophy, it's too dreadful — if something has happened to him — I shall never forgive myself!" She clutched wildly at Sophy's arm, her voice rising to hysteria.

Sophy disengaged the clinging fingers and took Mary by the shoulder, giving her a little shake.

"Stop lashing yourself into hysterics, Mary," she said, with as much quiet authority as she could muster. "Now just try to be calm and talk clearly. Something has happened to Jamie, I gather. Has there been an accident?"

"No — yes — I don't know — there must have been, oh, my poor little baby!"

Sophy looked at Philip in a mute appeal for assistance.

"Mrs Hanson, has Jamie run away? Is that it?" he asked.

"Yes, yes, I've looked everywhere about the house and garden and in the churchyard and inside the church, but he's nowhere to be found. And James has just gone into Tracey Nugent, so I came to you, Sophy. You always know what to do. You will find him for me, won't you?" Mary twisted a sodden handkerchief in her hands, tearing the delicate fabric into ragged shreds.

"Of course I shall find him," Sophy soothed, "but first you must tell me exactly where you have looked and what you have done to find him already."

"I sent the servants out, they're searching in the village now . . . "

"How long has he been missing?" Philip asked.

"Over an hour — I did not realise — I thought Jemima was playing with him in the garden, with the others, and she thought he was with me, though why she should think such a thing I cannot imagine, for I was feeding Baby and she knows I cannot abide the children by when I'm doing that. And then I went to see Cook about something — what was it? It has gone right out of my head, oh yes, the goose, she said the goose was not ready to be eaten and there was nought for it but to send for some butcher's meat instead . . . "

"Yes, yes, very annoying, but what of Jamie?" Sophy interrupted her.

"Jamie — I was just coming to that. You see, I was so long talking to Cook that it was not until past midday that I looked out in the garden and saw that he was not with Jemima."

"And when did you last remember seeing him?"

"Well, I started feeding Baby at about eleven, I remember that because . . . "

"It is now nearly half-past twelve," Philip said, glancing at the clock. "He could have gone quite a considerable distance in an hour and a half. But I would think that it is far more likely that he's hiding somewhere. So let us think of all the possible places nearby before we start sending out search parties into the woods — " He stopped abruptly, and Sophy, catching his eye, guessed immediately what he was thinking; mantraps. Her stomach heaved at the thought and she looked back at Mary, expecting her to relapse into her state of panic again. But Mary, happily, had not remembered the danger lurking in the woods of Tracey Manor, where the winding paths and ditches made a tempting exploring ground for a small boy.

"He climbed up into the belfry once," she was saying, beginning, under Sophy's steadying influence, to think clearly, "but James had the ladders taken away, so he cannot be there. And I looked in all the places he hides in about the garden. He must be about the village somewhere, but there are so many outhouses and pigstys and suchlike ... supposing he has got himself locked in somewhere and cannot get out? Or the river — he might have fallen in the river — he is forever asking to go down to the staithe ..."

"That's it!" Sophy exclaimed, and Mary gave a shriek of horror.

"No, no, not the river, the barges." Sophy hastened to explain. "He was telling me only yesterday how he wanted to be a sailor like Captain Ellard and go across the sea. There is a barge loading at the staithe now, is there not?" she asked Philip.

"Yes, the *Rosa*, but she was loaded when I came by. She may well have sailed now, as the tide's turned. She'll be taking the ebb downriver." And if Caleb Moore had been careless enough to let a stowaway on board, God Help him, Philip thought, though luckily Jamie was too young to make very much of what he might find. "Will you stay here with Mrs Franklin," he said to Mary, "and I'll go and hail the *Rosa*. Don't worry, it's my guess that if Jamie did get into the hold, he'll be yelling to be let out by now."

But Mary was quite unable to sit waiting in Thyme Cottage while her son was being carried out to sea. She insisted on going with him, and Sophy, seeing that she might be needed to prevent her from doing anything foolish, went as well. As soon as they rounded the bend in the street and had a clear view of the river, they saw the spreading tan sails of the *Rosa*, making good speed towards the sea with wind and tide in her favour. Already she was nearly half a mile out, and lengthening the distance evermore

193

rapidly as she caught the stronger flow of the tide in midstream. Mary uttered a faint scream and began to run, heedless of curious eyes, towards the staithe. The boys and the old man were still there, but otherwise the staithe was deserted. The five fishing-smacks that worked from the village were all out and the only boats moored up were a couple of small skiffs.

Philip questioned the possible witnesses. The old man was unhelpful. He had seen nothing, he maintained. The larger of the two urchins, however, recalled seeing something move on the barge, but he had been too busy fishing to really notice. He displayed his makeshift line and knotted rag of lugworm as proof.

"Did you not think to tell Caleb there might be someone on board?" Philip asked,

The boy shrugged. He had not thought it important.

"We still cannot be sure he is on the *Rosa*, but we can't let her go without finding out," Philip said, exchanging a glance with Sophy, begging her to keep

Mary quiet. Then cupping his hands to his mouth, he let out a roar that used to carry above the noise of battle. "*Rosa* aho-o-oy! Heave to!"

From the deck of the *Rosa*, the skipper raised his arm in a laconic wave, and continued on his course.

"Damn you for a stubborn, independent old devil, Caleb Moore," Philip muttered.

"Perhaps he did not hear you," Sophy suggested.

"He heard well enough. He just doesn't care to answer. An east-coast sailorman wouldn't stop for the Queen of Sheba if he didn't want to," Philip said, not without a touch of admiration. "Nothing for it but to go after him."

He untied the smaller of the two skiffs, pulled her alongside the staithe and jumped lightly on board. Before Mary could beg to be taken too, he had the oars between the pins and was rowing out into the creek, glancing over his shoulder occasionally to make sure he was on course.

"He'll never catch up now, it's too far," Mary wailed, wringing her hands. And Sophy, though she hastened to reassure her, was inclined silently to agree. However strong an oarsman he might be, there did not seem to be the remotest chance of Philip's overhauling the barge.

The two women watched in silence as the skiff left the sheltered waters in the mouth of Silver Creek and lurched over the waves of the Blackwater. Once into the main stream of the river, Philip rested on his oars and hailed the *Rosa* once more. This time, to the joy of the anxious spectators, the barge turned slowly into the wind. The sails swung, shivered, then filled again on the other side of the boat as she began to make way slowly upriver again. On the deck, a third figure appeared, much smaller than the two men sailing her.

"It's Jamie!" Mary squeaked, and, as if he could hear her, shrilled, "Oh Jamie, stand still, stand still! Don't fall in the water!"

The stretch of rolling grey-green water between the two craft narrowed, until at last the *Rosa* turned into the wind again to allow the skiff to come alongside. Caleb Moore, one foot on the bulwarks, regarded Philip with chalk-blue eyes in a tanned hide face.

"Wa-all, if it ain't the Shrimp!" he remarked. "Lost something, have you?"

"You'll be losing something if you get careless. This time it was just a small boy managed to get on board. Next time it might be a Preventy man."

Caleb transferred the wad of tobacco he was chewing from one side of his mouth to the other and spat expertly over the side.

"Since they gave you a command, you think you're next in line to God," he said.

Philip grinned. "Admirals come in between."

Ignoring this, Caleb jerked his head in the direction of Jamie, firmly held by the *Rosa*'s mate.

"One o'yours, is he? Just like you, poking his nose where it ain't wanted. You best keep a weather eye open for him in future. I'm getting too old to go playing nursemaid to skinny brats."

"I wasn't sailing these waters then, Caleb. He's the parsons's boy."

"That so?" Caleb studied a collier brig

with all-consuming interest. "Reckon his pa 'ud be passing glad to see him back again."

"Come on, Caleb, you don't want to end your career up before the beak for kidnapping, do you? Just hand him over and you can get on. You'll lose the ebb before you reach the spitway at this rate," Philip said.

"With a nice sou'westerly on our quarter? Do it under stays'l alone." Caleb dug in for a lengthy bargaining session. "Reckon there's some folks like to know the whereabouts of a certain feller with a stove-in head," he ventured.

"Aye, and the same folks would like to know who spirited him away too," countered Philip. In the same off-hand manner that Caleb adopted, he said, "There'll be a good lot of grain needing to be shipped off Creek End next year. Could be a nice regular run for someone."

Caleb snorted contemptuously. "Oh aye, if you don't swing first. Mind, if the rate's the same as it is for the lot I'm carrying now, it won't be worth my while, regular run or not."

"Conditions might have changed by then," Philip conceded. "Could be the rate might be different."

They regarded each other in silence for a minute, then Caleb gave a cracked laugh, showing his remaining brown-stained teeth.

"You'll do," he said. "Them fancy gold-laced bluebottles in the Navy ain't quite ruined you." He turned to his mate. "Here, Whitey, bring the lad over."

Jamie, who had been listening to this exchange in unprecedented silence, was handed over the side into the skiff. No longer a bold chaser of pirates, he clung monkey-like to Philip, sobbing with relief at being rescued. Philip waited for him to calm down, then sat him on the stern thwart and told him to hang on.

"We've got a rough passage back to your mama," he said. He shoved off and pulled the skiff round to head for the shore. "Mind you lash the hatch covers on in future before you hive off to the Plough and Sail," he called back.

Caleb raised his arm in a slow mock-salute.

"Aye, aye, Cap'n Shrimp, he retorted,

and set the *Rosa* back on her course.

It was a long pull back to the staithe with wind and tide against them. The little craft butted into the waves, occasionally throwing up sheets of white spray that whipped back, soaking Philip's back and catching Jamie unawares. Gradually they gained the smoother waters inshore, where the glistening mudflats were already showing below the saltings. Here they made faster progress as the force of the tide was not so strong, and at last pulled into Silver Creek and slid gently alongside the staithe.

It was a wet and unusually subdued Jamie who was handed up to a rapturous reception from his overwrought mother. Philip climbed up after him, made the skiff fast and regarded the reunion with an amused eye.

"A very touching scene," he remarked to Sophy. "The artful little imp must have slipped on board while Caleb and Whitey were in the alehouse. He's a brave little lad, though, he didn't start crying to be let out until they were well under way. Lucky he was discovered then, or I would never have been able to catch the *Rosa*."

"I doubt if he will do it again in a hurry," Sophy smiled, watching Jamie trying to wriggle out of Mary's suffocating embrace. "His father will be furious when he finds out. But you are wet through, you ought to go home at once and change."

"Of course, if you say so. I think certain other parties might be better off indoors as well."

Taking the hint, Sophy broke through Mary's transports at regaining her firstborn.

"Come now, Mary," she said, "Jamie is wet enough already without your making him any worse. He's quite safe and well, thanks to Captain Ellard, so had you not better take him home and change him into some dry clothes?"

"Oh — yes — of course — " Mary fluttered " — you're quite right. My poor little lamb! You're soaked to the skin? You'll catch your death of cold . . . !"

And clutching the little lamb by the hand, she hurried off up the street, still talking and exclaiming. Restored to dry land and safety, her son rapidly recovered most of his normal high spirits, to the point of attempting to explain how he had come to be a reluctant stowaway.

"I was looking for treasure," he shrilled, pulling on Sophy's arm to attract her attention. "It was a real treasure ship and I found it and I was going to tell Papa but then it went all dark and the pirates took me away."

"You'll have to wait till you are old enough to voyage on the Spanish Main before you can find treasure ships, my lad," Philip told him. "And if I ever catch you giving your poor mama such a fright again, I'll have you keelhauled then feed you to the fishes."

Jamie shrieked with horrified delight, but stuck to his story.

"There was treasure, I saw it," he insisted. "The pirates hid it. Lots of things."

They reached the gate of the parsonage before the argument could be taken any further, and Mary, recollecting at last the parts Sophy and Philip had played in the drama, thanked them both profusely, and begged them to come in and take some refreshment. Sophy refused, knowing that it would be difficult to get away under the circumstances, and Philip said that he had an engagement to ride with a certain young lady. Mary retreated into the parsonage, still voicing her thanks, and the other two walked on to Thyme Cottage. Sophy, who had been turning Jamie's words over in her mind, asked thoughtfully,

"What was the *Rosa* carrying in her hold?"

"The last of my surplus grain — why do you ask?"

"I was wondering what it was that Jamie took to be treasure."

"Oh, you know what a small boy's imagination is like. He had decided that the *Rosa* was a pirate ship, and so a heap of corn sacks was treasure. It's my fault, I expect. I shall have to stop telling him so many far-fetched stories about life on the Spanish Main."

But Sophy was unconvinced.

"I suspect there is more to it than that," she said. "Do you think there might have been contraband goods on board?"

There was a fractional pause, then

Philip said unconcernedly, "Highly likely, I should imagine. Old Caleb would sell his grandmother for sixpence."

"Then surely we ought to go to Sir Harry? This might be a link in the Shadow's chain!"

"Lay information against Caleb Moore? Never, upon my honour! He may be the wiliest old fox on the east coast, but he's fished me out of the water many a time, and he taught me more about working a boat than I ever learnt in the Navy. And as for him being connected with the Shadow — men like Caleb have been running in contraband ever since taxes were invented. The Shadow just distracts the authorities' attention from all the little boats that are still running the odd keg of brandy or chest of tea into every creek and landing-place in Essex. You're new to this area, Mrs Franklin, and you don't realise that smuggling is part of the way of life. When you have been here a while, you'll see that at times it is wise to be deaf and blind and most of all, stupid." He gave her a questioning smile and asked, "Does that shock you, Mrs Franklin?"

Sophy had the distinct impression that this was a test of her character, and thought carefully before answering. She decided that, however much respect she had for the law in most instances, smugglers came under the same heading as poachers, to be connived at so long as they did not get too greedy. She shook her head.

"No, I'm not shocked," she said. "I take your point. And it is right that you should be loyal to an old friend."

Ahead of them, the boy holding Dauntless was having difficulty in preventing the horse from eating the rose hedge. In fact, the bushes had a distinctly ragged appearance from having been used so often as fodder. Sophy gazed absently at the mangled flowers, thinking of another occasion when she had been involved with Philip's dubious acquaintances.

"By the bye, how is your Kingschurch friend? Is his head mending?" she asked.

"The last I heard, he was practically as good as new, thanks to you."

"And busy stirring up trouble again?"

"Quite probably, I should imagine."

Sophy smiled.

"You know, I don't think you're at all a suitable person to form riding engagements with my daughter," she said.

"How right you are, Mrs Franklin. You must not be deceived by my present respectable guise, it's all a lie and delusion."

"Yes, I'm beginning to realise that," Sophy replied thoughtfully.

6

SOPHY wandered through the small flower garden at the back of Thyme Cottage, breaking off the dead heads and pulling up the occasional weed. Her mother would have been pleasantly surprised to see her taking such an interest in growing things, she thought. She had despaired of Sophy's ever learning to control a household properly, and pointed out almost daily that a lady must be able to bake and brew, make jam and wine, raise poultry and concoct herbal remedies, even if she was lucky enough to have a housekeeper to see to these things for her, for she must then enquire that everything was being done correctly. Servants, she tried to impress on Sophy, respected a mistress who knew exactly how a task should be done and insisted on its being performed properly. But Sophy's heart had not been in the housekeeping lessons. She much preferred to cultivate her accomplishments and note down clever sayings in her quotation book. Now, she had to admit that the practical knowledge she had so reluctantly acquired was not only useful but enjoyable as well.

At the end of the path, where a hedge of quinces screened the kitchen garden and hen-run, she sat down on a white-painted bench and basked in the mid-morning sunshine. It was too hot for serious gardening. Too hot, indeed, for a lady to be out risking her fine complexion. But Sophy decided that she did not care if she became as brown as a gipsy. Closing her eyes, she drank in the scents of the garden — the fragrance of roses and honeysuckle and lavender, the rich smell of sun-baked soil, the occasional whiff from the pigsty, and drifting out of the open window of the kitchen, the savoury smell of the bubbling stockpot. Beyond the drone of insects and the trilling song of the skylark, shrieks could be heard from the parsonage garden, where a game of Walking the Plank was in progress, and up in the bedrooms, Susannah was putting her heart into her favourite lovesong as she polished the furniture. John Jennings was courting Susannah, taking her for long walks in the hayfields on her evenings off and finding various errands during the day that took him into the village to stop off at Thyme Cottage and drink flagons of home-brewed ale in the kitchen.

She ought to be happy, Sophy thought. She had Lucy, she had a charming house and friends who liked and respected her. So long as she was not extravagant, she had sufficient income on which to live very comfortably. But, in spite of all this, there was still a great yawning gap in her life, quite different from the one left by Jeremy. Indeed, he was rapidly fading into the past, a gaudy and unreal part of her existence from which she had emerged bruised and shaken, but a good deal stronger and wiser.

It was just as she was on the point of discovering what was needed to complete her life that Sophy's thoughts were interrupted by Susannah, hurrying towards her with a visiting-card in her hand. Irritated, Sophy asked sharply,

"When will you learn to use a salver, Susannah? If I've told you once, I've told you a thousand times."

Already flustered by an unexpected caller, Susannah became practically incoherent.

"Oh — oh ma'am, I'm sorry — I forgot — only there's this gentleman — he was very — and I said you wasn't likely at home, only . . . "

Sophy took the card and read it, and Susannah had the unusual experience of seeing her mistress's customary self-command completely shattered.

"Good God! Perry Allington *here*? I cannot, I will not see him, Susannah." She looked appealingly at the maid, aghast at having to face someone from a past that she had so lately thought had faded forever. "You must turn him away, at once. Say I'm not at home. Say anything, but get rid of him."

But it was too late. Sauntering through the flower garden, a picture of fashionable elegance from his carefully disordered hair to his tightly-booted feet, Peregrine Allington advanced towards her, supremely confident of an ecstatic reception.

Still reeling from the shock of seeing him again so unexpectedly, Sophy said the first thing that came into her head, not caring that it sounded downright ill-mannered.

"What in heaven's name are you doing here?"

Undaunted by such an inauspicious beginning, Perry made an exquisite bow.

"Ma chère Sophie," he drawled, "you devastate me. What should I be doing here but paying my respects — my sincerest respects — to the most beautiful lady of my acquaintance? You quite overturn me, ma chère. Do you not find it a pleasure to see me after so long?"

"Not at all," said Sophy bluntly. "But since you are here, I suppose you had better sit down." And steeling herself for a very unpleasant exchange, said to the maid, "Some Madeira, Susannah, and some ratafia cakes."

Perry looked doubtfully at the garden bench, dusted it with a snowy handkerchief and sat gingerly, crossing his dove-grey pantalooned legs.

"So this is where you have buried yourself," he remarked, looking around with undisguised amazement. "My dear girl, how can you bear it? The rustic squalor of this place quite takes one's breath away. The name alone. How can you live with an address like *Silver Creek*? It sounds as if you had been banished to the Colonies!"

"If you dislike it so much, why ever did you trouble to come?" Sophy enquired.

"Necessity, ma chère, necessity. I was positively hounded by the duns. It's a sad fact of life these days that tradesmen no longer seem to have any patience. Do you know, some of my bills were not even three years old? I really don't know what the world is coming to. But there you are, I had to make a bolt for it before I found myself incarcerated in a sponging-house, so I thought I might try my luck on Le Continent. You see me now on my way to Harwich, after which I shall no doubt find some nice fat pigeons all ready for the plucking amongst the honest burghers of the Low Countries. Yesterday I found myself in that terrible little place that goes by the name of Maldon. Not a single inn to be found fit for a gentleman! So I thought it best to travel on and see how the golden-handed Captain Ellard was enjoying playing Lord of the Manor, and incidentally avail myself of his hospitality for the night."

"*You* know Philip Ellard?" Sophy asked incredulously.

"But naturally — who does not? A gentleman of fame and renown is our gallant captain. Dear me — are you surprised? He has been playing a close game hereabouts, it seems. I confess I was sorely disappointed at his present circumstances, though. I expected to find him rolling in the lap of luxury, and instead he is living like a peasant in a ramshackle pile of immense antiquity and no comfort without even the pleasures of freedom, for he has his vinegar-faced sister with him. Dreadful female! How can a man bear to look at a countenance like that across the table each evening? And then he has not even the trappings of civilised country life. But one decent horse in the stables, and all he has to offer me to get to the posting-house this morning is a gig! I don't believe I have ever driven in such a vehicle in my life before. The degradation!"

He broke off his recital to favour Susannah with an appraising glance. "Ah,

Madeira. I am glad to find that you at least are not quite lost to all the finer points of living, ma chère Sophie." He took a taste of the wine, nodded his approval, and with his eyes following Susannah's rounded backside, remarked, "I suppose the brave captain has his pick of the wenches round here?"

"No doubt," snapped Sophy. "What time does your coach arrive at Tracey Nugent? You must not miss your connection with the packet ship."

"Not for another hour yet, chére. So kind of you to concern yourself on my behalf. Tell me," he leaned back, wineglass in hand, and rested his other arm along the top of the seat back, behind Sophy's shoulders. "Why is it that you bury yourself in this dusty backwater? You were always a very attractive woman. You could do very well for yourself in Cheltenham or Tunbridge Wells."

"I am perfectly happy where I am, thank you," Sophy replied tartly. "I have more real friends in this 'dusty backwater' than I ever had in any of your fashionable watering-places."

"Friends! Yes, I can imagine what they are like. There is a sporting squire, I suppose, who talks of nothing but hunting, and his horse-faced wife and no doubt a string of hopeful squireens and provincial misses. And a dull and dutiful parson and his dull and dutiful wife. There is the frightful Mrs Vye . . . not a very inviting scene, surely? Now, what can be the attraction? Is the parson a bachelor? Or perchance the squire's heir is of marriageable age? Or — can it be that the gallant Captain Ellard has taken your fancy? Is that it? Do you plan to be mistress of that draughty barn and the one-horse gig?"

To her profound annoyance, Sophy found herself blushing.

"Hold your tongue, Perry Allington!" It will get you into trouble one of these days!

Perry laughed softly.

"How splendid you look when you're angry! You know, Sophy dear, you are wasted in your rustic cottage. This is not at all the place to show you to your best advantage, you ought to be out in the world again."

His hand strayed over her shoulder and caressed her breast. "Do you not find the nights long and lonely?"

"Not so much that I need your company," Sophy retorted, jerking away from his embrace. "Really, Perry, you must be in Queer Street if you're willing to snatch at my small income. I could not even keep you in hats. Have you run out of susceptible young heiresses and gullible old ladies?"

It was a mistake to attack a self-esteem that had recently taken a good many knocks. Perry's well-schooled face did not betray the slightest ruffle of emotion, and only a very quick observer would have caught the momentary glitter of malice in his eyes. He drained his wineglass, sighed, and twirled it between his fingers.

"How I miss poor dear Jeremy on these little expeditions of mine," he remarked. "That seemingly transparent innocence of his was always such a help in lulling the fears of the wary. Nobody, looking at those clear boyish features would ever suspect . . . Such a good team we always made, it was a pity we could not work together more often, but then it is never wise to overplay a winning hand."

It took several seconds for the meaning of this little reminiscence to sink in.

"Just what are you implying?" Sophy demanded. And though she immediately assumed that anything Perry might say was twisted to his own ends, she could not suppress the beginning of a nagging doubt.

Perry affected his blandest air.

"My dear Sophy, I am not implying anything. Just voicing a few fond memories."

"They sounded like extremely slanderous memories," Sophy said suspiciously. "In fact, it sounded to me as if you were suggesting that Jeremy assisted in your card-sharping activities."

"You put words into my mouth," Perry replied, looking offended at such a slur on his honour. "I would never say a thing against the dear boy now he's no longer here to answer for himself."

"Jeremy was not a cheat," stated Sophy flatly.

Perry studied his immaculately manicured nails.

"Of course not, if you say so," he

agreed pacifically.

Sophy knew better than to question him further, however much she longed to force him to deny his infamous allegations. Rising, she said with frigid formality,

"Please do not let me keep you, Mr Allington. I have taken up far too much of your time already. So kind of you to call."

And since he could see very little point in staying any longer, Perry rose too.

"It has been such a pleasure to renew our acquaintance," he smiled. "I could not have hoped for a warmer reception."

The charade was spoiled by Lucy. Coming home from playing with the young Hansons, she spied the gig waiting outside the gate and naturally thought that Captain Ellard was visiting. Breaking into a run, she came through the side gate and scampered up the garden, calling his name, only to stop short on seeing not her friend, but a man whom she vaguely recognised and instantly feared. She shrank against her mother's protecting body and felt her reassuring hand on her head.

218

Perry's stage smile widened just perceptibly.

"Ah, so the gallant captain is the man, is he?" he enquired. And, with a heavily simulated sincerity, "Beware, Sophy dear, I should hate to think that an old friend such as yourself would be taken in by that gentleman's present pose as a respectable landowner. There is a great deal more to him than that."

"I am well aware of it," Sophy retorted.

"Are you indeed? I wonder. Are you 'well aware' of how he came to get his hands on Creek End?"

"I presume he bought it."

"Bought it?" Perry laughed incredulously. "Have you ever stopped to wonder with what? However successful he might have been, a naval captain is hardly likely to have made enough in prize money to buy an estate. He is not an admiral, you know."

Sophy was convinced that he was just trying to make trouble. In as disinterested a tone as she could muster, she said,

"It really is of no concern to me how Captain Ellard acquired Creek End, but since you are obviously dying to tell me, you had better do so before the words choke you."

But Perry preferred to sow the seeds of doubt and let them grow awhile untended.

"Oh no, I would not dream of giving away another man's secrets. I suggest you ask him yourself. You might be surprised at the answer. And now I really must take my leave. Take care of yourself, ma chère. No need to show me out, I can find my own way."

With which he made a graceful bow, and walked unhurriedly away with the air of one who owned the place.

★ ★ ★

In the blue saloon of Tracey Manor, the blinds were drawn against the beauty of the summer day. George lay on a sofa with a damp cloth across his eyes and a shawl about his shoulders, and Anna-Maria sat on a stool beside him, ostensibly reading aloud from *Julius Caesar*. They made a pretty picture, the affectionate sister distracting her afflicted brother with an improving example of great English literature. Even in the gloom of the shaded room, their golden heads and classic profiles immediately drew and held the eye. Reality, however, fell rather short of appearances. To start with, *Julius Caesar* concealed a work that would have been immediately confiscated, had Lady Isobel known it to be in their possession, and secondly, they disagreed violently over Anna-Maria's rendition of the piece.

In soulful, tragic tones, she declaimed:
"I saw the dungeon walls and floor
Close slowly round me as before,
I saw the glimmer of the sun
Creeping as it before had done . . . "
"No, no, no! That's not the way at all! Can you not get any feeling into it?" George demanded pettishly. "Good God, you sound like old Hanson droning on about the wages of sin. Here, give it to me. I can put more fire into it even with my head stuffed-up like this. I know what it feels like to be imprisoned.!"

"Lie down and be quiet!" Anna-Maria retorted. "You're supposed to be ill. You ought to be grateful to me, reading to you like this. And if anyone is a prisoner here, it's me, not you. You'll be going up to Cambridge in the autumn."

"Do you really believe that?" George asked, in the flat voice of utter dejection. "I don't. I shall drag out a useless, boring existence here, month after month, year after year, until I die of ennui. It's all right for you, you'll get married and go away."

"Go away! Oh yes, but how far? A couple of miles to Creek End. Very exciting!"

George was interested enough to tear his thoughts away from himself for a moment.

"I say, has he asked you?"

"No."

"Do you think he will?"

"I don't know. Perhaps."

"Would you like him to?"

"I — don't know." Anna-Maria fidgeted with the shawl draped about her brother's shoulder. "I like him," she said finally. "He's very charming, sometimes. But he's very *old*, he must be nearly thirty, and sometimes I can't follow a word he says. And besides, I don't know that I want to live at Creek End for the rest of my days and come to dinner here once a week." She sighed. "If only the Maceboroughs were to come down for the summer."

George sat up and blew his nose. "Funny sort of countess you'd make," he remarked caustically.

"Pig!" retorted his sister. "If you can't be nice to me, I shan't read to you. You can lie here and sneeze and snuffle by yourself, so there! I shall . . . "

"Hush, someone's coming!" George interrupted her.

In a flash, 'The Prisoner of Chillon' was hidden under a cushion and the invalid reclined again, obediently listening to a somewhat colourless declamation from Shakespeare. Lady Isobel sailed in, talking over her shoulder to Mrs Franklin.

"Alleluya! A messenger from the outside world!" George muttered under his breath. He threw off the degrading shawl, pushed his handkerchiefs out of sight and made an attempt to look fit and healthy.

Anna-Maria seized the opportunity to

escape, taking Lucy with her to see the litter of kittens the kitchen cat had recently produced, but George was subjected to the humiliation of hearing his mother detail to Mrs Franklin all his symptoms, his feverish headaches, his streaming nose, his continual sneezing, and all the many remedies she had tried to a greater or lesser degree of success. George crawled inside with embarrassment, for the very last person in whose eyes he wished to appear a weakling was Mrs Franklin. He glowered at his mother, waiting in vain for a chance to change the topic of conversation, until at last, recovering from a fit of sneezing, he interrupted her with,

"For heaven's sake, Mama, it's bad enough having to suffer all that without hearing you talk about it as well!"

Lady Isobel shot him a repressive look.

"We shall take that as not having been said, George," she replied, with dignity.

Sophy, anxious to prevent a family squabble breaking out, hastily asked George what his sister had been reading to him, and George, immeasurably grateful to her, kept up a discourse of *Julius Caesar* until a minor domestic crisis called Lady Isobel away.

"She will keep me here wrapped up in flannel waistcoats till I'm old and grey," George growled, as the door closed behind his mother. "It's infamous, the way I'm treated. I might just as well be in gaol."

"A fairly comfortable gaol," Sophy commented. She had learnt from past experience that sympathising with George served no useful purpose. It was better to try and turn his thoughts in a new direction.

"I don't care a fig for comfort, I want to see something of life. What was the point of sweating away at confounded Greek these past months to get to Cambridge if *she* won't allow me to go?" George asked bitterly. "I always go down with hay fever, every year. I shall be all right again in two or three weeks, and yet to listen to *her* you would think I had the plague. Only this morning she told my father to write to the college and say I would not be taking up my place. Ye gods! She treats me as if I were still in leading-strings."

Sophy could not help feeling sorry for him.

"Surely your father would listen to you?" she asked.

George shrugged his shoulders in contempt.

"Huh! My father indeed! My father may sound very impressive and look like the head of the family, but the person who really rules the roost is my lady mother. And it is her unshakable conviction that I shall expire the moment she lets me out of her sight."

"You will have to find some way of proving her wrong," Sophy said, though with no idea as to how he should do this.

George hesitated, thinking of his lifeline, his closely-guarded strategy for convincing the world that he was not just as good as, but better than, anyone who cared to challenge him. He had not spoken of it to a soul, not wanting to spoil the effect when all was revealed, and also, though he would not admit it, because he was afraid of being laughed at. But he wanted very much to bolster his standing in Mrs Franklin's eyes, and he was sure he could trust her not to breathe a word of it to anyone else. The prospect of someone to confide in, the chance of a word of admiration was irresistible.

"I intend to do just that," he said, with a knowing smile.

"You do?"

He nodded, almost regretting his rash decision, but realising that it was too late to back out now.

"I," he announced, rather loudly to cover his insecurity, "am going to capture the Shadow."

To his enormous relief, Sophy did not give an incredulous laugh. Instead, she looked rather impressed.

"That would be a heroic feat," she said evenly, disguising her disbelief. "But how are you going to set about it, when nobody even knows who he is?"

"I believe I know." George paused to give his statement full dramatic effect. "It is my conviction that the Shadow is none other than Richard Ellard."

Sophy forebore to mention that she had heard that particular theory before, from Mary Hanson, of all people, and that she had thought it rather far-fetched at the time. Instead, she pointed out the obvious objection.

"But Richard Ellard is dead. He was drowned in an engagement off Le Havre five years ago."

"He was not officially declared dead, only missing. His body was never found." George got up and paced about the room, his face animated with enthusiasm for his subject. "He could have swum ashore, he was a strong swimmer and the ship was sunk less than half a mile out. Even if he had been injured, he could have clung to a piece of wreckage and been swept in with the tide. It was nearly the end of the war then, remember, so the situation in France must have been chaotic, rife with rumours. He may have been captured and prevented from sending word home, or he may have been unable to frighten or bribe a fisherman to take him across the channel. But whatever happened, he could have made some contacts and learnt to speak fluent French, both of which would be very useful in setting up a smuggling enterprise."

Sophy could see several flaws in this

reasoning, but let him go on.

"Have you any real evidence?" she asked. "Anything that points to Richard Ellard in the way the Shadow works?"

"Plenty," George asserted. Now that he was getting into his stride, he was thoroughly enjoying himself. He stopped in front of the empty fireplace and ticked off his list of facts on his fingers. "Firstly, the Shadow must be an east-coast native. He knows the rivers and estuaries like the back of his hand and several times has slipped through the revenue men's fingers using tricks only a local man would know. Now, Richard and Philip Ellard come from somewhere on the river Crouch. Unlike some people," he explained, with bitter emphasis, "they did not have a mother flapping about them like a demented hen. Their father let them sail all round the Crouch and Roach waterways in a skiff, and they used to come up here to the Blackwater and further north to the Stour and Orwell on one of the barges. So they know the area well enough, and they know the barge skippers and fishermen who are likely to already be engaged in smuggling."

"But surely the Shadow is far more likely to be one of the bargemen with a sense of humour and a lively imagination?" Sophy objected. "They are an independent race, from what I have heard, and take a great delight in cocking a snook at authority."

George shook his head.

"No, no, that's not the answer. Witnesses say he is definitely a gentleman, well-dressed, well-spoken and able to throw off an apt quotation. And, what is more, his boat is not a fishing-smack or a barge, but a neat little cutter, thirty-five feet long and built for speed."

"But what about the witnesses that say he is a foreigner, a Frenchman or a Dutchman, according to who you listen to? And the size of him, too. I seem to remember somebody saying that the Ellards were remarkably alike, and yet the last report I heard of the Shadow was that he is a great tall fellow."

"That's easily explained," George declared with a dismissive wave of the hand. "He assumes a foreign accent with the intent of confusing people." The difference in height he could not find such a ready explanation for, so he skipped over it and went on to easier ground.

"Now, my next point is this — why should the Shadow wear a mask, as he is reported to do? Either because he would be instantly recognised by the men he deals with, or because he is hideously mutilated. Whichever reason, it could fit in with Richard Ellard."

Sophy thought that this would apply whoever the Shadow was, but it seemed too small a point to take issue with. George went on to his next piece of deduction.

"Thirdly, you recall the incident in which the revenue men were left reeling drunk while the Shadow sailed off with their seized cargoes? The man capable of doing that must have an incredibly hard head, and I have found out that Richard Ellard was famous for staying on his feet after all around him had drunk themselves under the table."

"I have yet to meet the man who is not reputed to be able to drink oceans of alcohol without visible effect," Sophy commented wryly. "It's the easiest way to recommend someone of whom nothing else can be said. I cannot think how many men have been introduced to me as 'a capital fellow, bruising rider and holds his drink like a gentleman'. Just as every girl you hear spoken of is the sweetest creature in the world and amazingly accomplished."

George drew breath to reply, and instead was seized with another fit of sneezing. He swore savagely into his already sodden handkerchief, apologised in some confusion, mopped his streaming eyes and picked up the thread of his argument.

"But a good many men are in reality overset by a couple of bottles, just as most girls are ill-natured and stupid. But I have been making enquiries about Richard Ellard, and he really could put down amazing amounts, particularly of brandy. So much so that he used to win bets on it."

A hazy picture of Richard Ellard began to form in Sophy's mind, a more reckless and flamboyant version of his brother, lacking Philip's basic stability. And, as she was thinking, George seized on the objection she should have been making and answered it himself.

"I know that separately these things do not count for much, but taken together, there cannot be many men to whom all of them apply." He began to pace about the room again, making Sophy feel tired just watching him. "What I intend to do now is to find where that cutter is hidden, and how the contraband is distributed. It must go out by sea somehow. The Shadow has never been sighted by the riding officers, and in any case the roads are so bad round here the stuff must be carried by water, just as all legitimate cargoes are. I think this is where the barges come into the picture."

Sophy listened for the first time with real interest. Wild theories about the Shadow's identity hardly seemed relevant to the real problem of catching him red-handed. But the idea that small boats might be used not only to bring the contraband in but to take it to the point of sale was quite likely to be correct. Barges going about their ordinary business of carrying farm produce and raw materials from all the creeks and landing places along the waterways would be unlikely to excite the interest of the revenue men, so the Shadow had only to run in a large consignment every so often and hide it in some remote part of the marshes, then redistribute it gradually through men like — Caleb Moore.

"You may well be right," she agreed. But even as she said it she knew she was not going to reveal the small piece of knowledge she had stumbled upon concerning Caleb's activities and his connection with the Ellards. She asked, "How are you going to set about searching out your information? There has been a reward of fifty guineas offered these six months past, but to no effect, and the barge men are a close-knit fraternity, they don't take kindly to outsiders asking questions."

George paused by the window, savouring the moment of anticipation before producing his trump card. Mrs Franklin had hit upon just the problem that was foxing everyone else, but he had the solution.

"There is one thing that works more powerfully on men's minds than money, and that is fear," he said with unconcealed relish. "I have found the very person to

234

gather all the incriminating details for me. Someone whom no smuggler would suspect, for he's as villainous as they are. And he will do what I ask, because I only have to report what I know about him to my father, and he will find himself committed to the next Assizes and transported to New South Wales. I have in my possession a knife belonging to him, that I found at the scene of Abel Harris's arrest. It's a distinctive knife, that several people in the village would readily identify, and it would instantly brand him as Harris's accomplice. And while I have it, he will dance to my tune, and I shall piece together each clue until I can lay a trap for the Shadow."

He came to an abrupt halt in front of Sophy, suddenly assailed with doubts as to her approval. He scanned her face anxiously for a favourable reaction.

Sophy stared back at him in genuine amazement.

"You have a diabolical mind, George Nugent," she declared, slightly stunned by this unexpected resourcefulness. "It is a pity you are destined to be a country squire. You would be better suited to the diplomatic service."

Taking this as a compliment, George sat down abruptly beside her. It had all gone fully as well as he had hoped, for he did not expect gasps of fawning admiration from Mrs Franklin. It was her cool, detached air that made her so different from the girls of his own age he affected to despise. But he did want to make sure of her approbation.

"You believe in me, don't you, Mrs Franklin?" he asked earnestly. "You are the only person I've told all this to. When I hand the Shadow into my father's custody, he'll have to respect me. He doesn't at the moment, while my mother keeps me tied to her apron-strings, but I shall prove to both of them that I'm more than able to look after myself."

Sophy was momentarily struck by the cowardly wish that she could be like Mrs Vye, repelling all but the shallowest of friendships. She had come to Tracey Manor in need of a practical, down-to-earth chat with Lady Isobel to dispel the confusion Perry Allington had thrown her into, and instead she found herself the confidante of George's dearest hopes, which put her into a very difficult position. For she was not at all sure that it was safe for George to go ferreting into the Shadow's organisation, and the use of blackmail, on reflection, was downright dangerous. But to say so to his face would only strengthen his resolve to go through with his design, and to tell his parents was unthinkable, as he had clearly divulged his plans to her in the strictest confidence.

"I'm sure you can look after yourself very well," she said carefully. "And you are certainly going to need your wits about you dealing with these characters. There is just one point that bothers me, though. If you push Abel Harris's accomplice too far, you might well find yourself knocked down from behind one day and thrown in the river. But if you were to let it be known that someone else is aware of your having that knife . . ."

"Oh no! That would never do. I couldn't possibly endanger you as well," George cried.

"But there would be no danger," Sophy pointed out. "You do not have to mention names, in fact it is essential that you do not. If this man knows that some unknown but responsible person is in possession of all the facts, he will not dare turn against you."

George stared at her, astonished as Philip Ellard had been at finding her to be an able strategist.

"Promise me you will do that?" she insisted.

George had only time to agree before his mother returned, marching into the room followed by two abashed-looking footmen bearing trays of refreshments.

"Upon my word, there are times when I despair of the lower orders," she declared, glaring at the unfortunate flunkeys. "Put those down, you dolts, and be gone with you. Now, Mrs Franklin, what can I help you to? Tea or lemonade? Or would you prefer some fruit from our succession-houses? The nectarines are particularly good this year, I must remember to speak to Hodge about them. Thank heaven the outdoor servants know what they are about, or I would never have a moment's rest. Well now, George, you are looking better. How is it that you always contrive to cheer him up, Mrs Franklin?"

"Did you know, Mama? Mrs Franklin is our good angel," George replied, watching Sophy's reaction from beneath his long lashes.

She frowned, suspecting sarcasm, but found that his expression was quite innocent. For five minutes or so he behaved impeccably, handing teacups and agreeing assiduously with all his mother's remarks, but the strain soon proved too much. On being told that peaches always brought him out in a rash he threw the offending fruit into the fireplace and marched out of the room. He regretted it the moment the doors slammed behind him, realising that he had acted like a spoilt child, but he could not bring himself to go back in and apologise, and spent a miserable half-hour loitering in the hall waiting to speak to Sophy as she left. His patience was finally rewarded with a friendly smile and a reminder to keep his promise.

He then escaped his mother's unwelcome

attentions by shutting himself in his room, where he unearthed the knife from its hiding-place and sat for a long time staring at it and weaving unlikely dreams of glory.

7

SOPHY was destined not to have a moment's peace that day, for no sooner had she arrived back at Thyme Cottage than a message came from Mary Hanson begging her to step along to the parsonage and give her opinion on the alarming spots the second youngest boy had developed. Sophy went, though not with very good grace, discovered that the child merely had a nettle rash, and was decidedly short with Mary. James Hanson was later regaled with the incident, much elaborated and with many exclamations of wonder, for Mary had been used to unending patience on Sophy's part. James suggested pacifically that Sophy might have had something on her mind. His wife looked at him in amazement.

"Sophy? Good gracious, no! What in the world could she have to worry about?"

James decided to call in at Thyme

Cottage after dinner, but by then Sophy made sure of escaping any further demands on her time by taking Shadow out for his evening walk. Had James known where she was heading for, he might well have gone after her, but as it was, he put off his mission till the next day and returned to listen to Mary's worries about the nettle rash.

For Sophy, looking out of her chamber window as she tied the strings of her bonnet, had determined to walk to Dead Man's Point. There were, she felt, far too many mysteries in the air, and this was one she meant to solve. She was sure the lights she had seen were not in the least supernatural in origin and no garbled tales of Ghost Ships and curses were going to prevent her. The fact that Philip Allard had also advised her not to go there only added to her purpose, for it seemed to her that the more she found out about him, the more unaccountable he became, and to investigate the so-called haunted spot just might clear up one unexplained part of his character.

When she reached the sea-wall she

stopped and took in the view. It was nearly low water and there was very little traffic on the river. The few boats that were out scarcely moved before the breath of breeze that hardly had the power to ripple the surface of the water. Visibility was poor, for a light mist appeared to be drifting slowly in from the sea. It was a peaceful scene, one which generally had the power to lift Sophy's spirits, but this evening it held no charm for her. Calling to Shadow, she started to march along the dyke, free at last to give full rein to the doubts and suspicions that had been nagging at her ever since Perry Allington's unwelcome visit that morning. For however much she told herself that he had only been trying to make trouble out of pique, she could not help remembering that, like all true gossips, his innuendoes always held a grain of truth.

So what, then, was the truth? Perry had implied that he and Jeremy worked some system of card-sharping together. She could well believe it of Perry. She had always considered him a bad influence and partly blamed him for Jeremy's death, since as his friend's second he could have patched up the quarrel before shots were exchanged. But she would not accept that Jeremy was a cheat. A gambler he had certainly been, and feckless and unreliable to boot, but Sophy could swear that he was never dishonest. And yet — during the last two years of their marriage, the more respectable people in the ranks of their friends had cooled, then dropped out of their acquaintance, leaving only the raffish element whom Sophy had mistrusted. Was this because of Jeremy's activities, or just coincidence? She decided that it was no proof at all, but still the nagging doubt remained.

And then there was the question of Philip Ellard. It was quite extraordinary that he should know Perry well enough to offer him a bed for the night. Sophy had always thought of him as a different character altogether from Perry and his type, and yet Perry had described him as 'a gentleman of fame and renown' and 'the golden-handed' Captain Ellard. And into her mind's eye drifted a little scene from the first time she had dined at Tracey Manor: Philip flexing his hands and saying that his luck was in, he could feel it at his fingers' ends. But it was ridiculous. He played an astute game of whist, certainly, but had none of the gamester's single-minded fanaticism. It was just another example of Perry's malicious tongue. He was probably jealous of Philip's owning an estate, however much he affected to despise the country life. As for Perry's hints that Philip had acquired Creek End in some underhand fashion, it just went to prove to what lengths Perry would go to discredit someone he bore a grudge against.

It was true, though, she conceded reluctantly, that Philip had some disreputable friends. There was the seaman she had helped to escape the law, and Caleb Moore, whom Philip admitted quite openly was a petty smuggler, and possibly there were others. And he had once said himself that she should not be deceived by his present respectable guise. But set against this was his collection of lame ducks, the tremendous mental and physical effort he put into making Creek End a success, his easy, affectionate way with Lucy and the Hanson boys, and above all his unfailing kindness towards herself, even to the extent of telling her about his disastrous marriage so that she might know she had a genuinely understanding friend in him. Taking all this together, she did not care two pins how he came to acquire Creek End. It was his now and she wished him all good fortune in it.

But even this was not the real cause of her present state of unease. 'Do you not find the nights long and lonely?' Perry had asked, homing in with unerring accuracy on her weakest point. For the past ten months she had hedged herself about with a protective air of cool detachment until she had successfully persuaded everyone, including herself, that this was how she wanted to be. Today's episode had forced her to admit that she did not like living alone, and yet what was the alternative? Certainly not to fall prey to a man like Perry Allington. She marched along the dyke with jerky nervous energy, eyes fixed on the ground in front of her feet, struggling with the conviction that the answer was tantalisingly within reach, if she could but grasp it.

It was still eluding her, though, when she reached the furthest limit of her usual walk, and it was with relief that she abandoned the effort of self-examination and gave her attention to the object of her expedition. Here was the landward curve of the sea-wall where Houselands Creek ran in towards Creek End House. Beyond the head of the creek, the sea-wall divided. It had once run round Dead Man's Point, the peninsula between Houselands and Dead Man's Creek, but a particularly ferocious storm ten years ago had broken it in two places, and instead of repairing the breaches, another wall had been built across the neck of the peninsula, leaving the land between the two walls to return to marsh. Just inside the very end of the old wall was a skeleton group of trees killed by the flood and bleached white by the salt water. Sophy decided to make these her objective, as the only distinctive feature in the flat landscape. She whistled to Shadow and set out along the old wall, conscious of a curious lagging in her footsteps. The dog gave a low whine and pressed against her, his tail clamped between his legs.

"Oh come on," said Sophy sharply. "Surely *you* have not been listening to village gossips?"

She went forward with an appearance of confidence that belied an inner unease. Shadow was not deceived. He hung back, his hackles rising, and only followed with the utmost reluctance.

The sea-mist was beginning to drift onshore, wafting across the water, obscuring the river then creeping over the marshes, a damp grey wraith, blotting out the world with its ghostly fingers. It was thicker in some places than in others, playing tricks on the eye, so that the skeletal group of trees seemed to appear and disappear as if by sorcery. It became unnaturally quiet, as the gulls and seabirds fell silent. Sophy shivered. There was no denying that there was something rather eerie about the place. And in spite of her severe admonitions to herself to remain calm and cool-headed, fear crawled up her spine and prickled the hairs on the back of her neck.

When she was within twenty yards or so of the trees, the mist cleared sufficiently for her to make out the swags of seaweed draped over the broken lower branches and something small and round hanging from a higher bough of the nearest tree. Shadow gave a strangled yelp and bolted back in the direction of home. Sophy tried to call him, but her voice sounded thin and muffled in the mist. For fully a minute she stood and stared helplessly into the swirling obscurity that swallowed him up, struggling with the instinct to follow him to safety. Then, fighting back the unreasoning alarm that threatened to take hold of her, she turned and went on until she came to the first breach in the wall.

It was dead low water, so the stream that drained out from the marsh had dwindled to the mere trickle of scum-covered water between mudbanks that gleamed brown-blue as the flanks of a whale. Rocks from the core of the wall, thickly overgrown with slippery bladderwrack, were still scattered over the gap, and it was possible, with care and concentration, for the sure-footed to cross from one side to the other without stepping into the mud. Gathering up her skirts, Sophy picked her way precariously from one rock to another, wobbling uncertainly at times and jumping the last yard or so. Taking in a long, shuddering breath, she scrambled up onto the wall again and looked at the trees. And this time there was no defence against the mindless dread that filled her.

For the object suspended from the rotting bough was a human skull, dangling at the end of a length of twine. As Sophy watched, it began infinitely slowly to revolve until it was facing her, and it was then that the full horror of the object burst upon her, transfixing her. It had eyes, and they were staring straight into hers. Sophy was held by the grisly object, a cold sweat breaking out all over her body, unable to move a limb. For an agonising age, the weird eyes bored into her, reducing her to a senseless quaking mass, until at last the skull began to move again, releasing her from its uncanny power.

Bereft of all thought, acting by instinct only, Sophy wrenched her horrified gaze away and fled, pursued by a scream that she failed to realise came from her own throat. She plunged headlong down the side of the breach, slipping on the rocks and lurching through the sucking, evil-smelling mud, and scrambled up the opposite side, cutting her hands on the sharp blades of coarse grass. Staggering to her feet, she made off along the wall, her legs leaden as if in a nightmare, miraculously escaping the ruts and holes that might have sent her sprawling. She ran until the breath tore at her lungs and rasped in her throat, forcing her aching limbs forward, heading blindly for home and safety. And then, beyond the pounding of blood in her ears, she heard the thud of hoofbeats, and someone calling her name. She reached the place where the sea-wall divided and hardly checking her speed, plunged down the landward bank.

★ ★ ★

It had been a long and frustrating day for Philip. He had set off hot-foot that morning on a tip that a bull of a certain strain he wanted was about to be put on the market. After riding hard across country he arrived just after midday only to find that he was not the only one to have been informed about the intending sale, and that the animal had been purchased by someone else the previous day. Now, coming slowly home on a tired horse, he looked back on an entirely wasted day, and thought that it would have been far better to have stayed at home and seen that poisonous Allington creature safely off the premises. Had he turned up on the doorstep today, he would have received very short shrift, and even yesterday Philip had only invited him in against his better judgement. But he had seen through the arrogant, self-assured facade that Allington adopted and recognised a man with scarcely a guinea in his pockets, reduced to desperate measures. 'There but for the grace of God . . . ' he had thought, and offered him bed and board for the night. And, after all, there was no harm done. The only other person to meet Allington was Charlotte, and as she disliked all his acquaintances on principle, it only served to confirm her poor opinion.

Approaching Creek End, he went over the familiar mental exercise of planning its defence against an unspecified enemy force. Breach the sea-wall and flood the lower meadows, strengthen the outer walls, board up the windows, rig traps and tripwires . . . But the real enemies were the creditors and mortgage-holders, and the only defence against them was hard cash. Philip reined in Dauntless and looked at the group of buildings composing Creek End, the old house itself, the stables and outhouses, the walled gardens, all casting long shadows in the evening sunshine. He was playing for very high stakes, and just occasionally his customary confidence failed him. But now was no time to suffer a loss of nerve, he told himself abruptly, and set Dauntless trotting down the last stretch of lane to the stableyard.

John Jennings came running out to take the horse.

"Give him a couple of days out to grass, John, he deserves a rest." Philip said, patting the horse on the shoulder.

"Aye, aye, sir."

"Did you get Mr Allington to the

Crown in time for the coach?"

"Oh yes, sir. Started off early so as to stop off at Thyme Cottage on the way."

"*What?* You let Mr. Allington visit ... My God, can't I trust anyone to act with a grain of responsibility? The moment my back's turned the whole place falls to pieces. I expected better from you."

The astonished John took this with a deliberately blank expression.

"I'm sorry, sir, but not having any orders to the contrary ... "

"All right, all right, never mind that now," Philip snapped, realising he was being unreasonable. "Get the bay out here, and look lively!"

"Aye aye, sir. With the gig, sir?"

"No, not with the gig, blockhead; saddled."

"But sir, he ain't been broke to the saddle."

"Well, he'll have to learn fast, won't he?" Philip replied. "If we haven't any tack, put this set on him."

And, as John ran to get the bay horse out, Philip began unbuckling Dauntless's girths. With a speed that would have compared well to a team of ostlers at a coaching inn, the harness was changed over and adjusted. Philip mounted the bay, which sidled rebelliously under the unaccustomed weight on his back, kicked him on and trotted smartly out of the yard, breaking into a canter once he reached the dusty lane to Silver Creek. John Jennings watched him go, then led Dauntless into his box grinning to himself. So that was the way the wind was blowing. Lucky for Mr Allington he was well on the way for Harwich.

Philip pounded towards Thyme Cotage, uncertain of his reception there. God only knew what sort of distorted tales Allington had passed on. It was typical of the man that he had not breathed a word about his knowing Sophy. If Allington had dared blacken his name an inch beyond the strictest truth, he would personally seek him out and silence him. Permanently.

At Thyme Cottage, Susannah told him that her mistress had gone out directly Miss Lucy was put to bed. Philip swore under his breath and asked if she knew which way Mrs Franklin had gone. Susannah did not. Remounting his horse, Philip rode down towards the river. Of all the routes she might have taken, the sea-wall was the most likely, and was easiest to check, for a person walking along it could be seen for miles around. If he drew a blank there he could start looking inland. But as he drew nearer the water, he realised that there was a mist drifting on shore, and by the time he reached the staithe it was so thick that, far from seeing for miles, he could not make out anything further than fifty yards away. He rode along the foot of the wall, growing increasingly uneasy as he progressed. If Sophy had come this way, why had she not turned back? It was not like her to go wandering about in a fog, and she must have seen it coming.

Then Shadow came pelting out of the mist and shot straight past him without the slightest sign of recognition, and Philip knew with a deadly certainty that something was wrong. He spurred on the bay horse, heading for the old wall, a dozen possible explanations of what might have happened chasing through his brain. Minutes later the dull silence of the shrouded marshland was rent by a thin high scream of terror. The bay threw up its head and nearly backed into the new drainage ditch, but Philip drove him relentlessly on until he came to the dividing of the walls. And there he saw her, running as if hounds of hell were behind her.

"Sophy!" he shouted. "Sophy!"

Flinging himself from the horse, he ran and caught her in his arms just as she reached the foot of the wall.

Sophy clung to him, gasping for breath, unutterably grateful for the solid security of another human being.

"The eyes!" she gabbled. "It had eyes — it looked right at me!"

"No, no, it did no such thing," he soothed, holding her close. "It was just your imagination."

"But I saw it — the skull — it was horrible — "

Her nerves crawled again to talk of it, but the irrational conviction that its power was pursuing her was beginning to ebb away.

"It's only the remains of some poor

long-dead fisherman," Philip assured her. "There were no eyes. It was just the mist, it plays strange tricks. If you saw it clearly, you would see there was nothing to frighten you. It was just the mist, and your imagination."

Slowly, she became convinced that he was right, and the terror drained from her, leaving her weak and trembling and feeling foolish at having succumbed to the very superstitious fears that she affected to despise. And as she regained the use of her senses, she became aware of the racing of Philip's heart beneath her cheek, his caressing hands, his voice, gentle and reassuring, close to her ear.

"You're safe now, my darling. There's nothing to harm you, nothing at all . . . "

She stiffened defensively and tried to pull away, afraid of breaking her carefully kept isolation.

"Of course — I — it was so stupid — " she faltered, trying in vain to keep her voice from shaking. "I'm all right now."

But Philip held her, weakening her resistance with the demand of his taut, lithe body.

"Don't shut me out now, my dearest

258

one," he begged. "I've waited so long for you. I can't go on without you now."

Sophy pressed both hands flat against his chest and leaned her forehead on them, not trusting herself to speak.

"Come on, Sophy, let go, give in, you can't keep yourself apart for the rest of your life," Philip insisted. "I love you, Sophy, I need you. I'm incomplete without you."

Sliding her hands inside his coat, Sophy surrendered at last to the hot wave of pleasure that engulfed her, and responded eagerly to his hungry lips. It was so obvious now what the great gap in her life was that she had agonised over so fruitlessly. The various parts of her existence, which before had only been a shapeless jumble, now fitted together smoothly with Philip as the keystone. Without him, life was meaningless.

"I love you too," she whispered. "It's just that — I was — afraid."

"Of what? Me?"

"No, no, of myself, of — committing myself to someone again. I can't go lightly into this. For me, it's all or nothing. No half-measure."

Philip pushed a strand of damp hair back off her face and traced round her jawline with a persuasive forefinger.

"It's the same for me, my darling. You, or nobody. Which is it to be?"

Sophy met his gaze, looking at his familiar features with new eyes. How odd that when she first met him she had not thought him at all handsome. She could not imagine anyone more attractive now, and she particularly liked the firm lines of his mouth, the way the creases at the corners of his eyes turned upwards when he smiled, and the perverse fashion in which his hair grew, never lying flat. It fitted with his character.

"For a long time," she said slowly, "my life's revolved round you, but I couldn't see it. It was — safer not to. But — " she smiled into his eyes, conscious of a golden glow of happiness spreading through her " — where's the charm in safety? From now on it will be you and me."

Philip wasted no further time on words. The fire that he had guessed lay beneath the cool exterior she presented to the world was all his now, the long wait infinitely worthwhile.

"Do you remember the day you first brought Lucy to Creek End?" he asked, much later. "And the mouse in the kitchen?"

"The day you gave Shadow to me?"

"That's right. It was then that I first knew that I always wanted to find you there when I came home."

They began, reluctantly, to wander back towards the village. Sophy laughed over the many times she had been unaccountably irritated at the Nugent's assumption Philip would marry Anna-Maria. Philip reminded her of the occasion when she had actually suggested that he should do so. It was not until they were over halfway to Silver Creek that the unwitting author of their present good understanding was mentioned.

"I had no idea you knew Allington," Philip said.

"He was a friend of Jeremy's. I had forgotten just how much I disliked him, it was a most unpleasant surprise to see him again. I thought I had escaped from that part of my past."

"People like him have a nasty habit of

reappearing when you least expect them," said Philip, with feeling. "But did he say anything about me at all?"

"Nothing to any purpose," Sophy replied, airily dismissing all her former doubts. "I never take any heed of his nasty pieces of gossip."

"So he did relate some tale against me?"

"Not in so many words. You know his way — a hint here, a suggestion there, but none of it of any importance."

Philip stopped and turned her to face him.

"It is of importance to me that you know the truth. So will you tell me, please, just what he did say?"

"He implied that you had come by Creek End in some underhand way, but that was all. He suggested that I should ask you, but it's none of my business and there is no need for you to explain anything."

"There was nothing underhand, it was all perfectly legal and above board, but it was unorthodox." Philip hesitated, then explained simply, "I won it."

Sophy stared at him.

"Won it," she repeated stupidly. But as she got used to the idea, she found that she was not so very surprised. After all, as he had neither inherited nor bought the estate, it stood to reason that he must have won it. Jeremy had been very fond of telling her, during their unprosperous periods, of how his luck was just about to change dramatically and that he would come home one day with the deeds of an estate in his pocket and they would live in luxury for the rest of their days.

"How very clever of you,"she said. "How did you do it, exactly?"

Philip laughed and hugged her.

"Darling Sophy, I might have known you would take it this way. No shocked amazement from you, no exclamations of horror at my walking off with someone else's birthright, just an interested enquiry as to how I did it. And the answer is: Hazard."

"Oh," Sophy said thoughtfully, as everything started to fit into place. "And that was how you met Perry Allington, as well?"

"Exactly. He is not a lifelong friend of mine, you understand, merely a passing acquaintance. But it just so happened that the night our paths crossed I did draw attention to myself in a rather dramatic fashion."

"I see. But go on — what did happen?"

They walked on again towards Silver Creek, and Philip recalled the night that changed the direction of his life.

"The strangest part was that I went out that evening without the slightest intention of playing any games of chance. I was just killing time in London for a few days before leaving the country for good — I already had a passage booked for America — "

"America?" This really did surprise Sophy. "Whatever for?"

"There was nothing to keep me here. There was only Charlotte left of my immediate family, I had no permanent home and I recently learned that Louise was dead and I was free to start again. So what to do? I had some money, but I was just one more half-pay officer amongst many with no other trade to my name, so I decided to look for a territory of my own in the New World. There I was, then, watching a new comedy at Drury

Lane, when I ran into an old friend. Afterwards, he took me to a club he knew of and I went along not meaning to stake more than a few guineas, as I had better ways of getting rid of my hard-won prize money.

"But I had some modest success, so I carried on, intending to pull out the moment my luck changed and, as is sometimes the case in gaming, found that because I was not particularly involved in the play, it went all my way. My principal opponent, however, was there hoping as a last resort to miraculously mend his fallen fortunes, and his luck was as bad as mine was good. In the end, when it was daylight and play had stopped at all the other tables, he ran out of cash. He should have cut his losses then, and gone home, as I tried to convince him, or at least gone on to IOUs, but instead he produced a rumpled sheaf of legal documents from his pocket and threw them onto table."

"'IOUs be damned,' he said. 'I've had enough of this paltry fifty guineas here and a hundred guineas there, you — ' well, he called me a lot of unsavoury names, none of them very original, ' — now we'll see what you're really made of. I'll play you for everything you've got, everything, I'll break you as you're trying to break me — ' and he ranted on for a while longer, and finally came to the point. 'I'll lay this, a house and seven hundred acres, to the last penny you have on you.'

"And he sat there staring at me with feverish intensity, while the sudden burst of talking that had broken out on his making the challenge died down. I was going to get up, pick up my winnings and walk out, but I looked at him and I thought, 'A man like that doesn't deserve his house and seven hundred acres. If he doesn't lose it tonight, he'll chance if again tomorrow, so if somebody's going to benefit, why not me?' So I agreed. It was only when I took off my signet ring and put that on the table that it came home to me that I might lose, and then it was too late to draw back. That was a very nasty moment. The whole room went deathly quiet, and the dice were thrown, and there it was, my fortune spelt out in little black spots. I'm not entirely clear what happened after that, except that my friend finally wheeled me back to my lodgings about midday."

To Sophy, it all sounded rather too much like one of Jeremy's fantasies to be true. But there was no reason to disbelieve a word of it.

"So several hours later you woke up with a sick headache, cancelled your passage to America and looked forward to a life of luxury?" she hazarded, going on what Jeremy's reaction would have been if the dream had ever come true. She might have guessed that Philip's response was quite different.

"On the contrary, I woke up with a sick headache, more determined then ever to leave. The whole adventure was a stock example of everything I wanted to get away from, so I tracked my opponent to his lodgings and tried to give the wretched deeds back to him. An estate in England was the last thing I wanted, I'd been busy severing all my ties from the moment I was set ashore. You should have seen the reaction it caused! You would have thought I was trying to seduce the man's wife in front of his nose, instead of returning his inheritance.

"He was one of those unstable, excitable characters and he took it as a slur on his honour that I should give back what I had won in a fair contest, but in the end after a great display of histrionics on his part, the truth of the matter began to come out: he was glad to be rid of the place, it was a millstone round his neck and he had always hated it. Once he had admitted that, I was able to come to a reasonable arrangement. I took over the property, but I also took over all the liabilities and debts connected with it. I later sent him five hundred guineas through a rather devious route, but he put it all on a horse and lost it, so after that I washed my hands of him. I've no time for people who wilfully ruin themselves.

"So there I was, with a property nobody wanted on my hands. I was going to sell the place to the first possible buyer, but when I read the deeds and saw just where it was situated, I had to come down and take a look.

"You remember what the weather was

268

like in 'sixteen, of course? No summer at all to speak of. I arrived here on an October afternoon, and it was raining, naturally, since it never stopped raining that year. They advised me at the Crown to take a horse, since the lane was impassable to wheeled traffic, and as I rode through the village and out to the house, it was obvious that the estate was practically bankrupt.

"The hedges straggled half over the fields, corn was left to sprout in the ear, there was hardly any livestock, the lower meadows were waterlogged — and then I came to the house itself. From the outside it was bad enough, with half the windows boarded up and the garden threatening to take over and cover it completely, but inside it was a wreck. The duns had stripped everything that could possibly be carried away and sold, the roof leaked in places and there were patches of fungus on some of the walls, but the moment I stepped into the old hall I was captivated.

"I walked round, thinking, 'This is mine. My house, my land.' The fact that it was all in the most appalling state

269

of neglect only served to strengthen the decision. I was on home ground, with the river forming one of the boundaries, and yet taming it and making it pay was as big a challenge as anything I might find in the New World. So first thing next morning I rode back into Maldon, found the attorney who handled the affairs of the estate and landed up to my neck in a legal tangle that I've been struggling to straighten out ever since."

"Not quite such a fairy story as the beginning seemed to be," Sophy said. "I wonder how many people, seeing the place as it was, would have sold up then? Especially knowing as little as you did about farming."

"You know me — contrary minded!" laughed Philip. "Besides, I wanted it, and what I want I usually get, provided I work hard enough for it."

"I can well believe that," Sophy replied, but with her mind only half on what she was saying. Now that Perry Allington's hints about Philip had proved to be at least partially true, what of his allegations about Jeremy? She did not want to live with an uneasy doubt about that.

"Philip?" she asked hesitantly. "Do you know — did your cousin say what the cause was of the — the duel?"

There was a momentary pause before Philip replied. For months he had waited for an opportunity to shake Sophy's blind faith in the late Franklin's integrity. Many a time, when some small thing occurred to trigger off a memory of him, Philip had watched her withdraw within herself, seen the shadow of grief descend upon her fine-boned features, and longed to tell her that Franklin was not worth mourning over, that he had been a third-rate confidence trickster, that he had been supremely fortunate to meet his end honourably, rather than languishing in Newgate, as would inevitably have been his fate. But now that it came to the point, he found that his desire to blacken Franklin's character had evaporated. He had after all won Sophy in the end, and surely it was kinder to leave her with her illusions? If he had been able to think well of Louise he would not have carried a weight of bitterness about with him for so many years.

"No," he said finally, "he did not say, and I did not enquire. I'm afraid I regard duels as a rather childish way of settling quarrels. Why do you ask?"

"It was just something Perry said, that's all."

"Listen, sweetheart, you told me that you never take any heed of what he says, so forget it. He should have been drowned at birth."

Sophy laughed weakly. The events of the day had left her feeling light-headed and it was oh, so wonderful to have someone else make judgements for her for once.

"Very well, I have forgotten it already," she said, and meant it. "Do you know, just at this moment I even feel well-disposed towards Perry Allington."

"I think I might even be able to meet him again without knocking him down, though earlier this evening, when I thought he might have ruined my chances with you, I could have cheerfully murdered him."

"Silly! As if anything he could say would come between us."

The outlying cottages of Silver Creek

loomed into view, insubstantial-looking in the shifting grey mist.

Now, Philip thought, comes the difficult part,

"Sophy darling, there is one more thing I have to explain," he said, stopping to watch her reaction more closely.

Sophy caught her breath in sudden apprehension. Was there, after all, to be a flaw in their new-found happiness?"

"That sounds a trifle ominous," she said, with feigned unconcern.

"It's just that we shall have to keep this to ourselves for a while, that's all."

"A secret romance?" Sophy laughed incredulously. "But why, for heaven's sake? We're both old enough to know our own minds, and hearts, and we certainly don't have to ask permission of anyone."

"Dearest, when I took on Creek End, I also took on a crippling weight of mortgages and loans, and two seasons is hardly time to start to pay them off, let alone get rid of them."

"But there was your prize-money, and all that you won the night you got Creek End — "

"A drop in the ocean," Philip explained. "It all went on repairs and equipment and new stock. I'm sitting on the edge of a precipice at the moment. I might well fall over if the harvest fails this year, and if that happens I don't want to drag you and Lucy with me."

Sophy laughed aloud with relief and kissed him on the lips.

"How like you to be so considerate. But it's not necessary, you know. There's my income, and I'm used to getting by on very little. We could go to America, as you planned in the first place. I don't mind working. I enjoy it."

"It might not be a question of America, and it's because you're used to 'getting by on very little' that I refuse to take away what you have," Philip reasoned. "Here you have some security. You must keep that, if only for Lucy's sake."

Sophy opened her mouth to protest, and hesitated. There was Lucy to be considered, but she had great faith in Philip's ability to hold on to Creek End for another season, and if the worst happened and the estate failed, she did not intend deserting him for the sake of security. There was no point, however, in arguing about it now.

"Very well," she agreed, "if it really is so important."

"Just till the end of the summer. It's not very long. Three months or so, that's all."

And later, when she hastened up to her room to change before Susannah could see her, Sophy gazed in amazement at the figure that she found in her looking-glass. A draggled girl stared back at her, her dress torn and muddied, her bonnet dangling by its strings, her hair coming down, and her face glowing with life. Sensible Mrs Franklin was practically unrecognisable. Slowly, she undressed, washed, and began to brush out her hair.

"Three months," she said to herself. "Not very long."

It was only when she finally climbed into bed that she questioned Philip's reason for secrecy. His mention of America disturbed her. What was the significance of his remark about possibly not going there? She was probably reading a good deal too much into a chance phrase, she told herself. She sighed as she lay back, her fingers linked behind her head, and relived the events of the evening, smiling to herself in the darkness.

8

THE long days of June and July danced by in a cheerful round of activity. The Families who had been in town for the winter returned and Lady Isobel, busily organising dinners and parties and picnics, had the pleasure of seeing her daughter become the acknowledged belle of the country for ten miles around. It was worth all the junketing about, in her opinion, to see Anna-Maria in the happy position of being able to take her pick of the eligible young men, and eventually settle within easy visiting distance. Had she been aware of Anna-Maria's intentions, she might not have been so complacent.

For Anna-Maria, as Sophy came to realise, was not quite the ignorant country girl that her wide blue gaze would lead the stranger to believe. She was quite sensible of her bargaining-power as a beauty with a considerable fortune, and she had set her sights on the Maceborough family.

The only cloud that troubled her horizon was the possibility that the Maceboroughs might not visit their Essex estates that summer.

"They have property in several parts of the country, there's no knowing which house they will choose," she said to Sophy, wrinkling her brow anxiously. "Or they might not go to the country at all, but take a house in Brighton for the summer. They move in a very fashionable set."

"I should imagine that if they were going to Brighton they would have gone by now," Sophy assured her. "But have you thought, Anna-Maria, what your father might say to your planning to marry into a family of Whigs?"

Anna-Maria smiled mischievously.

"Oh, I can get round Papa," she declared.

Sophy did not damp her hopes by pointing out that she might not succeed in captivating a young man who had been unsuccessfully pursued for several London seasons. There was no harm in Anna-Maria indulging in dreams of a brilliant match, and in the meantime nobody was going to be hurt in the game of deception they were all involved in. For both Anna-Maria and Philip found it useful to their own purposes to carry on a mild flirtation through the warm summer evenings that caused Lady Isobel to consider the very convenient distance of Creek End from Tracey Manor, and view with a critical air the many improvements still needed there.

Sitting in the shade watching cricket matches or playing dance music till midnight, Sophy often felt like a black crow amongst the girls in their white muslin dresses. Her feet longed to join in with the quadrilles and country dances, and it was difficult not to seek Philip's eye and exchange a smile that spoke of the 'chance' meetings they arranged on evenings when they were not claimed by some party or other.

She found herself becoming obsessed with a sense of wasted time. It seemed so pointless to be forever in the background, looking on with an indulgent smile at the fun and games of the young people, like some middle-aged matron. She wanted to jump back into the mainstream of life again, to be one of the participators, and the more so because this might be the only summer she was to spend in Silver Creek. If all went well she would be at Creek End next year but if not, then heaven only knew where she might be. There was even the possibility, though she did not like to face it, that she might be at Thyme Cottage whilst a new master ruled Creek End. It was all very well for Philip, she reasoned. He had given himself an active part to play in his game of deception, and he gave every appearance of enjoying it. Who would not, with Anna-Maria as female lead?

Sophy's constant companion through the endless hours when all the other young people were dancing was George. Much to the chagrin of a dozen or more pretty young ladies who would have been very happy to sit out with him, or better still take a moonlit stroll round the rose garden, George preferred to turn pages and keep Sophy amused by making caustic comments on their fellow guests. He had a facility for composing unflattering rhymes about an old lady's dyed hair or the receding chin of a vacuous young man.

"You ought to be a poet," Sophy told him, laughing inspite of herself.

George merely shrugged and began to talk of something else. He did indeed make frequent attempts at serious verse, but he was not yet ready to admit to it, partly because he was far from satisfied with the results, and more importantly because the greater part of it was addressed to Sophy.

About his efforts to track down the Shadow he was not so reticent. After pursuing a couple of false trails that his informant picked up in the Plough and Sail, he at last came upon a far more likely piece of information, and rode through the rain to Thyme Cottage to tell Sophy of it.

Sophy had been particularly hoping for a visit from Philip that morning, and almost told Susannah to say she was not at home when she saw him stepping up to the door. She thought the better of it at the last moment, as he had come out on a pouring wet day solely to see her. The moment he came into the front parlour, it was obvious that he had important news to impart.

"I'm really on his tail now," he exulted. "Just you wait! This is exactly what I have been looking for: a clue from a completely unbiased source. Couldn't be better! I've only to follow this carefully through and I'll have him by the heels."

"You are speaking of the Shadow, I take it?" Sophy said coolly.

"The Shadow, yes, I always knew I could do it! You'll never guess where I picked up this clue." He shook the rain-darkened ends of hair out of his eyes and sat down opposite Sophy, his hands clasped between his knees. "From the eldest Hanson brat — what's his name — Jamie."

Sophy immediately brought her full attention to bear on him.

"Jamie Hanson?" she asked. "What in the world does he know about the Shadow?"

The answer was just as she anticipated: Jamie had told him about the 'treasure' hidden in the hold of the *Rosa*, and George had immediately drawn the same conclusion as she had, namely that Caleb Moore was in league with the Shadow.

282

"You cannot build so much on the hearsay of a child," she protested, using the very same arguments that Philip had employed. "You know what a small boy's imagination is like. A sack of corn can be transformed into gold doubloons with no effort at all. He stole on board looking for treasure and inevitably he found it."

"But did you ask him exactly what he found? I did, and it was rolls of lace, he was absolutely sure of that. There were kegs as well, though he did not count them as treasure. But I'll lay my life they were full of contraband brandy, and that they were put on board by the Shadow or one of his accomplices the night before the *Rosa* sailed."

Sophy thought rapidly. She had gone along with George's unlikely ambition in the past as she had not much faith in his ever finding out anything that would lead him to the Shadow. But now it seemed he had discovered a smuggler, the very one, as luck would have it, who was connected with the Ellards. And then it occurred to her that George very probably did not know that.

"The goods need not necessarily have

been put on board here at Silver Creek," she pointed out. "They could have been picked up anywhere along the coast."

George leaned forward, his face alight with excitement.

"But the *Rosa* came direct from London," he said. "My informant found that out for me. Calem would not have been conveying brandy out from the capital, so he must have got it from somewhere very near here."

"He could just as easily have met with a French boat on the open sea," Sophy objected. Then, testing the extent of his knowledge, she said, "Even if he did pick the contraband up here, it does not prove that he is in league with the Shadow. Men like Caleb Moore have been smuggling from time immemorial. I expect he does run in the odd keg of brandy or roll of lace every now and again, but quite independently of the Shadow or anyone else."

George jumped up and flung over to the window, where he stood tapping his fingers on the sill. He had arrived full of his latest achievement, secretly hoping for at least a glimmer of admiration, and instead his pet theory was picked to pieces.

"Why are you so set in proving me wrong?" he demanded. "I will do it, you know. I'll catch the Shadow if it's the last thing I do."

"That is what worries me," said Sophy. "And I am not trying to prove you wrong, I am merely looking at all possible objections to your idea, so that you don't go flying off on another false trail."

Chastened, George returned to his seat with a muttered apology.

"Tell me, what do you intend to do next in the light of this new information?" Sophy asked him.

"Keep a close watch on Caleb Moore," George replied, brightening up again. "It may be that he has nothing whatever to do with the Shadow," he conceded, "but on the other hand, he may lead me straight to him. The *Rosa* is due at Heybridge in the next day or so, with a cargo of timber. My informant will be down there, watching his movements and listening in on his conversations in the Old Ship. He may already have contraband on board then, in which case my theory must be wrong, but I think he'll call in here at Silver Creek on the way out, and I'll be ready for him."

"You will put him under arrest?"

"No, no, of course not. If Caleb's just a pawn in the game, as I suspect, he must sooner or later make contact with the Shadow, or at least the next link in the chain."

Sophy was sceptical. She was still not convinced that the Shadow was Richard Ellard or that Caleb Moore was anything other than a small independent smuggler. But she felt that it was not at all advisable for George to mix with such characters with only the dubious support of a blackmailed poacher. He would be no match for someone like Caleb.

"You had better be careful, in that case," she said. And seeing him bridle at the hint of a suggestion that he might not be able to look after himself, added hastily, "if you are seen doing anything at all unusual about the village, you will immediately arouse suspicion. You are too well-known to start frequenting the staithe or the Plough and Sail without a plausible reason."

"I take your point," George agreed reluctantly. "But I mean to go on with my investigations. Perhaps I shall have to rely on the services of my poacher until I am sure of my quarry."

"I think you would be more certain of success that way," Sophy agreed, relieved to have postponed any direct action on his part for a while. She wondered if she could persuade him that it would be better to enlist the help of the revenue men, but then there was always the remote chance that Philip's brother was involved, in which case she did not want to be party to his arrest in even the smallest way. All in all, she wished George had not made her his confidante in this, for it left her with very little scope to act as she wished.

George, meanwhile, had got up again and was fidgeting about the room.

"Would you — would you be concerned for me if I went out to take the Shadow single-handed?" he asked, with unusual diffidence.

"Of course I would, George. He must be a desperate character, and he would be fighting for his freedom, if not his life."

"I am a crack shot, you know."

"I do know, I've seen you shoot the pips out of a playing-card many a time." But that, she knew, was quite different from injuring a man badly enough to disable him before he can put a shot through you. The Shadow, whoever he might be, was not going to submit tamely to a slender boy waving a pistol. But it was no use at all telling George that.

"Perhaps you could teach me to handle a gun," she said, suddenly struck by a new line of thought. If she did find herself in the New World, it would be very useful to be able to shoot passably well. America was an uncivilised place, by all accounts. "You never know, I might have to defend myself against the Shadow," she explained glibly.

George was overjoyed at such an opportunity to reverse their usual roles.

"I shall be delighted," he assured her. "When would you like to start? Today? Tomorrow? You only have to say and I am entirely at your service."

"Not today," said Sophy, slightly taken

aback by such fervour, "today I am — occupied, and in any case, it is raining. Tomorrow is Sunday, and the day after I shall be sailing with Ph — Captain Ellard in the race. Tuesday, perhaps."

She looked at him anxiously to see if he had noticed her slip of the tongue, but luckily George was too concerned with arranging the earliest possible date to take in such details, and for the remainder of his visit he talked on happily about how he proposed to undertake her instruction. He left in the best of spirits, reflecting that there was only the rest of that day and the horrors of Sunday to be got through, for the race promised to be good sport.

The race in question had been organised by Philip. He had a couple of friends staying with him, forcibly retired naval officers like himself, and the proximity to water was too much to resist. Fishing-smacks were hired for the day, a course worked out and half the village staked their shirts on one contestant or another.

When Philip first suggested that Sophy might like to come, he meant it as a joke, never thinking she might take him seriously. He soon discovered his mistake. Sophy overruled his objections with a dismissive wave of the hand.

"I'm never sick, I do not mind discomfort, my complexion will not suffer irreparable damage from just one day on the river and my reputation for sense and propriety is high enough to stand one unconventional act at least," she said, implying that there was an end to the matter. And to press the point home, she asked him what she should wear.

Philip lowered his voice to a stage whisper.

"Inexpressibles!"

For a moment, Sophy thought he was serious. He returned her shocked gaze solemnly, not a muscle moving. Then it dawned on her that she was being teased.

"Idiot!" she exclaimed, hitting him. "I'd like to see your face if I did. Now make a sensible suggestion."

"Oh, I don't know — something warm, it gets chilly on the water. Something fairly old, so that it won't matter if it gets wet or dirty. And no wide-brimmed hats, they might get blown away."

On this scant advice, Sophy finally decided upon an old round gown with skirts short and wide enough to allow free movement, the black wool pelisse she had worn the very first day she came to Silver Creek, a serviceable pair of half-boots and a black straw bonnet with a minimum of trimming. Not the height of fashion or elegance, she thought, letting her imagination run on a stylish adaptation of a naval uniform, but it would do well enough for just the one occasion.

Fierce competition raged amongst the young men of the neighbourhood to be taken as crew on one of the boats, and after it became known that Philip was taking a lady passenger, even fiercer but more subtle warfare was waged amongst the girls angling for invitations. Some doubts were expressed as to the propriety of gently-reared females taking to the water, but as Lady Isobel pointed out, if Mrs Franklin was going, there could surely be no harm in it. Philip resisted with difficulty the opportunity of employing underhand tactics and handicapping his rivals with excitable and faint-hearted passengers, and instead recommended a couple of tough, cheerful girls, well-known for their exploits on the hunting field. Several pretty noses were put out of joint as a result.

Monday produced ideal conditions for sailing, with a good westerly wind and fitful sunshine.

"Capital," said Philip, surveying the sky. "A run down and a beat back, that should sort us out nicely. It will freshen up later, though. Anyone with a weak stomach had better back out now."

If he hoped to discourage amateur crews, whom he regarded as something of a liability on such small boats, Philip failed dismally. Nobody was going to give up before the race began. A noisy concourse of local gentry crowded the normally quiet track leading to the staithe, and waved and laid bets as the competing teams were rowed out to the waiting boats. Sophy, caught up in the excitement of the occasion, waved back to Lucy and only just stopped herself from joining in with the cheerful defiance that was bandied back and forth between the rival craft.

"Do you think we shall win?" she asked Philip.

"Win? Of course we shall. I'll never be able to show my face in the village again if we don't!"

Sophy had been looking forward to this day from the moment she had been invited. Up till then, her only nautical experience had been a gentle drift along a quiet inland river on a punt, so she welcomed the chance of finding out what it was like on a real boat. It would give her some idea, if only a very vague one, of the world in which Philip had spent over half his life.

The smack they were to sail in, patriotically named *Britannia*, had been specially cleaned up for the occasion, and lay ready with her sails bent on. Sophy managed to scramble aboard with some semblance of dignity and sat in the stern taking in the distinctive boat smell of tar, paint, shellfish, damp hemp and bilgewater, and watching as Philip went into action. As the *Britannia*'s skipper,

'Bandy' Coates, hoisted the sails Philip gave his crew, Henry Nugent from Farthings, a quick introduction to the craft that left the boy bemused. Ropes were not ropes, but sheets, shrouds, halliards, or painters; there were blocks and cleats, a boom and a bowsprit. Henry looked helplessly at Sophy, who smiled back her encouragement.

"You'll learn," said Philip cheerfully. "Just remember to duck when we go about, or you'll crack your head on the boom."

None the wiser for this piece of advice, Henry stood by the sheets he had been assigned to and hoped for the best.

The mooring was cast off, the sails trimmed and the *Britannia* began to make way slowly out of Silver Creek towards the river. It was a tricky operation, Philip explained, as the channel was narrow and the tide falling. If they touched one of the mudbanks now, they might well be aground there for the next twelve hours, ignominiously stuck in full view of the village.

Bandy Coates nodded in agreement.

"Hev to stand drinks all round at the

294

Plough and Sail if that happens," he informed them.

But he was confident enough of Philip's ability to keep them out of trouble to let him negotiate the creek, Sophy noticed, rather than pilot the smack out himself, as the other two skippers were doing. She reflected with admiration on Philip's retentive memory, for he could not have had much, or indeed any, practice lately, being so taken up with the affairs at Creek End.

Once all three craft were out in the main channel of the Blackwater, there came the sharp crack of a single gunshot from the shore. Of one accord, the boats turned downriver, sails let out to catch the following wind. The race had begun.

"Can I not do anything to help?" Sophy asked. "I feel somewhat superfluous here."

Philip promptly produced a battered brass telescope from the pocket of his coat.

"You can be the lookout," he said, handing it to her.

Sophy squinted through it, sweeping

inexpertly round the moving horizon.

"What do I look out for?" she queried. French frigates? Pirates?"

"Thass the only enemies we got now, missis," Bandy told her, pointing downriver. "Fool Preventy cutters."

Sophy smiled to herself, remembering a sharp exchange between Philip and his sister on the subject of the village fishermen's manners. Philip admired their independence. Charlotte found their lack of respect for their betters insolent in the extreme. What would Charlotte say to being addressed as 'missis', and without so much as an 'if you please'? She followed Bandy's direction and focussed on a neat red and black painted craft on the south side of the river. As she grew accustomed to compensating for the movement of the *Britannia*, she was able to make out the smart red and blue uniform of the cutter's crew, and even the iron guns she carried.

"Thass the *Badger*," Bandy volunteered, "out from Bradwell."

"I hope we're not carrying contraband today," Sophy smiled. "It would ruin our chances if we were stopped and searched now."

Bandy grinned.

"Be worth it to see their faces when they found they were accusing a lady like you of freetrading!" he declared. "And Nugent's boy, too. Never live it down, they wouldn't."

Sophy turned and looked back at Silver Creek as it slid away behind them. With the wind at their stern it did not feel as if they were going very fast, but she found that if she gauged their speed by watching one particular landmark they were actually making quite good progress. Searching the shoreline for such a landmark, she came upon the trees at Dead Man's Point, and suppressed a shudder of sick revulsion. The terror of that evening had been masked by the subsequent events, but fear remained. Even as she recalled it, however, the practical side of her mind noted that the point did make an excellent site from which to signal to passing shipping, commanding as it did a long stretch of the river. And behind it was Dead Man's Creek and a whole maze of fleets and waterways that would make an ideal hiding-place. But no, not even the most hardened of felons would use that evil spot as a headquarters.

As Sophy was coming to this conclusion, Philip was taking steps to keep *Britannia* in the race with a fighting chance. Slowly but inexorably, one of their rivals was pulling ahead, and they were only just keeping up with the other.

"Thass orl right," Bandy assured him. "*Britannia*'s mebbe a sight slower in a following wind, but wait till we're beating back to windward. Knock them others into a cocked hat, she will."

"Not if we're so far behind that we're pushing the flood before we get to the turning-point," Philip argued. "Haven't you got a bigger stays'l stowed away somewhere?"

"Reckon I might have," Bandy conceded.

"Look lively, then, and get it out! This is a race, not a pleasure cruise. My reputation and the fortunes of most of the inhabitants of Silver Creek are at stake. And you, Henry, bring the stays'l down and for God's sake freeze on to both ends of the halliard. If you let one go you'll have to climb up the mast after it."

Bandy disappeared into the sail locker and Henry, desperately anxious to prove himself useful, tested the bewildering selection of cordage attached to the mast until he found the right one. Philip took immediate advantage of the opportunity to exchange a few words with Sophy in private.

"Enjoying it, my love?" he asked.

"Mmm, yes, every minute," she sighed, resting her head on his shoulder. And she meant it. She had taken to the water as readily as a duck, revelling in the rolling green seas, the lift and surge of the boat, the breeze at her back. "If only it were just you and I, sailing off into the blue, it would be perfect," she said.

"You wouldn't find it very comfortable, living on a boat this size."

"I wouldn't mind that. I'm used to making homes in odd places, I adapt very easily," Sophy assured him. Then added, pressing the point home, "So does Lucy."

"Patience, sweetheart. Just wait till the autumn and you can try adapting to living at Creek End."

"It's not easy to have patience when I meet you in company nearly every day and have to act like a mere friend while inside I'm longing to touch you."

"And it's even less easy for me, believe me. There's nothing . . . " he broke off, releasing her suddenly as Bandy emerged from the sail locker bearing the larger staysail.

There was a flurry of activity as the sails were changed and the new one lashed onto the boat hook to keep it 'goosewinging' on the opposite side of the craft to the mainsail, thus catching every available puff of wind. Henry was set to see that the wind did not 'back' the sail, and Bandy took up position in the bows to watch the progress of the opposition. Henry, eager to learn more about the mysteries of sailing, kept up a constant stream of questions, to which Sophy listened with just as much interest. There was more to it, she soon realised, than simply hoisting the sails and pointing the boat in the right direction. And if it required skilful knowledge in daylight, what must it be like at night, navigating the tortuous creeks and channels of the river? Small wonder the revenue men had little success in their attempts to catch the Shadow.

"Looks like old Caleb Moore lying up off Mill Creek," Bandy remarked.

Sophy got out the telescope again and trained it on the barge in question. From a distance, one barge looked very much like another to her. But sure enough, this one had the name 'Rosa' painted on her bow. And with a jolt she remembered George's discoveries and his plan to use Caleb.

"I suppose he's waiting for the tide to take him up to Heybridge," she ventured.

"How on earth do you know what his movements are?" Philips asked.

"Oh, one hears these things," Sophy said airily, playing for time. She was caught in a conflict of loyalties. George had spoken to her in strict confidence, and she was fond of him an in elder-sisterly fashion and sympathised with his efforts to prove himself. But Caleb was an old friend of Philip's, and there was still the remote chance of the Shadow being his missing brother. Under her breath, for Philip's ears alone, she said, "Certain persons are very interested in Caleb's movements."

Philip appeared unconcerned.

"That's old news," he said.

"But with this rumour about the Shadow's identity that's going around, Caleb might be under more suspicion than usual, if it were also known that he was connected with you and your — your brother."

"So somebody has been regaling your ears with that tale, have they? It's odd how nobody has yet had the courage to repeat their suspicions to my face. But at least I can rely on your not believing that Dick is returned from the dead and masquerading about the coast as a smuggler."

Sophy felt a twinge of guilt at this, and avoided making a direct reply. Instead, she stuck to her original purpose.

"It doesn't do to rely on the discretion of a six-year-old boy."

Philip reached for her hand and pressed it swiftly.

"You don't have to worry about old Caleb," he said lightly. "He's far too cunning a fox to be caught at this stage of his career." And, dismissing the subject, he glanced up at the masthead. "Just look what that boy's done to the flag — it's a disgrace to a well-run boat. Would you mind taking the helm for a minute while I fix it? Just hold her steady."

And before she could reply, Sophy found herself holding the tiller and invested with the responsibility of steering *Britannia*. The boat moved beneath her like a live thing, and Sophy, watching the sails anxiously, failed to notice the speaking exchange of looks between Bandy and Philip as he dipped the flag once, twice, three times before it set to his satisfaction.

"A slovenly ship is an inefficient one," he remarked severely to the downcast Henry.

He resumed this place and released Sophy from her temporary command.

"That's better," he said. "Well done, First Lieutenant Franklin, you can go off watch now."

Sophy smiled and touched her hat.

"Aye, aye, sir."

She glanced aloft at the cause of

the trouble, and it seemed to her inexperienced eye that the flag looked just the same as it had before, but she did not betray her ignorance and say so.

By the time Sophy spotted the turning-point, a marker buoy that had been placed the day before, it was evident that *Britannia* still had a very good chance of winning. The other two smacks were well ahead, but the tide was still ebbing and they would make scarcely any progress back upriver until it began to flood, by which time *Britannia* would have closed the gap and be in a good position to take over the lead. Philip decided that now was the time for luncheon. Once they started beating back against the wind, they were going to be quite busy.

Henry, who had been noticeably quieter for the past half-hour, gave an involuntary groan at the thought of food. The uneasy motion of the boat as the following seas surged under her stern was beginning to turn his stomach. Philip, seeing sweat breaking out on the boy's white face, had a remedy to hand.

"If you would be so kind as to look in the right-hand pocket of my coat, Mrs

Franklin, you'll find a flask."

Sophy, who had been using his coat as a cushion, did as she was bid. As she drew out the silver flask, a piece of folded paper came with it, which she caught and, not thinking, pushed into her own pocket as she handed the flask to Philip.

"Here you are, Henry," Philip said, pouring out a generous measure. "If that doesn't cure you, nothing will. Best Jamaica rum, and not a penny duty paid on it. Don't look so downcast, lad, even Lord Nelson used to take twenty-four hours to get his sealegs, so they say. Care for a drop, Bandy?"

"Thankee, sir, don't mind if I do." Bandy raised the flask, said, "Damnation to the Preventy men," and took a long swig. "Begging your pardon, missis," he added belatedly.

"Perdition to the government," Philip responded. "Hm, not a bad drop of stuff, that. Now, Henry, if you cannot stand watching the rest of us eat you had better take yourself up to the bows and tell me if I'm about to hit anything. Bandy, the hamper, please."

It was a convivial party that rounded the marker buoy and set to catch up with the leading boats. Sophy noticed the change in the feel of *Britannia*. Instead of wallowing lazily, she now danced over the short, steep waves, leaning over with the force of the wind. It felt as if they were going much faster than before, and a new air of purpose settled over the boat as they began to work as a co-ordinated team. With every tack in their zig-zag course against the wind, they gained ground on their rivals. Philip was enthusiastic in his praise of the boat.

"You're right, Bandy, she sails a good three or four points closer to the wind than the others. Handles almost as well as — as a revenue cutter."

Bandy grunted contemptuously.

"Knock spots off 'em any day," he asserted.

Before long, they drew level with and overhauled the nearer smack, and set their sights on the leading craft. Henry, in full possession of his sea legs now cheered wildly.

"I say, this is first-rate sport. Even beats hunting," he declared, raising his voice against the roar of the wind in his ears. "Don't you ever miss the sea, Captain Ellard? It must be a dead bore farming after commanding a ship."

"There are few things more boring than blockading enemy ports for weeks on end, and the channel ports in winter in particular. It's cold, wet, uncomfortable and monotonous and I'm thankful not to be doing it any more. But cruising around the Caribbean taking prizes — that, as you put it, was first-rate sport."

"You could buy a yacht," Henry suggested eagerly. "Then I could crew for you."

"A yacht?" Philip laughed. "I wish I could afford such an expensive toy! No, what I would like to buy is something rather like that — "

He pointed astern to a sturdy two-masted vessel that buffeted easily through the waves, overhauling them by degrees. Sophy, who had been listening with intense interest, surprised Henry by airing her knowledge. "A brig," she said.

"That's right," Philip agreed. "A nice, well-found trading craft would be a very useful possession."

Sophy would have liked to pursue the subject further, but casual conversation was out of the question as they began to challenge the remaining smack for the lead. The two boats jockeyed for position, coming hair-raisingly close at times in an effort to steal the other's wind or force her to bear away. Weaving amongst the rest of the river traffic, colliers from the Tyne, barges laden with goods from London, smacks coming home with holds full of oysters and a storm-damaged barque limping up to Maldon for repairs, Philip finally succeeded in shaking off his rival. A jubilant chorus of 'Rule, Britannia' was borne over the waves to the unfortunate losers.

Philip's prediction of the wind's freshening proved to be all too accurate. *Britannia* heeled over at an angle and kicked up spray as she cut through the white-crested waves. Henry looked admiringly at Sophy, braced against the slope of the deck, riding easily to the lift and fall of the plunging craft.

"I trust you are not too frightened, Mrs Franklin?" he asked solicitously.

"Frightened? Me?" Sophy laughed.

"Not in the least. I am finding it all most exciting and exhilarating. It takes a good deal more than a puff of wind to make me afraid." She glanced at Philip as she said this, remembering when she had been terrified out of her wits, and met with an answering smile that told her his thoughts were also turned to that evening, and its felicitous outcome. If Philip had dispelled the terror of Dead Man's Point, how could she feel the slightest fear of wave and wind when he was in command?

She watched him covertly, both his strong hands resisting the kick of the tiller, his face creased against the sun as he looked up at the set of the mainsail. Carefree, confident, he was in his element here. On the estate, he was constantly frustrated by the slow rate of progress, by the resistance to change on the part of tenants and labourers, whereas at sea, problems demanded instant decisions and gave immediate results.

It occurred to her that when he had said that if Creek End failed it might not be a case of emigrating to America, perhaps he had meant he had it in mind

309

to go back to sea as master of a trading vessel. If so, she was ready to go with him. Given the choice, she would prefer to help him build up Creek End, for she was a country girl at heart. But she had spoken the truth when she had said that she adapted easily and was used to making homes in odd places, and she was certainly not going to choose to stay in the security of Thyme Cottage if to do so meant losing Philip.

Henry, pursuing his own line of thought, broke into hers.

"I'm sure my sisters would be making a deuce of a fuss by now," he said. "They're always squealing and sqeaking over something or other. But then they would not live alone as you do, Mrs Franklin, with nobody but a maidservant to protect you."

"Protect me from what?" Sophy asked. "The only danger in Silver Creek is the possibility of a bull getting loose, or perhaps," she smiled, letting her imagination run wild, "perhaps the notorious Shadow might try to take me hostage. But in that case I shall be able soon to protect myself, for

310

your cousin has promised to teach me to shoot."

"My sisters — " Henry began, but he was obliged to break off and jump to the foresheets as Philip sang out, "Ready about — lee-oh!" and swung *Britannia* onto the opposite tack. He slipped on a rope as he scrambled to sheet the sails on the other side of the boat, and Sophy, practically without thinking, caught hold of the snaking rope, hauled it tight and secured it neatly round the cleat, working side by side with Bandy. Triumphantly, she grinned at Philip."

"Carry on like that and I'll sign you on as third hand," he laughed.

But when he sent Henry and Bandy forward to change the large staysail for the smaller one, she found he was not altogether pleased with her scheme for self-defence.

"If you really want to learn to handle a gun, I can show you," he told her.

Sophy looked at him sharply, surprised that he should take it so seriously.

"To tell the truth, the thought never occurred to me until the other day. I just said it to sidetrack George from — some other subject," she explained.

"That boy spends a good deal of time at Thyme Cottage."

Light dawned on Sophy.

"Why, I do believe you're jealous! There is really no need — you must know you can trust me."

Philip reached out and touched her hand.

"I would trust you with my life," he said. "But George Nugent has nothing better to do than moon about the place looking like Childe Harold and imagining himself in love."

"With me?" Sophy laughed incredulously. "Oh come, I'm six, no, seven years older than him."

"And more bewitching than all the younger misses put together," Philip insisted. "I've seen the way he looks at you."

"Oh, nonsense, it's entirely in your imagination," Sophy retorted, though charmed by the compliment. "You're a terrible tyrant, and I shan't pay any heed to you. You have your lame ducks and so I'm entitled to mine, and George is one of them."

"It seems to me sometimes that you have taken half of Silver Creek under your wing. You're Anna-Maria's 'good angel,' James tells me you're going to organise this Sunday school of his, Mary Hanson cannot get through the day without your assistance in one form or another, not to speak of the practical help you give about the village. Is there room for me as well?"

Sophy glanced briefly forward where Bandy and Henry were engaged in bending on the sail, then turned and kissed him in a way that left him no room for doubt.

"I could take all of Silver Creek 'under my wing' as you put it," she whispered, "but there is only you in my heart."

There was no further opportunity to talk after that. They soon had to negotiate the narrow channel into Silver Creek, and once they neared the village an enthusiastic crowd gathered to welcome the victors home. A great many people who should have been busy working contrived to appear on the staithe to cheer as *Britannia* came alongside and small boys competed for the honour of catching the mooring ropes and making her fast. A holiday atmosphere pervaded the village as winnings were collected from those who had been rash enough to back one of the losers, and the Plough and Sail did a roaring trade.

Lucy, wild with excitement, raced to meet her mother, closely followed by Susannah and Polly, Polly's children and a gaggle of escaped Hansons. It was a noisy and cheerful concourse that processed back through the village to Thyme Cottage, Sophy still rolling slightly as she tried to regain her landlegs. Then Philip hurried back to the staithe to greet his opponents, and Sophy, after seeing that cakes and lemonade were dispensed to the party of children that seemed to have gathered, retired to the luxury of a hot bath.

The party that evening at Creek End was a lively affair, attended by everyone remotely connected with the race. Philip's cook excelled herself in providing a celebratory feast, and the wine, which Sophy rightly suspected had had no more duty paid on it than the rum Henry had drunk to such good

314

effect, flowed freely. A rowdy game of charades followed and the evening was rounded off by dancing to the music of Zacchy the fiddler. Even after the respectable families had departed, a hardcore of revellers remained, as Charlotte Vye informed Sophy afterwards with a disapproving sniff.

So it was not until the next day that Sophy discovered the piece of paper she had inadvertently slipped into her pocket. Not recalling at once where it had come from, she unfolded it curiously and spread it out. It transpired to be a radical news-sheet, extreme to the point of republicanism and rejoicing in the name of *The Scourge*. Sophy recalled that its editors had recently been imprisoned for sedition. The crude cartoon of the Regent crushing his subjects underfoot whilst guzzling a gargantuan spread and fondling his latest mistress, accompanied by inflammatory articles, made her understand why the authorities had hastened to silence such a subversive paper. But what really attracted her attention was not the newsheet itself but the marginal notes.

For odd lines and significant paragraphs were marked in red ink, and remarks such as 'Good point', 'Wrong' or more often just 'No!' scribbled in Philip's handwriting.

When Sophy handed it back to him, Philip merely remarked that rags such as that gave the Radical movement a bad name, but Sophy was not altogether convinced by his apparent lack of interest. She had not forgotten the evening she helped the Kingschurch rioter escape the law, and though she told herself that she was making mountains out of molehills, yet she could not quite dispel the suspicion that there might be something more to Philip's insistence on secrecy than he cared to admit.

9

"MRS FRANKLIN! Oh, Mrs Franklin, you'll never guess, they're coming, they really are . . . "

Anna-Maria burst into the back parlor at Thyme Cottage, breathless with excitement, flushed from having ridden fast across the fields from the Manor. Sophy was glad of a visitor at any time, and doubly so today as Philip was away seeking advice on drainage from a farming friend in the fen country. With a knowing smile, she bade Anna-Maria be seated. It was not difficult to guess the cause of such agitation.

"And what has happened to bring you here in such a hurry?" she asked.

"They're coming, the Maceboroughs, in two weeks' time. Isn't it exciting? I was beginning to think they were going to stay away all summer." Anna-Maria took off her plumed riding hat and shook her tangle of corn-coloured curls.

"We only heard this morning," she went on, "when the bootmaker's boy delivered George's new top-boots, and he said that his cousin, who's a housemaid at Witherington, had told him they were all working like slaves up there as word had come the family was arriving in a fortnight."

"And will your mother call on them?" Sophy asked. She was not at all sure whether the Nugents were on visiting terms with their august neighbours. It seemed likely to her that the Maceboroughs would bring their own amusement with them in the form of a houseparty, rather than deign to mix with the local gentry.

"She hasn't in the past," Anna-Maria admitted. "Well, you know what my father's like. He cannot abide absentee landlords, and he says the Maceboroughs are a pack of Whig mushrooms," she laughed and gave a creditable imitation of Sir Harry. "Bunch of upstarts! Second earl — what's that? Nothing, doesn't mean a thing. Just a bone flung to them for licking the boots of the government." Resuming her own voice, she continued, "But I shall find a way round that, never fear. Mama is going to hold a ball for me on my birthday! Isn't it wonderful? But, Mrs Franklin, you must help me. Do please say you will, I shall be absolutely lost without you."

"Of course I shall, Anna-Maria, though I don't see why my help is needed. It seems to me," Sophy commented dryly, "that you and your mama have things pretty well organised between you."

"That's just the trouble! I can probably persuade Mama to send an invitation to the Maceboroughs, but you know what her idea of a ball is like. If she arranged a horrid, old-fashioned country affair I should just die of shame. The Maceboroughs are used to the most fashionable London entertainments. I just couldn't bear it if I thought they were laughing up their sleeves at us."

"If the Maceboroughs turn their noses up at your parents' hospitality, then they are not worth inviting, in my opinion," Sophy told her candidly, then seeing the girl's face fall, she relented. "I'll see what I can do," she promised.

"Darling Mrs Franklin!" Anna-Maria jumped up and gave Sophy an ecstatic hug. "I knew I could rely on you. I know rank and wealth aren't everything, really I do, but when a chance like this comes along, it would be foolish to throw it away, surely?"

Sophy smiled. Put like that, Anna-Maria's logic was unanswerable, but she still disliked the idea of running after a family who might hold such a high opinion of themselves that they despised the Nugents. Over the past seven months, she had grown very fond of Sir Harry and Lady Isobel. Reactionary old die-hards they might be, to use Philip's description, but they were intensely loyal and you always knew just where you stood with them. Of late, she had come to appreciate that more and more, as a contrast to all the little plots she had become involved in to a greater or lesser degree.

Anna-Maria's desire to ally herself to the Maceboroughs did not bother her too much, but George's dangerous game of Shadow-hunting did, and in particular the part she had played in using her knowledge of his plans to warn off Caleb Moore weighed on her conscience. For that promising trail had gone completely cold, and she was sure it was because of her hint to Philip. She had in part betrayed George's trust, even though it was for a good reason.

But if this caused her anxiety, it was nothing to the nagging worry about Philip and his affairs. There was nothing she could lay her finger on, just a number of small disconnected circumstances, straws in the wind, that led her to wonder if there was more to his radical views than just talk, and that he might be actively involved in some way with other extremists. And the fact that he did not tell her what was going on hurt her and made it all the more difficult to talk openly to him about it. The nearest she had ever come was to mention his notes on the copy of *The Scourge* and then he sidetracked her with outrageous condemnation of Lord Byron's 'Manfred', which only served to annoy her.

She brought her attention back to the present with a jerk. Anna-Maria was looking at her anxiously as the silence lengthened.

"Yes, yes of course," she said. "You're

quite right." And as Anna-Maria relaxed, she added thoughtfully, "I think I shall order a new gown for this ball of yours."

"Oh yes, you must. I shall get mama to go into Colchester," Anna-Maria took her up with enthusiasm, "and you can choose from the shops there. What shall you have? Black gauze? I suppose I shall have to wear white. It's such a bore."

"No, not black," Sophy said, thinking aloud. "It will be over a year by then — it's time for a change . . . "

★ ★ ★

Sophy ran her eye over the superb selection of fabrics in the draper's establishment. The rainbow choice of colours was bemusing. Blues, greens, pinks — her gaze lingered on a flame-red silk, but went reluctantly on. Not flame-red, that was going too far. But not a dull, demure half-mourning, either. No boring dove-greys or lavenders: if she was going to leave off her black, she was going to do it properly. She spied a pretty, warm peach colour, and pointed it out to the draper, who sent an assistant scurrying to fetch it down.

"A wise choice, madam," he declared, unrolling the bolt of fabric with a flourish, spilling the river of subtle pink-gold over the counter. "The very finest Spitalfields silk, beautiful quality, and just the shade to flatter any complexion . . . "

His flow of sales talk was not needed. Sophy was already decided. Anna-Maria fingered the silk and gave a sigh of envy.

"It's quite, quite beautiful. I think one of the best things about being married must be the right to choose one's own clothes."

Sophy refused to rise to this. A coolness had arisen between them over the subject of Anna-Maria's new ballgown. As Lady Isobel had elected to stay at home at the last moment because of her worry over George's latest indisposition, Anna-Maria expected to have all her own way. She was mistaken, though, and excessively disappointed to find that Sophy insisted on her buying white muslin and satin.

"You don't want to ape London ways, Anna-Maria," she explained.

"He — they — the Maceboroughs have seen nothing but overdressed young ladies all winter. Your attraction lies in being different."

"A fresh simple country girl," Anna-Maria replied, with more than a touch of her brother's caustic tone. "Well, I'm not simple!"

"No, indeed," Sophy soothed. "Natural, rather. Unspoiled."

Anna-Maria was unconvinced. Sophy merely held her counsel, bought her peach-coloured silk and some cream gauze, and made her way to the dressmaker's. Once she had explained the style she had in mind for Anna-Maria, and the dressmaker had draped and pinned the fabrics and exclaimed ecstatically over every aspect of the idea, the girl came to see that Sophy was right. And having realised it, she was unstinting in her praise.

"It's going to be lovely, the most beautiful dress in the world! You have such good taste, Mrs Franklin, I shall always, always listen to you in the future." She chattered on for a while longer, parading this way and that before the looking-glass, then finally turned her attention to Sophy. "But what about your gown? Have you decided how to have it made up?"

Sophy explained, but added, with a conspiratorial smile, "But this is to be a secret, mind, between you and I. Nobody else must know."

Anna-Maria nodded, giggling.

"Won't they all be amazed to see you?" she said, genuinely unconcerned that Sophy might steal some of the attention at what was supposed to be her big occasion.

"I hope so," Sophy smiled.

She stroked the shining folds of peach-coloured silk, wondering if, like Anna-Maria, she was counting too much on one evening. There was only one person she wanted to amaze, but it seemed unlikely that she would change his mind on the question of secrecy simply by her putting off her mourning. It was worth trying, however, and at least she would be able to dance again.

"Come along," she said briskly. "There's a good deal more to be done yet."

When Sophy and Anna-Maria returned

to Tracey Manor, pleasantly weary and laden with their own purchases and commissions for Lady Isobel and Mary Hanson, they found that Philip and his sister had been invited to dinner. Anna-Maria, full of the days' excitements, rattled on at length about the pattern, quality and quantity of every piece of fabric and trimming she had bought, not caring that most of her audience did not share in her enthusiasm. Mrs Vye disapproved of such frivolity, George was already sick of everything to do with the projected ball, Philip and Sir Harry were more interested in the finished effect of a dress than the minutiae of its construction, and then it was not so much the dress itself but the woman inside it that mattered. None of this in the least affected Anna-Maria's flow. When she had finished with her own purchases, she started on Sophy's.

"And just wait until you see Mrs Franklin's gown," she began, heedless of Sophy's frantic silent signals across the table, "it's going to be the most . . . "

"Hush!" Sophy interrupted her. "It's meant to be a secret, remember?" And

326

she gave a forced little laugh to try and show that it was really of no importance.

Anna-Maria clapped a hand over her mouth.

"Oh, how foolish of me! I quite forgot!" she gasped, but recovered herself with admirable presence of mind and struck out on an allied subject. "Just think how provoking," she said to anyone who cared to listen, "Mrs Franklin had some beautiful Valenciennes lace, but it got mislaid when she removed to Thyme Cottage. Can you think of anything more annoying? And it would have been perfect for the new ballgown."

"I was very fond of that lace," Sophy said, "it always used to set off my favourite dresses."

In fact, it had not been lost, but sold, one of the many luxury items sacrificed to pay off Jeremy's last debts. She had only mentioned it in passing, but now Anna-Maria was turning its loss into a major tragedy.

"But it's really of no importance," she said. "The gown will look just as well without it." And deciding that the company had been bored for quite long enough with descriptions of finery, she began to ask about the prospects for a good harvest.

During the next couple of weeks, she asked the same question of everyone in the neighbourhood who might have an intelligent opinion on the subject. She pretended to the casual, polite interest of an outsider, but listened with the intensity of one whose future depended upon the answer. But nobody was bold enough to tempt fate at this time of the year by forecasting a good yield. The grain looked fine enough, to be sure, but anything might happen to destroy it: fire, flood, incessant rain, even hail. Anything was possible. The most hopeful comment she heard was 'middling fair'. And as the fitful August sun gradually turned the barley, the oats and the wheat from green to gold, the hopes and ambitions of Sophy's many confidantes began to ripen.

Mary Hanson, torn between pride and distraction, let it be known that she was expecting yet another addition to the Hanson household. This time, she told Sophy, she was sure it was going to be a dear, quiet little girl, like Lucy. Catching the sound of Lucy screaming like a shrew at Johnny, Sophy wondered if her friend was harbouring ludicrously false hopes, but hastened to congratulate her all the same. George, recovering slowly from a summer cold that settled, as usual, on his weak chest, was driven by his antipathy to the fuss about the ball to pressing his accomplice harder still for information. News of the Shadow's activities had been very thin for several weeks, and rumour had it that something big was in the offing. At last George was rewarded with a clue that led in the direction of Dead Man's Point. Sophy, to his surprise, was vehement in her opposition to his having anything to do with the place, so to stop her worrying he half-promised to take any firm evidence to the revenue officers, and went ahead with his investigations without letting her know what he was doing. Her evident concern served to bolster his confidence in attaining the second of his dearest hopes, the one which was rapidly overtaking the first in order of importance.

At Creek End, word arrived from

329

Doctor Vye that he had completed his travels for the time being and was planning to be home sometime in September. His wife made no outright expression of pleasure, but her manner was noticeably more conciliating. Even when Philip was unexpectedly called away to attend to some unspecified business in London, she only remarked mildly to Sophy that she supposed he must have his little jaunts up to town every now and again. For once, it was Sophy who saw other reasons for his departure. She read the newspapers with much greater attention than Charlotte Vye and knew that there was a meeting of stockingers due at Nottingham, to be addressed by the great orator, Henry Hunt.

She was certain that Nottingham and not London was Philip's destination, and it was just one more worrying example of his lack of trust in her. Sometimes when she lay awake at nights, brooding over his deception, her own words to Charlotte Vye came back and mocked her, 'No good ever comes of trying to chain a man to your side. It only breeds resentment.' So easy to say, so difficult to adhere to. Why was it, she wondered, that she had managed to turn a blind eye to Jeremy's behaviour during his unexplained disappearances, and yet found it so hard to do the same with Philip? Perhaps because she was convinced Philip was involved in a far more dangerous game than a trip to the races, perhaps because she loved him more. But turning it over in her mind, she knew that the reason was because he was deceiving her as to his real activities. If he would but tell her . . .

All in all, it was difficult to muster up the right degree of pleasure when Anna-Maria confided, three days before the ball, that the Countess of Maceborough had written to Lady Isobel accepting the invitation on behalf of herself and her family and friends. Sophy felt that the only person in the district who was as far as ever from attaining her heart's desire was herself.

* * *

In the early hours of the morning, two days before the ball, anyone keeping a close watch on the street in Silver Creek might have caught sigh of a strange figure. He came from the direction of Creek End, keeping close under the hedgerows, and was clad in a long black cloak, with his face hidden by the shadow from his ancient tricorn hat. He held by the bridle a sturdy grey donkey that the gardener at Tracey Manor would have recognised, for it was generally employed in pulling the heavy roller that gave the lawns their bowling-green smoothness. On this occasion, however, it was engaged in a rather more mysterious occupation, for strapped onto its back were two kegs of best French brandy.

The man in the black cloak paused under the protective cover of an outhouse and looked swiftly up and down the street. Anyone out at that time of night would be up to no good and, therefore, only too glad to mind his own business, but there was no need to blunder about taking needless risks. Only a hunting cat disturbed the stillness, and man and donkey, two moving shadows, slid across the street to the churchyard. Here the donkey was tethered beneath the yew trees and relieved of half its burden. It stood cropping the tough, late summer grass whilst its temporary master heaved one of the kegs onto his shoulder and made his way towards the parsonage. He trod softly, keeping to the lawn so that his footsteps did not crunch on the gravelled path, and with infinite care set the keg down in the porch. Reaching into his pocket he brought out an envelope, and checked with difficulty by the dim light of the stars that it was the right one before placing it on top of the keg and securing it with a large stone. This done, he walked swiftly back to the waiting animal, smiling to himself in the dark.

So far, so good. He untied the donkey and proceeded on his silent course up the street with further unsolicited gifts. Brandy for the landlubbers, best Jamacia rum for the seafaring gentleman, and now a present for the Lady in Black. He considered again the question of the message that was to accompany the small package. 'She walks in beauty' had of course been the obvious choice, but he disliked the obvious, and only lack of time had prevented him from looking up anything more original.

He went past Thyme Cottage and left the donkey by the footpath leading to Tracey Manor. Letting himself in by the back gate, he brushed past the runner beans and the artichokes, and skirted the pigsty, heading for the herb patch. Sage, rosemary, marjoram — the pungent scents rose on the night air and he touched their leaves — thyme. Stooping, he thrust the package under the spreading, fragrant plant, then turned to rejoin his accomplice. From the footpath, he looked back at the cottage, his gaze lingering momentarily on the upper widows, blank and shuttered against the night. Then, clicking his tongue softly at the donkey, he set off on the most difficult part of the journey, beset as it was with the hazards of keepers and mantraps. But the dangers only made the prospect of success more tempting. Sir Harry Nugent would rest at nothing to find who had invaded his domain and escaped without detection. By noon the whole of Silver Creek would be swarming with revenue men, baying like a pack of hounds on a hot scent, but all to no avail, for by then their quarry would have moved its lair and set up a new base further downriver. Laughing inwardly, the man in the black cloak made his way towards Tracey Manor.

* * *

Sophy stood in the pantry, surveying her stocks of food. She was not concerned with what was needed for immediate consumption, but with the growing store of home-produced fare saved against the winter months. The soft-fruit season was already over, and there to prove it were jars of redcurrants, blackcurrants, strawberries, raspberries, gooseberries and cherries, made into jams, jellies, cordials and preserves. The peas had been dried and now the runner beans were being salted down in the large stone jars, but the real defence against winter famine would start in three or four weeks' time. Then the orchard fruits and the blackberries and quinces would be ripe, the root vegetables would have to be lifted and the messy process of pig-killing gone through. And, at the end of it, would she even be here to enjoy it all? She hoped not. In fact, whatever happened, she did not intend to still be at Thyme Cottage after September. But in the meantime, she had to behave as if she would be, a necessity endorsed by a sneaking superstitious feeling that if she did not prepare for the winter, she would not only find herself still here, but with a bare larder as well. Now, looking at how much she had accumulated already, she decided that it was time to start drying herbs.

She took a basket and walked down the garden, past Lucy who was grubbing under the quinces in search of snails, and took a critical look at the herb patch. The tarragon and borage were just right, and she picked a generous bunch of each. The thyme — she ran a hand over the bushy plant — the thyme needed another week. It was best gathered just before it flowered. And then something very odd caught her eye. Under the herb was a small package, wrapped in oiled cloth. Picking it up, Sophy drew breath to call to Lucy and show her the treasure, then saw that there was also an envelope, addressed to her in an unfamiliar, backward-sloping hand. Consumed with curiosity, she broke the seal and found that instead of a letter, the paper contained four lines of verse.

'She walks in beauty, like the night
Of cloudless climes and starry skies;
And all that's best of dark and bright
Meet in her aspect and her eyes.'

Sophy stared at it for fully a minute. There was no mistaking who had left the gift, and the audacity of it at first staggered and then amused her. Her immediate instinct was to keep it strictly to herself. She took a furtive look around the garden. Josh Greenways was hoeing the lettuces with his back to her, Lucy was squatting on the path arranging her snails in a line, Susannah and Polly were both at the front of the house cleaning windows. Sophy placed the package in her basket and covered it with the bunches of herbs, then walked back to the house, forcing herself to move without undue haste.

Once indoors, she unfolded the oiled cloth and tore at the brown paper inside. A final layer of tissue opened to reveal a roll of lace — yards and yards of finest

337

Valenciennes, three inches wide, and very similar to the length which she had been forced to sell. Hard on the heels of her amazement at the coincidence came the suspicion that it was not a coincidence at all. And if it were not, it all but proved George's theory about the Shadow's identity. Sophy sat and looked at the delicate, finely-worked festoons, thinking how well the lace would look on her new gown, and how Philip would expect her to protect his brother. But Philip had always maintained that Richard was dead, and her duty as a law-abiding citizen lay in surrendering contraband to the revenue officers. Reluctantly, and still partially undecided, she rolled the lace up as tightly as possible and put it into a reticule. Then she called Lucy, changed and set out to pay a morning visit on Lady Isobel, taking her booty with her.

Tracey Manor was in a state of uproar. Sophy and Lucy had hardly stepped inside the entrance hall before Anna-Maria, pink with excitement, burst through the morning-room doors and clasped her arm.

"Oh, Mrs Franklin, you'll never guess

what's happened . . . !"

Sophy's first thought was that the Maceboroughs had come to call, which suited her purpose admirably, as it meant it would be next to impossible to reveal her find. But Anna-Maria soon dashed that hope.

"It's the Shadow, it's so funny, he left my father a present! But do come in and see the sport, you'll never guess what came with it — my father's in such a taking . . . " She ushered Sophy into the morning-room, where Sir Harry was pacing up and down, George was leafing through a book with the most irritating suppressed grin on his face, and Lady Isobel was looking from one to the other with unconcealed annoyance. They all looked up when Sophy entered, and all started to talk at once. Lady Isobel eventually cut through the confusion.

"For shame! What will Mrs Franklin think of us? Sit down, my dear, and Anna-Maria shall ring for some refreshments. George, you will kindly not interrupt when your father is speaking."

George snorted and picked up a companion volume of the one he had been looking at. Sir Harry thrust a piece of paper into Sophy's hands.

"See here, Mrs Franklin, you're a lady who reads a good deal," he said, "what d'ye make of that?"

Sophy looked at the thick, expensive sheet, a twin of the one concealed in her reticule. On it, in a backward-sloping hand, was written:

'Here is a dear and true industrious friend,
Sir Harry Nugent, new lighted from his horse . . .
And is this not an honourable spoil?
A gallant prize?'

Studiously avoiding George's eye, as she knew that a glance from him would release the laughter that shook her chest, Sophy acknowledged her ignorance.

"It sounds like something from Shakespeare," she said, an irrepressible smile tugging at the corners of her mouth, "but I could not tell you exactly which play. One of the histories, probably."

"That's what I thought," George commented. "I'm trying to find it now."

Now was the moment to reveal her

own 'honourable spoil,' but she let it pass.

"But what is it all about?" she asked, with convincing innocence. "Anna-Maria mentioned something about the Shadow."

"Damned rogue left a keg of brandy at the door — begging your pardon — a keg of contraband brandy, with this," he waved at the paper, "this piece of confounded impudence. Gallant prize, I'll give him gallant prize! I'll see him swing for this, by Jove!"

Sophy could not resist stirring up a little more trouble.

"But it is not so impudent, surely? He calls you a 'dear and true industrious friend'."

"Damned insult! Begging your pardon. I'm no friend to a confounded smuggler. Sent for the revenue officers, and a lot of use they'll be, bunch of old women scared of getting their feet wet. They're about as good as a damp powder horn. Couldn't arrange an orgy in a whor . . ." he broke off abruptly in some confusion and was rescued by his wife.

"And how is little Lucy?" Lady Isobel enquired with blighting brightness. "I

341

hope you are learning your letters nicely? How does she go on, Mrs Franklin?"

A stilted conversation about Lucy's education was interrupted, much to everyones relief, by the arrival of footmen with trays of refreshments, and soon afterward, more interestingly, by James Hanson.

He came into the room looking rather more harassed than usual, and accepted coffee from Lady Isobel with a distracted air. Before he could state his reason for calling, however, he was asked his opinion of Sir Harry's message.

"*Henry the Fourth, Part One*," he responded promptly. "From the first scene. It should be Sir Walter Blunt, in place of Sir Harry Nugent. It would then scan properly, as you see." And having started speaking, he brushed aside the general admiration of his learning and continued, "It is something of a relief to me, I must confess, to find that you have had one of these — ah — communications, Sir Harry. Was there by any chance an — ah — unsolicited gift accompanying the verse?"

"Brandy, d'ye mean? Contraband?"

"Just so, Sir Harry, just so. It came as something of a shock when I was informed that it had been found in my porch this morning. Mrs Hanson is most distressed, she takes it to be in the nature of a threat and was loath to have me leave the house at all today. So I must put it to you in the strongest terms, Sir Harry, that every effort must be made to bring this — this scoundrel to book."

Sophy had never heard him speak so forcibly before. Sir Harry assured him that the revenue officers were on their way to Silver Creek at that very moment, but spoilt the effect of his statement by repeating his personal opinion of their abilities. Sophy asked if she might see the message the Shadow had left at the parsonage, and frowned over the fifteenth-century English.

'A Better Priest I trowe that nowher noon ys.
He waited after no Pompe and reverence,
Ne maked him a spiced conscience
But Christes loare and his apostles twelve,
He taught, but first he folwed it by inselve.'

"Chaucer?" she guessed. "*The Canterbury Tales?*"

"Yes, yes, 'Parson of a Town'," James Hanson replied testily. "But what it is hardly signifies. The fact that this rogue can roam freely about, menacing the law-abiding population of the district, is a disgrace. Whoever rids us of his presence will be doing us all a great service."

Sophy stole a glance at George, and caught an expression of smug self-satisfaction on his face. He was already, she could see, imagining the praise that would be heaped upon his head when he brought the Shadow to justice. In the meantime, she found James Hanson's reaction hysterical in the extreme. She, a widow living alone, had not felt threatened by the smuggler's gift.

"Menacing is putting it a little strongly, surely?" she asked. "Judging by the quotation, our free-trading friend has a high opinion of you. Does it not occur to you that it might all be in the nature of a joke? A rather childish joke, perhaps, but harmless enough."

Only a lifetime's ingrained habit of

politeness and deference to ladies prevented both Sir Harry and James Hanson pouring scorn on the very idea. They regarded the Shadow's activities as a flouting of authority, an attempt to prove that he could do whatever he wished with impunity. Sophy's theory they treated as ill-timed frivolity, to be expected from a mere female, who of course could not understand the issues involved.

"It would be interesting to know if Captain Ellard has had a similar communication," George said thoughtfully, with the air of one who is presenting an important clue to the assembled audience.

Sophy could guess exactly which direction his reasoning was taking him, and pulled the strings of her reticule more tightly shut. As if in answer to his query, a knocking at the front door heralded another visitor, and Philip was presently ushered into the morning-room. Sophy stared fixedly at her hands, momentarily deaf to all but his voice, hoping for a sign, just a tiny signal in his greeting, that set her apart from the rest of the gathering. He was evidently in tearing good humour, she could hear the suppressed laughter in his voice.

"Quite a crowd, upon my word!" he was saying. "I'll wager I can guess what brings you all here today." He paid his respects to Sir Harry and Lady Isobel, then teased Lucy about her snails, asking if she was entering one for the Derby this year. Sophy permited herself to look up, and caught his eye for a split second before he launched into an explanation of his reason for calling.

"There's never a moment's peace these days," he said. "I no sooner get back from town than I find that smuggler fellow's been leaving his inimitable calling-card. A cask of rum, no less. So here I am, entrusting it to your care, Sir Harry, which is particularly public-spirited of me as I'm almost out of the stuff at home. And what do you think of this?" He produced a sheet of paper from his inside pocket and read,

"I fear thee, Ancient Mariner!
I fear thy skinny hand!
For thou art long, and lank, and brown

346

As is the ribbed sea-sand."

He looked round, waiting for the laughter he expected, but found that the faces around him registered only shock, anger or consternation. Sophy's expression he could not read. She seemed to have developed an intense interest in her hands. Surely she was not taking it seriously?

"Damned impudence!" Sir Harry exploded. "Who does the scoundrel think he is, insulting respectable folk like this? Look at what he left for me, and for Hanson. Let him see your one, Hanson. What d'ye think of that, hey? Damned insults!"

Philip read rapidly through the two sets of verse, an irrepressible grin spreading over his face.

"I think it has all the hallmarks of a man enjoying a good joke," he said. And as Sir Harry turned yet redder, he laughed and clapped him on the shoulder. "Come on, where's your sense of humour? The fellow's a showman, a play-actor, we can at least try to enjoy his attempt at entertainment. What shall we do to him when he's caught? I suggest we dress him as a maid and take him to the hiring fair."

There was a strangled snort from the other side of the room. Sophy, her arm round Lucy, was rocking back and forth, gasping for breath.

"Oh dear — I'm so sorry — it's just so funny — I'll lend you a bonnet to make him look his best — "

Lucy, though not understanding the joke, giggled happily in response. Anna-Maria and George joined in, Sir Harry suddenly threw back his head and gave a below of mirth, and even Lady Isobel and James Hanson permited themselves to smile.

"That's rich! We'll do it, by Jove!" Sir Harry declared. "And as from today the reward for his capture is going to be a hundred guineas, from my pocket. By thunder, it will be worth it to pay the rogue out."

"And I'll make it up to a hundred and fifty," Philip responded. "That should tempt the most loyal of accomplices."

There was general agreement to this. On a rising tide of optimism, everyone knew that it was only a matter of time now before the Shadow got his just deserts. Only George was confounded by this new turn of events. He was not dismayed when Philip produced a gift from the Shadow as well, for it was likely that Richard had included his brother in his recipients to allay suspicion. But when Philip volunteered to add to the reward fund, George's theory began to show serious cracks.

Philip turned to Sophy.

"But did our audacious friend not leave anything for you, Mrs Franklin?" he asked. "He has visited every other prominent person in the neighbourhood."

The reticule on Sophy's wrist felt as if it had gained a stone in weight. Now would be a splendid opportunity to reveal its contents and amaze the assembled company, as the gift of lace must surely have been a coincidence. But still Sophy was reluctant to relinquish it. She looked Philip straight in the eye.

"I suppose he is too much of a gentleman to give presents to ladies to whom he has not even been introduced," she said.

And this time, everybody laughed.

349

10

EXCITEMENT at Tracey Manor was running at fever pitch. Activity started in the kitchens at dawn, where dinner for thirty and supper for one hundred was being prepared. Mountains of food had already been stored in the spacious pantries, but there was still the bulk of the work to be done, not to speak of the usual demands of breakfast, luncheon and meals for the servants' hall. By the time George made his appearance sometime after nine o'clock, the task of reorganising almost the entire ground floor of the house was well under way. Wherever George went, he found somebody busily preparing for the ball. In the south drawing-room, the furniture had already been cleared and now half a dozen housemaids were polishing the floor for dancing. The morning-room, where he often lounged for an hour or so before deciding what to do, was in the process of being set out with card tables.

The breakfast-room was being cleared away and the dining-room undergoing a last dusting. The library was cluttered up with furniture from the south drawing-room, and in the blue drawing-room his mother and sister were consulting lists, ticking off jobs done and making last-minute changes to the seating plan for dinner. Even the gun-room, his retreat in times of crisis, only served to remind him that his promised birthday gift, the latest model of a detonator shotgun from Manton's, had not yet been delivered. Knowing his luck, it would not even arrive in time for the opening of the shooting season.

The whole house was alive with excited, busy people going about the task of preparation for the ball. George could hardly move without colliding with somebody bearing flowers or silverware or gilded chairs. Even his father was engaged in his effort towards the evening's success, although he was not in evidence. He had retreated to the cellar with the butler to choose the wines, a long and exacting process involving tasting all the bottles concerned to make sure they were entirely suitable for the occasion. Everyone in the house, from his mother to the scullery maid, had something important to do, except for George. He was merely in everybody's way. That was bad enough, but worse still it was all for the purpose of a ball, which of all forms of entertainment was the one he hated the most. He went out to the stables, only to find that all the riding horses had been turned out to grass to make room for the carriage horses that would be arriving in the evening. He sent a groom to catch the wildest youngster for him, and wandered back towards the house, brooding over the horrors of his existence, and swiping the heads off the flowers with his whip.

It was then that Lady Isobel happened to catch sight of him in his riding dress and opened the windows of the blue drawing-room to call to him.

"George! George dear, you're not going out, are you? Do you think that's wise? You don't want to tire yourself before this evening."

George lashed viciously at a rosebush, sending up a shower of pink petals. A sweet cloying scent filled the air, catching at his throat.

"Yes, I am going out, and what's more, I might not come back," he retorted.

Lady Isobel's expression stiffened.

"George, you will kindly come here when I am speaking to you," she said.

Slowly, he approached the house, every line of his body speaking rebellion.

Even Lady Isobel sensed the gathering storm, and dropped her tone of command.

"I would be obliged if you would stay in today," she said, with a palpable effort to use some tact. "I never know when I might need to consult you on some matter."

"Consult me? That will make a change. I can't remember ever having been listened to in my entire life. If my opinion mattered at all, this whole farce would never have been started."

Lady Isobel cleared her throat. Anna-Maria looked from her mother to her brother anxiously. She did not want anything to spoil the evening upon which so much depended.

"George need not come to the actual dance if he if does not want to, surely?"

she asked. But nobody heard her.

"What do you mean by 'this whole farce'?" Lady Isobel was saying.

"You know very well what I mean. This confounded ball. It happens to be my birthday as well as Anna-Maria's, in case you don't know. Everyone seems to have lost sight of that small fact. The whole house is turned upside-down for her, and I just have to conform, as usual. Nobody thinks of what I might feel. Oh no, I'm just George, I just have to be quiet and do as I'm told, like a good little boy."

"Just at this moment," his mother replied, "you are behaving like a spoilt little boy."

"It really doesn't matter what I do or say, does it?" George questioned bitterly. "The result is just the same. I'm kept here like a — a parrot on a perch with a chain round my leg, expected to bow and say 'Good morning' for the benefit of visitors."

Lady Isobel said, "Really, George — " with heavy patience, but her son was getting into his stride. He had been working up to this for the past fortnight and nothing was going to stop him now.

"You go to all this trouble," he waved an arm expressively at a troop of gardener's boys bearing plants in from the hothouses, "all this expense. I can't even get a horse to ride, they've all been moved down to the lower pastures. And what for — to get Anna-Maria off your hands. I don't begrudge that, don't think I do, but I fail to see why you do all this for her, and nothing for me — " And as if in answer, he felt the first warning tightening of his chest, and broke out in a fine sweat of panic. To suffer an attack now would just about put the seal on his imprisonment.

"If you are referring to Cambridge, than maybe we might consider it next year, if you are stronger," Lady Isobel conceded. She, as much as Anna-Maria, wanted to keep the peace today. In the interests of the great occasion, she would even make some form of compromise with her son. But George was not to be put off by vague half-promises.

"And maybe we might not," he flung back, mimicking her tone of voice with biting accuracy. "This year, next year, sometime, never. It's always the same, isn't it? Empty words, just something to keep me quiet. Perhaps it would interest you to know that I am not concerned about going to Cambrdige any more. You can't use that as a carrot for good behaviour, it no longer has any effect. I've something altogether different in mind now, something that will take me far away from here, and you won't be able to raise a finger to stop me."

He paused, his rapid shallow breathing whistling over his bared teeth as he grinned provokingly at his mother, watching for her reaction.

"I really cannot think what you are talking about," Lady Isobel said with repressive dignity. But her eyes were wary.

"I really cannot think what you are talking about," George repeated. "I'll tell you what I'm talking about, mother: Sophy Franklin. I shall marry Sophy Franklin and we shall go away, far, far away from here, we shall travel to the south, to where the sun is always warm . . . "

356

"George! George, you can't. You don't mean it . . . "

Lady Isobel's voice was thin and weak with shock. She reached out towards her son with a hand that trembled slightly. George felt a tremor of dismay at what he had done. She seemed to have aged before his eyes.

"Oh, yes I do, every word. We shall go to Italy, Albania," he began to elaborate, covering up his misgivings, "the Isles of Greece, Turkey. We shall be away for years and years. Perhaps we shall never return. Perhaps . . . "

"You can't do it," his mother stated, "you're too young."

"I'm exactly the same age as Anna-Maria, and yet she's not too young. That's what all this farce is about, is it not? To throw my sister at the head of the Maceborough heir? If she's old enough to be married, so am I."

Back on the safe ground of facts, Lady Isobel recovered some of her accustomed authority.

"You are under age as far as the law is concerned," she declared. "You need your father's consent."

George laughed in her face.

"In this country, maybe. But not if we were to go abroad first. We would have no trouble in finding some foreign priest willing to perform the rites."

"Your father would cut off your allowance," Lady Isobel countered desperately. "You would have nothing to live on."

"Sophy has money," George replied airily. "It costs next to nothing to live abroad, and in any case our needs will be very small. We shall take a tiny white villa overlooking the sea, and we shall live on grapes and wine and love — " he flung wide his arms, riding a wave of exultation. He would carry it through. He really would. From a long way away, it seemed, he heard his mother saying, George, I cannot possibly allow you . . . " Laughing, he began to stride back towards the stables. "Just you try and stop me!" he cried.

By the time he reached the yard, he was fighting with each wheezing breath to force air into his closing lungs, but even this was not going to stop him. It was now or never. He mounted the skittish chestnut colt that the groom had just brought up from the pasture and erupted through the gateway, gravel scattering from beneath the horse's hooves like grapeshot.

★ ★ ★

Sophy was very tempted to take the cowardly way out and escape from Thyme Cottage before the inevitable confrontation with Lady Isobel. The fervid scene with George had left her wrung out like a dish-rag. If she could have given George some honest reason for refusing him, she might have felt slightly better about it. If she could have said that she was determined against marrying again, or alternatively, if she had been able to admit to there being someone else, then she could at least have let him down gently. But as it was she was forced into using vague, empty excuses, until George was convinced that she could see nothing of any good in him. Reassuring him on that head without raising any false hopes left her more emotionally drained than she could remember having been since Lucy's illness.

And now there was Lady Isobel to cope with. No doubt she would come sailing in, ready to do battle with the scheming woman who was stealing her innocent lamb. And of course, it would be easy enough to deflate her in one short sentence by saying that she had no intention of marrying George. But she felt she must make Lady Isobel see that she had to give her son a chance to grow up on his own. That much Sophy owed him, and to do it she would have to make Lady Isobel really worried about the possible alternatives.

She had no time to work out any definite strategy before a rumble of wheels outside heralded Lady Isobel's arrival. She had come in state, in the family coach, and marched into the parlour with all guns blazing.

"Well now, Mrs Franklin, I don't know how far this affair with my son has gone, but I am telling you here and now that it has to stop," she stated, refusing Sophy's offer of a seat with a dismissive wave of the hand. "It is absolutely unthinkable that he should go running off to foreign parts. His health would never stand up to the strain."

"I hardly think that could be the case," Sophy replied, forcing herself to speak with cool confidence. "A warm climate is probably just what he needs. It would do him the world of good to live by the Mediterranean. Far more than continuing here for another winter in the damp air from the marshes. A few months, or years, in Italy or Greece would make a new man of him."

"Stuff!" Lady Isobel snorted. "You know nothing at all of the matter. George has a very delicate constitution. It is only because of constant care and attention to his wellbeing that I managed to rear him at all, and if you imagine I am going to let you undo all my years of devotion by encouraging him in this lunatic scheme of marrying and going to live like a foreign peasant, you are very much mistaken. If you go through with this, you'll be the death of him, you mark my words!"

Sophy looked faintly amused.

"Is that not a little extreme?" she remarked. "There are doctors abroad, you know, and they must be reasonably competent, or there would not be so many foreigners."

"You are a hard, unfeeling woman, Mrs Franklin, to tear my son away from his family like this. If you had any true affection for him, you would never have let matters become so serious.

Sophy swallowed nervously. She had hoped the exchange of views would not descend to a personal level. Once that was reached, things might be said that could not be easily mended.

"On the contrary," she said, with far greater calm than she felt, "I have George's best interests very much to heart."

"Ha!" Lady Isobel was unconvinced. "You are taking advantage of a boy's foolish infatuation. It will burn itself out in a matter of weeks, just you wait and see!"

"George does not think so," Sophy replied.

"No, of course he does not *now*. But what will it be like in a couple of years' time, hey? Tell me that. And besides, what about the difference in your ages?

You must be at least eight years older than him, and a widow to boot."

"Six years," Sophy corrected frostily. "And if George does not mind, I fail to see why it should concern anyone else."

Lady Isobel changed tack.

"If you will not consider George, you might at least have some feeling for his father. It will break Sir Harry's heart if he goes."

"It will break George's heart if he does not," Sophy countered. The knuckles of her tightly-laced fingers turned white with the effort of keeping her hands still. She sensed that Lady Isobel was nearing the end of her points of debate, but she was a long way yet from winning.

"I know exactly why you persist in continuing with this," Lady Isobel declared. "You are after his money and position. You want Tracey Manor." She advanced to within inches of Sophy, her head thrust forward. "But you'll get nothing out of it, believe me. Sir Harry will disinherit him."

Sophy ran her tongue over her dry lips and willed herself not to back away. The sheer physical presence of the older woman was intimidating.

"I think not," she replied. "Unless I am mistaken, the estate is entailed."

For an endless, nerve-cracking minute, she held Lady Isobel's infuriated glare, and watched her expression change from outrage to desperation.

"But — but — you can't do this — " she spluttered. "You can't take George away from us — our only son — he's far too young — "

Sophy let drop the charade of opposition. "I do so agree with you," she smiled.

It took some while before Lady Isobel realised just what she had said.

"You mean — are you telling me — that you are not intending to elope with my son?" she said slowly.

"Good heavens, no! The very idea!"

"Well, thank the — it's not that I have anything against you personally, Mrs Franklin," she hastened to explain, now that the danger appeared to be over, "dear me, no. Nothing at all. It's just that — you must understand — it is too soon for George to be making such an important decision — "

"Of course, of course I understand

entirely," Sophy assured her. "George is but eighteen, and an immature eighteen at that." And having soothed Lady Isobel's fears, she slipped a sly thrust under her guard. "But unfortunately one cannot guarantee that the next person to take his fancy will see it in the same light. A pert tradesman's daughter, for instance."

Lady Isobel's jaw dropped.

"Do you really think he might?" she exclaimed horrified.

"Nothing would be more likely. Young men of George's volatile temperament are only too apt to fly from one unsuitable attachment to another, particularly when they have nothing else with which to occupy themselves."

"Yes — " Lady Isobel turned the awful possibilities over in her mid. "Yes — but my dear Mrs Franklin, what is to be done?"

Sophy allowed herself to breathe a great sigh of relief.

"I don't know about you, Lady Isobel, but I feel a considerable need of something to calm the nerves. This morning's events have been something of a strain. Would you care for a glass of brandy? Or shall I ring for tea?"

"Brandy," said Lady Isobel, and sat down abruptly.

Sophy poured out two generous measures and handed one to her guest, restraining the hysterical impulse to say 'And not a penny duty paid.' She had recently come to an amicable arrangement with Bandy Coates over the supply of tea and alcohol to Thyme Cottage.

"Now then," she said, as the fiery liquid glowed pleasantly through her agitated system, "what are we going to do? It's quite clear that George cannot remain here, it would pose a very awkward situation for all concerned."

"I suppose you are right," Lady Isobel said heavily. "But the question is, where is he to go . . . ?"

Sophy sipped her drink and held her counsel, waiting for Lady Isobel to find the answer herself.

"I have never been happy about his going up to Cambridge," she went on. "There's no knowing what he might get up to. One hears such tales. Just look at what happened to the Carfews' boys — but I don't suppose you know them. And yet, it is not too far away."

"Hardly any distance at all, once you reach the turnpike," Sophy agreed. "And it's not as if there will be nobody there to keep an eye on him. Doctor Vye will probably be home for the new term and I'm sure you must have other acquaintances there as well. As for getting into scrapes, he'll do that wherever he is. Witness today's episode."

Lady Isobel was nothing if not decisive. Her back regained its usual ramrod straightness, her mouth its lines of determination.

"You are quite right, Mrs Franklin. It's the only solution. I shall speak to Sir Harry about it the instant I return."

"I'm sure you won't regret it," Sophy said. "George is a clever young man, you know. He has a sharp brain but he has not been taught how to use it properly. It would be a pity to see that go to waste. If he has the benefit of studying under some of the best scholars in the land, I think he might well surprise you."

"I hope you're right, Mrs Franklin, though I fear the surprise might not be a pleasant one. However, we shall see."

As Lady Isobel rose to take her leave, Sophy steeled herself to make a sacrifice in the interests of a problem-free evening for the Nugents.

"I think it might be better," she said, unsuccessfully trying to keep the regret out of her voice, "if I stayed away tonight."

"Nonsense!" Lady Isobel exclaimed, then stopped short as concern for her son and gratitude to Sophy battled for precedence. "At least," she went on, less forcefully, "perhaps it would be a little difficult if you were to come to dinner, but on no account must you miss the ball. Anna-Maria depends upon your coming."

Sophy smiled wryly. So she was no longer a hard, unfeeling woman, but back in her usual role of sensible Mrs Franklin, confidante and friend. Perhaps tonight Lady Isobel would see her in yet another light. And she walked thoughtfully upstairs, took down her new ballgown and began to sew the Valenciennes round the flounced hemline.

At half-past eight that evening, she crept into the nursery to see if Lucy was sleeping. The child stirred and her eyes flickered open, focussed and widened in delight. She sat up, instantly awake.

"Mama! You look beautiful. Like a princess!"

Sophy laughed and revolved slowly to show off her finery. The peach-coloured gown was a triumph, a confection of silk and gauze trimmed with deep flounces, knots of palest green ribbons and the Shadow's delicate creamy lace. Gone was the widow's cap and plainly-dressed hair-style, and in its place a cropped and curled head set off with green ribbons and peach silk roses. A gold locket, an ivory fan and green satin slippers completed the effect. Sophy bent and kissed Lucy, tickling her nose with an exotic waft of frangipani.

"Cinderella's going to the ball, sweet-heart," she said.

"Ooo! Shall you meet a handsome prince?"

"I don't know, pet. Would you like it if I did?"

Lucy nodded enthusiastically.

"Oo yes, then we could all live in a palace."

"Well, don't depend upon it, darling. Princes are few and far between these days. Snuggle down and go to sleep, Susannah will be here to look after you."

She covered the child up, kissed her cheek and made her way downstairs to await the arrival of the Nugents' coach, not without a tremor of trepidation. Yesterday, on the anniversary of Jeremy's death, she had shed some tears of nostalgia for the good times they had shared, but today she was finally casting off his influence and deciding her new life. No more retreating behind the cover of a black veil.

At Tracey Manor she had to wait in a queue of carriages to alight at the front door. Everyone who was anyone for ten miles around had been invited and the house was alive with music and lights and laughter. Sophy felt a surge of nervous excitement as her name was announced and she walked into the transformed drawing-room, to be received by her hosts. Sir Harry gave a roar of amazement on seeing her.

"Mrs Franklin, by Jove! Well, well, you could knock me over with a feather! I'll tell you something, that foolish boy of mine has very good taste. Are you going to give me the pleasure of dancing with you later on? Got to get in now, you see, before all the younger fellows have a chance."

Lady Isobel's reaction was more restrained.

"Very nice, my dear, very proper," she commented, taking in Sophy's attire with one appraising glance. And inclining her head confidentially towards Sophy, she went on, "I would be very much obliged to you, Mrs Franklin, if you would find out something about that gentleman over there for me."

She nodded in the direction of Anna-Maria, who was deep in conversation with a curly-haired young man with military side-whiskers, an eye-patch and an empty left sleeve. Oblivious to their surroundings, he and Anna-Maria were utterly engrossed with each other, a small intense island of happiness amongst the chattering, superficial throng.

"He came with the Maceboroughs, and his name is Major John Smetterton," Lady Isobel said. "But I would like to know a little more."

Sophy said she would see what she could do. Small wonder Lady Isobel was so interested. Sophy had never seen such a promising case of love at first sight.

She moved on into the ballroom, searching for familiar faces. George, she was relieved to discover, was nowhere to be seen. She caught sight of the Hansons, and was about to walk across and speak to them when Philip appeared at her side.

"Sophy! You are quite stunning. You make the Maceborough females look like a bunch of frights. But what are you up to? First you don't attend the dinner and now you appear fit to make a killing at Almacks."

Sophy smiled radiantly. She had meant to be cool and distant with him this evening, but it was next to impossible when he was practically eating her with his eyes.

"Does there have to be an explanation?" she asked. "I just got so bored with black. You're looking very elegant yourself this evening. Such a magnificent waistcoat! I suspect you're something of a dandy at heart."

Philip grinned and glanced down at the garment in question, a rather splendid affair of blue and white striped brocade. But he was not easily sidetracked.

"You won't escape so readily," he said. "You still haven't explained why you stayed away from the dinner. There must have been some reason."

"Oh, nothing you need bother your head about."

Philip's expression sharpened with suspicion.

"Sophy, you are up to something."

Sophy straightened an imaginary wrinkle in her glove.

"Well now, and if I am, it's only what I've learnt from you, General Ludd. You're the master of deception, are you not?" She looked past him at some people she knew on the other side of the room. "Oh, there are the Passinghams, I must just go and have a word with them. Will you excuse me?"

He laid a hand fleetingly on her arm, the only contact he would risk in public, but it was enough to bring Sophy up short.

"Not until you've promised me two dances, Mrs Franklin. I've jigged around with country lumps these eight months past while you've thumped away at the piano. Tonight you and I are going to show everyone how a waltz should be performed.

"Are we indeed?" Sophy's feeble attempt at defying him began to crumble. She had come with every intention of playing the game by his rules this evening, dancing with everyone else and merely finding time for the odd friendly word when her attention was not called for elsewhere. But she did desperately want to dance with him.

"Oh — very well," she agreed, giving in. And she persuaded herself that it would bring home to him even more strongly what he was missing.

She found no shortage of partners to aid her in her plan. Even the two Maceborough brothers found her worthy of their notice. They spent most of the evening dancing or talking with members of their own party and regarding the rest of the company through their quizzing-glasses with supercilious smiles. Sophy's immediate reaction was to turn them down, but then she reflected that to be seen with the most distinguished guests would not go unnoticed by Philip, so she agreed to one dance with each of them, but with an air of condescension that left them in no doubt that it was she who was conferring the honour.

In between dances, she managed to elicit some information on Anna-Maria's major. He was, she discovered, one of the myriad Maceborough connections, a second cousin. He had belonged to a Light Infantry regiment and fought his way virtually unscathed right through the Peninsular War only to lose an eye and an arm at Waterloo. His immediate prospects were respectable, but hardly brilliant, for he was about to take up the job of looking after the Maceborough interests in East Anglia. Sophy relayed all this back to Lady Isobel, who expressed restrained enthusiasm.

"Acceptable," she commented. "Not a great match, but she could have gone farther and fared worse. Not," she added hastily, "that anything might come of it. But one does like to be forewarned."

Philip, on coming to claim Sophy as his partner, was asked his opinion.

"Smetterton? Very pleasant fellow, for a redcoat," he commented generously. "By far the best of that particular bunch."

He chuckled as he led Sophy onto the floor.

"God knows what Sir Harry's going to make of it. Smetterton's an out-and-out Whig. But no doubt Anna-Maria will find a way round it. By the by, do you know what's the matter with young George? He looks as if he's touched bottom on a lee shore."

Sophy's conscience gave a sharp knock. In the excitement of the evening, she had half-forgotten George, thinking that he had stayed away from the ball. If he was here watching, though, her present behaviour must be acting like a twist of the knife. She sighed. "I rather think he has," she said.

But it was too late to change tactics now. The band was striking up a lilting, irresistible waltz, and Sophy succumbed willingly to its magic. From the very first step she and Philip moved as one, perfectly in time, each knowing instinctively what the other was about to do. Sophy sang as she spun in dizzying circles, moving effortlessly, it seemed, a foot above the ground. The green silk walls of the room, the cascade of lights, the multi-coloured throng of the other dancers coalesced into an indistinct blur, until the only reality was herself and Philip and the music. She floated down to earth again slowly, the enchantment dissolving in the polite, kid-gloved applause that greeted the conclusion of the dance.

"That was — indescribable," Philip declared softly. "However am I to wait till the next one?"

The answer quivered unspoken in the space between them: why wait?

Philip was torn between caution and desire. The soft promise of her body, so tantalisingly close to his, was an open invitation to cast aside the facade of indifference he had maintained so carefully. But with it would go Sophy's protection. To leave now, together, would be certain to arouse speculation. Even as he wavered, the dance floor was clearing, leaving them exposed to curious glances. Abruptly, he began to steer Sophy back to her seat at the side of the room.

"I see you found your lace," he remarked in his company voice.

"Yes, it was not lost at all, merely mislaid," Sophy replied, a brittle, frigid smile masking her sense of rejection. She trotted out her prepared explanation. "I found it stuffed into an old reticule. Was that not extraordinary? I have no recollection at all of having put it there."

"Extraordinary," Philip echoed.

Already he was regretting his decision, and now before he could change course the Maceborough heir was approaching to claim Sophy for the quadrille. She left without another word, seemingly as disdainful of him as of her new partner. Recollecting his social obligations, Philip sought out Anna-Maria, who had promised him the dance some days beforehand. They were probably the most uncommunicative couple in the room, exchanging only the briefest of disconnected remarks, whilst her eyes unashamedly followed Major Smetterton,

378

and Philip kept a more covert watch on Sophy.

Another two dances brought the hour round to midnight, and the guests moved into the panelled dining-room for supper. Sophy, intent on exacting revenge for all the hours she had spent quietly observing while Philip danced attendance on Anna-Maria, overacted her part, sparkling brilliantly before a bemused audience of admirers. Philip watched her as she leaned forward, emphasising some point she was making with spiky, nervous gestures of her hands. His supper partner, an undistinguished young lady anxious to make the most of her opportunity, asked him earnestly what his most frightening experience had been during his years in the Navy, and he almost forgot himself so far as to relate a tale he reserved for male company: that of being laid out by a half-empty gin bottle wielded by an irate whore who objected to his press-gang taking her client. Hastily, he substituted one of his Caribbean adventures.

Supper over, the company drifted back into the ballroom to be entertained with songs from the more musically-inclined young ladies while they recovered their strength.

Philip sauntered across to where Sophy was sitting, and bent down, pretending to retrieve something she had dropped.

"Come outside, you ravishing creature," he whispered, "before I create a public scandal. I'll wait for you in the Italian garden."

Sophy nodded vaguely, studiously avoiding his eyes. She gave him five minutes of suspense, wondering if she was coming, then slipped out to join him.

★ ★ ★

The day that had started badly and become rapidly worse was now turning into a protracted nightmare for George. When he left Thyme Cottage, he wanted never to see Sophy or even hear of her again, and yet when he learnt that she was not to attend the dinner, he could not imagine how he was to get through the evening. He drank heavily through the interminable length of the meal, but this only deepened the black depression that gripped him. Released at last from the dining-room, he was shyly approached by a girl who had adored him from a distance for months and had at last summoned up the courage to speak to him, and was so savagely cutting that he reduced her to tears of despair. Finding that hurting someone else did nothing to help him, he retreated to his room with a decanter of brandy, meaning to obliterate all recollection of the disastrous day. But through the open windows came the rumble of carriages arriving, the excited chatter of expectant voices, the persuasive lilt of dance music. Somewhere down there was Sophy. Drawn irresistibly by the memory of evenings spent talking to her whilst the others jigged around, George went back downstairs.

What he found there was beyond his worst fears. Sophy the remote and unattainable dark star was just bearable, for though she could not be his, at least he could be sure she belonged to nobody else. But Sophy laughing and sparkling, hardly still the entire evening, smiling into the eyes of every man she danced with, was unendurable. To watch her waltzing with Philip Ellard, the pair of them moving as one, as if they had practised every day of their lives, made him feel physically sick.

By the time supper was over, he had seen as much as he could take. He left the sweating, gibbering rabble and went outside. He shambled across the lawns with no clear purpose in mind other than to get away from the ball, but even beyond the light streaming from the open french windows, the persistent sound of a piano sonata pursued him. He made his way round to the side of the house, and the accommodating privacy of the rose garden. Here the full moon silvered the formal pattern of the flower-beds and cast shadows of black velvet under the arbour and trellised alleys. The scent of roses hung in the soft summer night. It was the perfect setting for vows of eternal love, and sure enough, he came across two pairs of lovers in the whispering darkness. Sickened, he wandered towards the Italian garden, hoping there to find only the silent company of the statues brought back by his grandfather from the Grand Tour.

At first he thought he was alone. Only the classical figures stared blindly into the middle distance, and at the far end of the long, rectangular canal the fountain's spray shivered in the moon's reflection. The air was slightly damp, and clear after the cloying closeness of the roses. George reached out to touch the cool calves of a marble Juno. Italy! He supposed this was the nearest he would ever get to it. And then beyond the curtain of water a movement caught his eye, the pale shimmer of a woman's dress against the shadow of a man's coat. Embarrassed he turned to go, but above the murmur of the fountain's fall came the sound of their voices: a gasp, a low laugh of pleasure, an urgent plea, "Sophy, Sophy my love . . . "

Without thought, he marched to the end of the canal to confront them.

"So!" he hissed. "This is why you refused me! How long have you been deceiving me this way?"

They did not jump apart, but turned slowly to look at him, resentful of the intrusion. And to his despair, he found that his rival was Philip Ellard. He was doubly betrayed. They stood before him with all the unspoken strength of a couple against a single outsider. He wanted to flee, but some inner compulsion made him stay and confirm that all was lost.

"And this is why you went on pretending to encourage me — you were acting as a spy," he accused, gathering momentum. "Everything I said, all my plans, went straight to *him*!"

"No! No, I did nothing of the kind." Sophy spoke with low, desperate urgency, but even as the denial left her lips, she remembered the warning she had given about Caleb Moore. "You must understand . . ."

"Understand! I understand it all now. And to think I trusted you . . . !"

"Hold your tongue!" Philip Ellard's quiet command cut across his rising tide of invective. "You have no right to speak to Mrs Franklin in that manner. I know nothing of your affairs and I care less, so kindly take yourself off; your presence is decidedly unwanted just now."

Sophy drew breath to speak, but before she could do so, George was jabbing an angry finger at Philip.

384

"I'll break you!" he threatened. "I'll find that brother of yours and I'll make sure you're implicated!"

Philip let go of Sophy and took a menacing step towards George, who held his ground, instinctively putting up his fists. Sophy clutched at Philip's arm, begging him to stop. George was half a head taller, but no match for Philip's strength and experience. In one movement, Philip shook her off and gripped George above the elbows, pinioning his arms to his sides.

"You will keep my brother out of this," he stated, speaking with slow emphasis. "He died so that people like you could sleep easy in their beds. Now go, and leave the grown-ups to their own affairs."

And George finding himself released as suddenly as he had been captured, stumbled away.

Philip watched him out of the garden, then turned back to Sophy.

"That boy is becoming a positive bore," he remarked dispassionately.

He was not prepared for Sophy's reaction.

"It's all your fault," she accused. "This

385

need never have happened if it wasn't for this ridiculous charade you're making us play. Don't you care that he's been hurt?"

Philip did not point out that he had warned her.

"He'll get over it," he said reasonably. "We all go through it: puppy love. Like the measles."

"Thank you!" Sophy snapped. "I appreciate being likened to a case of measles!"

Philip held her close, stroking the unfamiliar curls.

"Calm down, sweetheart, it's not worth quarrelling over," he soothed. "You've had a difficult day, I can see that, but it won't look half so bad in the morning."

"Don't patronise me!" Sophy responded fiercely. "And don't ruin my hair, either!"

"I am not patronising you."

"You are. You treat me like a half-witted child. You tell me nothing. I am tired of all this petty deception, and I am sick of your pointless game of secrecy. It's so — so unnecessary!"

386

"It is necessary, darling. I told you why, I thought you agreed with me. And it's not for much longer now. A month, five weeks at the most."

"Till after the harvest?"

"Exactly."

"And why then, precisely?"

"Sophy, I did explain." An edge of exasperation crept into Philip's voice."

"Yes, but you only told me half the story." For weeks she had kept her growing fear to herself, but the strain of the day's events had finally worn her down. "You may fool everyone else, but not me. I saw through your so-called business trips a long time ago. Don't forget I know all about where you were when you were supposedly at a wedding at Cheltenham. And the other journeys as well — you've been all over East Anglia, and in these last few days you went to meet Henry Hunt. It only needs a bad harvest, and there will be riots again, and who better than you to fan the flame?"

She stopped abruptly, relieved to have it out in the open at last, but unsure of his reaction. Philip was looking at her with an odd half-smile.

"Well?" she said.

"So — you suspect me of inciting revolution, do you?" he asked slowly. "And me a quiet, respectable land owner? Would I not be working against my own interests?"

"It makes a perfect cover," Sophy pointed out.

"Running with the hare and hunting with the hounds? That's a dangerous game."

"You enjoy dangerous games."

"You know me too well.

"So you don't deny it?" Sophy spoke carefully, pressing her point home.

"Listen, my darling," Philip spoke carefully, choosing his words. "If — *if* — I was involved in what you suspect, I would not want to run the risk of having you forced to give evidence against me, or worse still, perjuring yourself for my sake. Far better that you should be kept in ignorance, and that you are not seen to have any connection with me. Think of Lucy, if you will not consider yourself. You have to protect her. Surely you realise that?"

Reluctantly, Sophy agreed. She could

see the sense in his reasoning.

"But why must you get embroiled in such a desperate plot? Why not get out of it now, before there's any trouble?" she pleaded. "Why not leave it to someone else?"

"And desert the cause?"

"Cause?" Sophy snapped her fingers contemptuously. "*That* for your cause! It's you that I care about, you and me."

"So do I, my only love. You above all things. I only said 'if', remember. I expect the greatest danger I shall incur in the next few weeks will be that of cutting my foot off with a scythe, so stop worrying. Trust me, Sophy, for just a little while longer."

Sophy sighed. She had flown to meet him on wings of joy, but now the mood had dissolved completely, leaving her flat and weary. Unheeding, the fountain played on, a gentle, soothing fall into the lily-cluttered canal. In the house, the orchestra was striking up again. Another waltz.

"I suppose we had better go back inside," she said dully.

11

AFTER the frivolity of the ball, the most vital part of the year's work got under way. The Lord of the Harvest was chosen from amongst the casual labourers and rates of payment negotiated with the farmers, and each morning the village was roused by a boy with a tin horn, blowing the peremptory call to work. Throughout the long hours of daylight the swinging scythes sliced through the standing corn, the men working with slow, inevitable rhythm across field after wide field. In their wake came the women, binding and stacking the sheaves, and with them a motley band of children, helping or hindering according to age and ability, playing, shouting, carrying draughts of ale to their sweating fathers and looking after the squalling babies. Feuds and tussles that flared through the rest of the year were buried in the all-important task of ensuring a good harvest. Anxious eyes scanned each threatening cloud, for a week of rain or even one bad hailstorm could mean the difference between wealth or short commons for the large farmer, solvency or the debtor's gaol for the small man, and a full belly or starvation for the labourers.

Philip was up each morning to see the gaily-painted wains rumble out of the yard at the heels of the great Suffolk horses. He worked through the day, a rather eccentric figure in a Panama hat he used to wear in tropical waters. The harvest afforded a watertight excuse for avoiding Sophy, and allaying any suspicions that might have been aroused at the ball. For the first weeks or so, she brought Lucy and the Hanson boys out to watch the progress of the work, but after a while she seemed to take the hint and stayed away. When the tide was up in the evening, he would plunge into the rolling grey-green river and slough off the day's accumulation of dust and grime, and sometimes, shaking the water out of his eyes as he surfaced, or lying back and letting the waves carry him along, he would see her silhouetted against the sky, alone but for the spaniel that ran ahead of her along the sea-wall.

Sophy would understand, he was convinced. The scene at Tracey Manor had just been the product of an exceptionally difficult day. Soon he would be in a position to live at Creek End in the manner for which it was built. He would open up the new wing, clear the gardens, turn the Suffolks out of the stables and set up a carriage. No more camping out, nothing but the best for Sophy. If all went well for the next three or four weeks . . .

At Thyme Cottage, Sophy busied herself with her own harvest, throwing her energies into bottling, drying, preserving and salting. Polly and Susannah found her unusually short-tempered, and exchanged speaking looks behind her back. Sophy's life seemed to have suddenly become restricted, though in reality she had simply lost patience with her friends and acquaintances. Mary Hanson could talk of nothing but her condition, Anna-Maria's conversation was restricted to a recital of her John's virtues, and although Sir Harry and Lady Isobel welcomed her at Tracey Manor just as heartily as they had ever done, visits there were necessarily strained.

None of this would have mattered if it were not for Philip's apparent defection. Sophy was not deceived by the demands of the season. He had been just as busy during haymaking, and yet he had still found time to see her. She began to think that next year would still find her in Thyme Cottage. Bankruptcy she could have coped with, or emigration, or even another woman. But what could she do with a man with a cause? On Sundays she watched him covertly from her pew across the aisle and two further back than his, until she was sure he could feel her eyes on him. An invitation to dinner at Creek End one Sunday produced no explanation, for Charlotte Vye played chaperone with unwavering adherence to duty.

At last the final field at Creek End was cut, and the terret-shaped corn dolly made from the very last sheaf. The Lord of the Harvest led the Horkey Load through the village with a flower-crowned girl riding on top of the stacked wain, and the villagers lined the street to throw buckets of water over the wheat. Susannah, dressed in a cast-off gown of Sophy's much let out at the seams, went off to the Horkey Supper with John Jennings, stiff and sleek in his Sunday coat.

As the evening began to draw in, Sophy knelt on the window-seat of her bedchamber, opened the casement and leaned out, breathing the damp air. The copper-coloured shield of the harvest moon hung low in the darkening sky and there was a faint, unmistakable tang of autumn in the scents of the garden. And across the still, shorn fields came the persistent beat of the tabor and shrill warble of the reed pipe, the scrape and skirl of Zacchy the fiddler. In the coach house at Creek End, specially cleared and decorated with flowers and greenery, the supper with its age-old traditional toasts and songs must be coming to an end and the dancing starting up.

Sophy hoped that Susannah would not burst out of the gown. She rested her chin on her hand. Next week, she reflected, Susannah was to marry John and would move into the rooms above the stableyard. Later on, perhaps in the new year, Anna-Maria would no doubt marry her major, after a great deal of fuss, preparation, planning and rejoicing. Doctor Vye would soon reappear and carry Charlotte back to Cambridge, preceded by George. And sometime in the early spring Mary would give birth to her baby and it might even be the girl she so wanted. It was time, Sophy decided, for action. Tomorrow she would go to Creek End, and see if Philip's promises had any substance to them.

A rude shock awaited her. Philip was not there.

"But where has he gone?" she demanded of his sister.

"I have no idea," Charlotte replied, putting aside a length of fringe of a particularly ugly shade of puce. Sophy had often wondered just what she did with all the yards of fringing she manufactured.

"Do you know when he will be back?" she asked, fighting to keep an edge of desperation out of her voice.

"In a few days, I should imagine, but I cannot be certain. My brother does not see fit to inform me of his movements." She fixed Sophy with an uncompromising eye. "But if I were you, Mrs Franklin, I should not build too many hopes on his return. My brother has an unfortunate habit of saying rather more than he means."

"And what, precisely, do you mean by that?" Sophy snapped.

Charlotte assumed an irritating, knowing expression.

"I am well aware what's going on," she said, "and I think it's disgusting." Her gaze travelled pointedly to Sophy's waistline. "I should imagine you've good reason for wanting him to come home soon."

Sophy flushed hotly, bereft of speech.

"I've known for a long time," Charlotte went on. "You really weren't very clever. Ever since the spring, Philip has been turning down evening invitations and going out for solitary walks instead. It did not take me too long to discover who it was that he was meeting. And at that ball you really gave yourself away. You may enjoy the patronage of the Nugents and organise the Sunday school and be renowned for good works, but I have always seen through you."

"I — " Sophy found her tongue at last, "I do not intend staying here to be insulted." She turned to make for the door, but Charlotte blocked her path.

"You are always very free with your advice, Mrs Franklin, now let me give you some. You would do well to give up any idea of marrying my brother. You must realise that if he had any serious intentions, there would have been none of these clandestine meetings. I've seen it all happen before. He's never really loved any one since his wife died."

This last pronouncement was produced with the air of one letting off a bombshell.

Sophy met her gaze steadily.

"It may surprise you to learn that I have known about Louise for a very long time," she said, trying in vain to still the tremble in her voice. "In fact I have probably heard a fuller account than you. And, as to the rest of what you have said, I don't believe a word of it. You may choose to give me advice, but I do not have to act on it. Good day to you."

She marched out of the house and took the long way home along the sea-wall, needing time to regain her customary calm. Tramping angrily towards the river, she tried to banish Charlotte's words from her mind, telling herself that the woman was to be pitied. Some failure, some great disappointment in her life had embittered her, making her see only the worst in everything. She was not to be regarded. Reaching the top of the dyke, she slowed her pace and took several deep breaths of sea air. On the river the usual boats were going about their business, and she recognised the *Rosa* making her way up to Heybridge. Sophy began to wonder just what Philip was up to this time. And then she stopped dead in her tracks, struck by a blinding revelation. Fool! she raged at herself. Idiot! It was so obvious, why had she not seen it before? Why did not everyone else know, for that matter? There was nothing she could do now but wait.

And wait she did, for four more days, days made even more anxious by yet another burden. Lucy fell ill again and was fretful and feverish, demanding all her attention. Sophy could not leave her to go out and gather the sparse news of the neighbourhood, and the only piece that made its way to her was that there was a suspected case of smallpox in the village. Desperately worried, Sophy watched for the first sign of a rash. It seemed that the pattern of last year was beginning to repeat itself.

During the night of the fourth day, Sophy woke suddenly from a disturbed and uneasy sleep and lay listening, convinced that something was amiss. A squall of wind was blowing the first autumn leaves off the trees, but no more sinister sound broke the profound quiet of the night. Sophy waited, expecting to hear Lucy cry out. Often she woke a few minutes before the child, as if some extra sense knew she was needed before even Lucy was aware of it. But the cottage lay supine, as soundly asleep as she was awake. Goaded by a vague but persistent suspicion that all was not well, Sophy slid out of bed and felt for her slippers.

Not bothering to kindle a light, she padded across the familiar room and made her way along the landing to Lucy's nursery. Drawing back the curtains, she peered at the child. The racing clouds exposed the face of the moon briefly, and by its light Lucy could be seen soundly slumbering, her arms flung wide above her head in the total abandonment of childhood to sleep. Sophy laid a hand lightly on her forehead and felt only a healthy warmth. The fever had gone. It had, after all, been only a mild childish ailment. She stood studying the curve of her dark lashes against her soft cheeks, the vulnerable line of her half-parted lips. But even through the relief of Lucy's recovery, Sophy could not shake off the feeling that someone close to her was threatened by an unnamed danger. Slowly, she let the curtain fall and crept back to her own chamber.

She was about to climb into bed again when a noise outside arrested her in the act of reaching for the blankets, and set her heart racing in apprehension. There was something happening out there. Catlike, she padded over to the window and twitched the curtain aside a fraction. The moon had disappeared again, and it was difficult to make out anything beyond the dark shapes of the rose bushes swaying in the wind. And then the sound came again — a cough, quite definitely a human cough. Sophy strained her eyes. Across the street, something moved stealthily, then melted back into the shadows again. Probably a hunting cat, Sophy reasoned. She shivered. The nights were growing cold, she ought to go back to bed. And yet — and yet she stayed, the unease she had woken with growing stronger by the minute.

She stiffened, catching her breath. Someone, no, more than one, several people were making their way along the street from the direction of the staithe. They moved silently, in a bunch, not attempting to hide, as if they made a nightly habit of patrolling through the village. Nearer they came to Thyme Cottage and nearer, soundless as ghosts. The scene took on an unreal quality, as if the band of men might disappear into thin air. Sophy stifled the urge to cry out, to break the unnerving quiet.

"Now!"

The barked order rent the silence, and the scene exploded into animation. From every side, from the hedgerows, from under the walls of the cottage, from the front garden of Thyme Cottage itself, dark figures sprang forward and fell upon the men in the lane. The night was filled with shouts and curses as the brawl swayed this way and that. Sophy could just make out the shape of a tall hat being knocked off one of the nearest struggling figures. Dragoons! It was an ambush, a well-planned trap, and this time the revenue officers had called in reinforcements. They meant to win.

From somewhere in the middle of the fray, a different voice shouted another order.

"Scatter! Cut and run!"

The moon came out at that instant, lighting up the skirmish with the silver intensity of a stage setting, glinting on sword-point and cutlass-blade, flashing fleetingly on white neckcloth and gold braid, highlighting the fall of a cudgel, the slump of a wounded man. Transfixed, horrified, Sophy watched as the smugglers, outnumbered, fought their way out of the deadly trap and took to their heels, each with a half a dozen assailants in pursuit.

The tide of the battle began to move up the lane, away from Thyme Cottage. Sophy changed her vantage-point to the other side of the window. And then two men broke away from the main bunch and circled warily, sword-blades at the ready, right in front of Sophy's gate. For a nerve-stretching moment each waited for the other to make the first move, and as they did so, Sophy identified one as a revenue seaman by his striped jersey, and the other was scarcely visible even by moonlight, as he was dressed entirely in black and part of his face was obscured by a mask.

Sophy was quite unconsicous of the pain as her teeth bit into her knuckles. Shaking, she watched the duel. The revenue man lunged forward, knowing his enemy, eager to claim the reward: the Shadow parried the blow with a grating clash of steel, sidestepped and attacked. For fully a minute he seemed to have the upper hand, to be driving the seaman back against the rose hedge. But then he stumbled on the rutted lane, the point of his sword ran into the ground and he was forced to let go as the toe of the seaman's boot crunched into his wrist. The cutlass-blade was already slashing down on him as he shot forward, head down, and butted his opponent in the stomach. The revenue man staggered, gasping for breath, and before he could straighten up the Shadow drove two heavy blows at his head and felled him.

Panting, he retrieved his sword and looked round for the next attacker and as he did so, two shots rang out and he lurched forward, his hand clutching his thigh. Sophy cried out feebly, horrified at the turn of events. There was no hope of escape how. But even as she despaired, she saw that there was still a chance. Before the Shadow could hit the ground, another man emerged from the darkness and, heaving him upright, began to haul him away from the fray, whilst a third figure covered their retreat. The fight was breaking up. As the smugglers made their bid for freedom Sophy caught sight briefly of what looked like the revenue officer, running back towards the staithe and issuing orders as he went. Pairs of seamen made off between the cottages, evidently seeking to flush out any smugglers who might be hiding. The dragoons seemed to have disappeared. For several age-long minutes nothing happened, and all that Sophy could hear was the retreating sound of the search. She stayed at her viewing-point, shaking with cold and apprehension.

And then quite close to Thyme Cottage a shot shattered the air and shouts and running footsteps crashed through the neighbouring gardens. As they seemed to head for the pasture at the back of the village, a solitary figure could just be made out, limping painfully along the street away from the staithe, keeping close under the straggling rose hedge. Just as he reached the front path of Thyme Cottage his injured leg gave way and he fell awkwardly, caught his head against the iron gatepost and crumpled onto the ground.

Quicker than thought, Sophy sped across the room to the closet, tearing off her nightcap as she went. Her questing fingers closed round the old black pelisse and fumbled with the loops from which it hung. Desperate in her haste, she tore it off the pegs and raced for the stairs, thrusting her arms into the sleeves and almost tripping at the awkward turn halfway down. In the hall she paused, doing up the buttons. Not a fold of her white cambric nightdress must show to betray her. With infinite care, she slid back the bolt on the front door, opened it a fraction and peeped out. There was nobody in the immediate vicinity of the gate, and she would have to take the risk of anyone looking up from the fray just at the crucial moment.

Head down, she pelted for the gate, wrenched it open and grasped the unconscious man under the arms. His head lolled sideways as she backed through the gateway and Sophy grunted with effort, the muscles of her arms and back protesting. She had not realised just how heavy a helpless adult could be. The short journey back up the path seemed to take an age — the scrape of the man's boots sounded loud as gunfire. Up the shallow step into the porch. One more heave and they were over the threshold. A last effort and his feet were clear of the door and she could shut it — carefully, carefully, for a hasty slam would ruin everything — and they were safe.

Sophy leaned her back against the door, panting with exertion, then smiled, feeling again the thrill of facing danger and overcoming it. The Shadow had slipped the net once more and she, Sophy Franklin, was responsible for a first-class sleight-of-hand trick. But her triumph was short-lived. Susannah, creeping downstairs with a candle in her hand, brought her sharply back to the grave realities of the situation.

"Lord save us, ma'am! What's going on? Why — ow!" her gaze dropped from Sophy to the man sprawled in the narrow hall and her hand flew to her face. It ain't — is it? *Him*, right here?"

"It is," said Sophy, with an admirable parody of her usual calm manner. "Don't just stand there gawping, girl, open the door into the back parlour and make sure not a glimmer of light can be seen from the garden. Quick!"

Long training of instant obedience, whatever the circumstances, prompted Susannah to do as she was bid. As soon as the parlour curtains were held firmly against the windows with books and ornaments, Sophy dragged her burden in and laid him on the worn carpet, snatching up a cushion to place under his head. Then, taking the candle from Susannah, she made a swift survey of his injuries, the blood draining from her face as she did so. There was a gash on his head where he had hit the gatepost, what looked like a nasty chest wound and as far as she could make out, a shot-gun ball embedded in his left thigh.

"Oh, sweet Jesus!" she whispered. "What are we going to do?"

With shaking fingers, she reached out and peeled the blood-soaked mask off his face.

Susannah gave a squawk of disbelief. "Lord save us — 'tis the captain!"

12

"OPEN up in the name of the King!"

The roar reverberated through the cramped rooms of Thyme Cottage, backed by a fusillade of fist-beats on the door. For a moment Sophy knelt, transfixed with horror, unable to move. They had seen her! Fear pounded through her, paralysing all thought.

"Open up!"

Susannah squeaked with fright, and Sophy jerked into action, a plan already beginning to form in her brain. If she could only keep her head, all was not yet lost. The essential thing was not to give way to panic.

"Stay here and keep him quiet!" she hissed at Susannah, and bolted from the room, clutching at the hampering folds of her nightgown as she leapt two at a time up the stairs. Crossing the landing, she began to tear off the pelisse she had donned so hastily, dropping it on the floor of her bedchamber. The hammering on the door grew more demanding as she searched frantically for her nightcap in the dark. Finding it at last, she clapped it over her hair and tied a hasty knot before dragging back the curtains and flinging open the casement. Kneeling on the window-seat, she leaned out, took a deep breath and let fly.

"Stop that at once! At once, do you hear! What in heaven's name do you mean by rousing my house in this fashion, and at this unearthly hour? Has a respectable citizen no rights? What is this country coming to when a decent, God-fearing, law-abiding widow is treated in this way? It's a disgrace!"

The assault on the door ceased abruptly, and four upturned faces stared at her with a variety of expressions ranging from scepticism to open curiosity. Rather belatedly, the officer sketched a salute. Sophy's heart sank as she saw a shotgun over his arm and recognised his broad, pugnacious features. It was Lieutenant Forster, the man who had been tricked over the shipment of brandy.

He always went hunting smugglers with a sporting gun.

"My apologies, ma'am, but this is a very serious matter," he stated, not the least affected by Sophy's tirade. "I require to search this house."

"Over my dead body! What do you take me for, sir, that you expect me, a respectable, unprotected female, to let you and your band of ruffians in at the dead of night? I've never heard of such a thing!"

"Madam," Forster was clearly impatient of delay, "a notorious and desperate smuggler is at large somewhere in this village. He has not been found in the streets or gardens, so it is clearly my duty as a servant of the Crown — " he laid stress on these words " — to start searching in every one of the dwellings before looking further afield."

"Are you seriously suggesting that *I* am harbouring a felon in my home?" Sophy could hear her tone of voice becoming more like Charlotte Vye's by the second. "I beg you to consider, sir, whom you are addressing."

"When you have been in the service

as long as I have, ma'am, you suspect everyone. Magistrates, parsons, members of the nobility — they're all of 'em more than likely to be in league with the smugglers. So if you would be so kind as to let me in, it will save me the trouble of having to break down the door."

Sophy bit her lip, her mind a terrifying blank. Blustering was not going to work. There had to be a reason for not letting the men in, when they were combing every other house in the village. She swallowed hard.

"Under no circumstances," she began, "under no circumstances am I going to allow anyone into this house — " And at the moment Lucy, woken by the noise and frightened by the sound of her mother shouting at strange men in the middle of the night, let out a thin, penetrating wail. Inspiration dawned on Sophy. "My daughter is sick of the smallpox and if you do not care whether you disturb a desperately ill child, you might pause to consider that the malady is highly infectious."

"Mama, Mama!"

Lucy's cries became fretful. Sophy prayed that Forster had not already had smallpox.

"My garden and outhouses you are welcome to search," she put in, as Forster hesitated. "Far be it from me to obstruct the course of the law. I hope you meet with success. It's high time these rogues were caught and severely dealt with!"

She stopped herself just in time from making an oblique reference to the ludicrous episode with the brandy. To antagonise the officer now might be fatal. Forster continued to scrutinise her expression for some unwary slip that could betray her. Sophy stared back, her fact stiffening with the effort of maintaining the mask of sincerity.

"I trust you will know me again?" she enquired at length.

At last a brief look of discomfiture crossed the lieutenant's alcohol-reddened features.

"Go through the gardens," he barked over his shoulder at his men. "Sheds, outhouses, pigsties — leave not a stone unturned." To Sophy he tipped his hat. "Servant, ma'am," he growed, and made off round the side of the cottage. Trembling from head to foot with the sudden release from tension, Sophy slammed the casement shut.

"Unmannerly boor!" she flung at the space where he had been, her voice sharpened with tears.

Lucy cried out again, and Sophy hastily pulled herself together. Brushing a hand across her eyes, she hastened to reassure and settle the child, then hurried back downstairs. Susannah, white-faced, was still kneeling by an unconscious Philip. Sophy lit another candle and thrust it into the girl's hand.

"Fetch a bowl of water, and bandages and old linen," she whispered. "But be quiet as you can. They're still outside."

Susannah nodded dumbly and went.

Sophy sank to her knees and took Philip's limp hand between both of hers. What was to be done? If she kept him here she ran a grave risk of his being discovered, and she would be unable to give him the nursing he needed if she had to present a normal facade to the world. Besides, he required the skill of a surgeon, and to call one in was impossible. She could contact Caleb Moore, possibly through Bandy Coates, and have him taken to the sawbones who had patched up the rioter. But of course, that wounded rioter had not been connected with the Kingschurch affair at all, she realised. He was another member of the smuggling gang.

She forced her mind back to the problem in hand. It might be days before Caleb was in the Blackwater area again, and even if he was sailing upriver at this very moment, Philip's prolonged absence would have to be explained. His movements had coincided with the Shadow's on too many occasions. This time it would be sure to be noticed. Somehow she had to get him back to Creek End with a plausible reason for having been shot. Who would be likely to attack a well-liked landowner in the early hours of the morning?

Outside she heard the infuriated clucking of the disturbed hens as their house was invaded. And the answer came to her: a smuggler on the run might do it, especially if he wanted to steal a horse.

Philip began to stir at last, mutter

incoherently. Sophy leaned forward, trying to make out what he was saying.

" . . . mizzen blown away . . . douse that fire . . . Cartwright? Have we captured her, or has she sunk?"

"Just be still," Sophy soothed. "All's well."

His eyes slowly opened and stared, blurred and uncomprehending, at the ceiling.

"Sophy?" he muttered. "She mustn't know. What's she doing here?"

"I live here, and I do know, but it doesn't matter. Just stay quiet, don't try to talk."

He turned his head towards the sound of her voice and made an effort to focus on her face.

"Must get out of here," he declared, starting to ease himself up. "Forster, out for my neck . . . mustn't know you . . . hell's bells!" He stopped short, grimacing with pain, and before he could get any further, Sophy caught him by the shoulders and forced him to lie down again.

"Hush — Forster's outside looking for you. Lie still, for heaven's sake, I don't want you bleeding all over my carpet."

Philip gave a twisted smile.

"Yes, ma'am."

Susannah reappeared, a bowl of water in her hands and bandages and towels over her arms.

"Good," Sophy approved. Now that the immediate danger was over, she was feeling more in command of the situation, and the practical task of patching Philip up also helped her to calm down and think clearly. The chest injury turned out to be less serious than she had feared, but the shot in his leg worried her greatly. It was essential that a skilled surgeon took it out as soon as possible. To this end she made no attempt to clean and dress the wounds properly, but merely staunched the flow of blood.

"As soon as Forster's given up, I'm going," Philip insisted, watching her pale, intent face thrown into contrasting planes of light and shadow by the single candle.

"No . . ."

"Yes. I tried all along to keep you out of this, I'm not having you involved now, just when it's most dangerous. Ye gods! What a time to get myself shot. They were waiting for us, they must have had a tip-off. Someone's been talking." he wandered off the point, saying the first thing that came into his head in an effort to take his mind off the throbbing agony in his leg.

Sophy finished strapping him up.

"Is that any easier?" she asked anxiously.

"Much better," he lied. She had not been taking the slightest heed of what he had said about leaving.

"Listen," she said, still speaking scarcely above a whisper for fear of being heard outside. "You cannot stay here, and neither can you just go out into the night and take your chance. And it's no use trying to get to that man you sent your colleague to before. Even if you managed to get on board a barge tonight, you'd be in a high fever before you arrived. What I think is the best course of action is this: we must get you to the other side of Creek End, where the track leads down from the turnpike, and leave you there. You'll be found as soon as the labourers start coming in to work, and you must say that you were riding home when you were set upon by the

Shadow and his accomplices, and they made off with your horse."

Philip found her hand and squeezed it.

"When in trouble, just ask Sophy," he said. "Sore heads, lost children, injured smugglers — Sophy knows the answer."

She frowned, not sure whether he had spoken with sincerity or sarcasm.

"Is there something wrong with it?"

"It's a magnificent scheme, darling. I wish I had thought of it myself. But I'm not sure I can get that far." It was over a mile to the cart-track, and the dragoons were out scouring the countryside. If he had some sort of a crutch he might make it, provided he kept to the hedgerows.

"I thought of that. I'll take the Hansons' horse. Do you think you could ride, if I led the beast? He's generally very quiet."

Philip drew a breath of protest, then stopped as he heard the scrape of a boot outside the window. Footsteps thudded round the side of the house.

"They're going," Sophy breathed.

She stood up, listening intently, then crept out of the room and made her way upstairs to the spare front bedchamber. Here she risked a peep out. Yes, all four of them had gathered in the lane, and presently they were joined by half a dozen others, shaking their heads. The smugglers had evidently not gone to ground in the village. Forster led them back down the lane towards the staithe.

Sophy went downstairs again and sent Susannah back to bed. There was nothing else she might be needed for. Susannah gave a knowing grin and went.

"They've gone from the garden. They went back to the creek, I think."

"They're after the boat. Forster must think we doubled back and are getting away by sea. Or if not, that the boat's unguarded and he can seize it and claim a cut of the cargo."

"Then now is time to take the horse, while they're occupied.

"Sophy, no!" Philip half-rose and gripped her arm. "Horse-stealing's a capital offence. You must not take such a risk."

"James Hanson would never press charges against me," Sophy maintained. "And if he did, he would have to go through Sir Harry. It's perfectly safe. Can you really see Sir Harry sending me up to the Assizes? Anyway, I'm going, and nothing you can say will stop me."

Philip held her gaze, anxiety gradually mingling with wonder as he saw she meant every word.

"Is there nothing you cannot cope with?" he asked softly.

"I couldn't face the world at all without you."

Philip released her and looked away. Perhaps she was right. Perhaps it was the only way. "Very well," he agreed reluctantly. "If our luck holds we might be deported on the same convict ship. Listen — this is important. Some of my men might well be in hiding out there. If they are, they'll help you. The countersign is 'Moonshadow.'"

"Countersign?"

"Yes — " he was beginning to have difficulty in following the thread of what he was saying. "We use the French, 'Qui vive?' just to confuse matters. The answer tonight is 'Moonshadow'. Do you follow?" He was not quite sure whether it made sense himself.

"I understand."

"Carry on then, Lieutenant Franklin. The ship's yours."

Sophy slipped out of the back gate of Thyme Cottage ten minutes later, dressed in her mourning to blend in with the night, and armed with a lump of meat to appease the Hansons' guard dog. Clouds covered the moon now, and she picked her way carefully along the edge of the pasture, keeping close under the irregular line of hedges and fences that bordered the cottage gardens. From the direction of the staithe she could hear the sound of Lieutenant Forster and his men at work, but otherwise the whole village seemed to be quiet. To Sophy's over-sensitive ears, it was a sinister, watchful silence, as if a hundred suspicious eyes were following her progress. The nerves down her spine pricked with every sigh of the wind in the hedgerows. She had not gone more than fifty yards before she saw something move ahead of her and froze, every sense straining to penetrate the darkness and make out what it might be. The black shape stopped as well, and out of the night, music to her ears, came a hoarse whisper, "Qui vive?" spoken with an unmistakable Essex accent.

Limp with relief, Sophy licked her dry lips and gave the countersign.

"Strike me dead, if it ain't the widder lady!" came the disconcerting reply. "How's the captain, missis? Hurt bad, is he? We had to leave him and draw them damn revenue men off, and when I got back I saw you'd got him."

"Bandy Coates!" Sophy hardly had time to be surprised before she realised that it was perfectly obvious that Bandy was one of the gang. "The captain's well enough to be moved, if I can but get a horse for him. Is it safe between here and the parsonage?"

"Safe as the Bank of England." Bandy gave his peculiar cracked laugh. "Horse-stealing now, is it? A fine dance you led old Red-nose Forster! I ain't seen better play-acting since the mummers last came round." He cackled again with unholy glee at the revenue man's routing, then applied himself to the problem in hand. "What's the plan, missis? Going to get him off to Pagglesham? There's a boat lying off Dead Man's Creek, if you can reach it."

Sophy felt sick at the very thought.

"No . . . !" she said faintly.

"You don't want to fret about that ole skull out on the point, missis," Bandy reassured her. "Thass only bits of glass he's got for eyes. Just hung up there to put the wind up folks as goes nosing around where they ain't wanted, he is."

"Oh — yes — " Of course it was. Like everything else about Philip's organisation, it was so obvious now that she could not imagine how she could have been so blind and stupid not to have guessed it before.

"I have a better scheme than that," she explained, "but it is essential that we hurry. We must get the horse and be out of the village before Forster comes back."

"Right you are, missis. You and me'll give parson's nag a bit of exercise."

At the Hansons' stable, they met with a setback. The potting-shed, where the tack was kept, was locked.

"We'll have to manage without," Sophy whispered. "You keep watch and I'll take the horse."

424

The dog, chained up in the yard, gave a menacing growl, but was partly soothed by Sophy's familiar voice and finally won over by the meat. Sophy opened the stable door, speaking softly to the gentle bay cob, and caught his halter as he turned his head towards her. Obediently, he followed her out, his hooves thudding dully on the beaten earth. She led him through the garden, and was about to make for the back gate when Bandy appeared at her side.

"Revenue men — pair of 'em," he hissed. "Wait till I draw'em off, missis, then run like hell."

Sophy had just time to agree before he disappeared in the direction of the churchyard. Moments later, ghostly moans arose from amongst the gravestones, followed by the shouts and curses of the revenue seamen as they dodged and stumbled in pursuit of their prey. With a brief but fervent prayer for Bandy's safety, Sophy tugged at the cob's halter and raced past the churchyard and on towards Thyme Cottage. Twice she tripped, but was saved by the horse flinging his head up and stopping before he trampled on her. She sent silent thanks to James Hanson for owning such a reliable beast. At her back door, she tied the horse to a rose bush and left him placidly chewing the last of her blooms while she went indoors.

Philip was already on his feet, swaying slightly, as she entered the back parlour.

"Heard you coming in," he said. "All's well?"

"Yes, for the time being, but we must get away fast. Bandy Coates is keeping two of them busy, and there may be more on their way."

"Good. If you would take a chair out as a mounting-block, I'll take my leave."

It took a moment for Sophy to grasp the full import of this remark. When she did, she stopped abruptly in the act of picking up a chair and declared,

"You are not going alone!"

"Oh, yes I am. I absolutely forbid you to come. You've done more than enough for one night."

Sophy bit back a sharp rejoinder, replying mildly that she had done nothing out of the ordinary, and took the chair into the garden. Philip wondered at so easy a victory, but when he hopped outside, leaning heavily on Sophy's shoulders, he found the reason for it.

"The animal's not harnessed."

"No," Sophy replied blandly. "I apologise for that but the potting-shed was locked."

Philip staggered, so heavily that Sophy had difficulty in holding him up.

"What is it? Are you all right?"

"Yes . . . yes . . . " Philip gasped, flinging his arm across the cob's back and leaning against him. "Quite all right . . . " To her relief, Sophy realised that he was laughing. "I surrender, you're incorrigible, you'd make a far better free-trader than I. Come on, help me up on this beast if you will be so kind, then you may set course for Creek End."

The way to the cart-track was fraught with difficulties. They avoided established lanes and footpaths and kept close under the cover of the hedgerows, which meant taking long detours round stubble-fields and pastures from one gateway to the next. Often Sophy would stumble in the confusing darkness, and Philip, desperately anxious for her safety, insisted that they stopped at any suspicious sound or movement. At what felt like the hundreth false alarm, Sophy lost patience.

"We'll not get there before dawn at this rate," she protested.

"Hush!" Philip whispered urgently. "Listen: hoofbeats."

Sophy strained to hear, and sure enough, caught the thud of hooves and the jingle of harness. She pulled the horse closer to the thick hedgerow and stroked his nose with a hand that shook slightly. A barbed hawthorn branch jabbed her in the small of the back and the long, dew-covered grass tickled damply round her legs. The cob shifted, resting one hind-leg. And then, opening the gate they had gone through themselves only minutes before, she spied two horsemen, darker shapes against the cloud-covering night. They trotted across the field, not hurrying, the white facings and gold braid of their uniforms looming pale, the chink of bit and stirrup and sabre ringing loud as church-bells in Sophy's over-sensitive ears.

Almost opposite the silent watchers

they reined in, and Sophy held her breath, certain that they had been discovered, wondering what was the best course of action. She sensed rather than saw Philip measuring the range for an accurate shot. And then, in the wood bordering the other side of the pasture, something stirred and the dragoons spurred their horses in the direction of the sound. Sophy took back all her former curses on the hunting animals that had caused their earlier delays. They had served their turn admirably now.

"Close," Philip commented. "By Jove, I'd like to know who informed against us. I'll have his guts for whip-points."

Sophy shivered. She had a horrid feeling he really meant it. It brought home forcibly the fact that fifteen years spent fighting Napoleon must have hardened him to most forms of violence.

"I doubt if anyone is going to admit to it," she replied.

"I'll find out, never you fear. Come on, the coast's clear. We shouldn't have any more trouble from them for a while."

Two stubble-fields more, and they came upon the track that led from the turnpike to Creek End.

"Listen," Philip said, as they paused by an elm tree growing by the track. "We can turn those redcoats to good account. Get me down, and the bandages off me, then we'll fake a scuffle and fire a couple of shots. You take the pistols and the horse and hide in the next field. When the dragoons arrive I'll direct them towards the turnpike, and once they're gone you make off home. No coming back to see if I'm all right, understand? It takes more than this to finish me off. Don't take the horse right back to the Hansons', turn it loose. Somebody will find it and return it. Do you follow?"

"Yes," said Sophy, "but . . . "

"No buts, just do as I say. If you please."

Sophy agreed, and was just reaching up to help him off the horse when a movement further down the track caught her eye.

"Someone's coming," she breathed.

Philip followed her gaze.

"Not the revenue, they hunt in pairs. Might be one of ours, might be just a poacher. Can't take any changes." He thrust a pistol into Sophy's hands. "Get down and crawl to the hedge, then get round behind him. If he's with us, all's well, but if not, I'll keep him talking and you hit him really hard with the butt. Can't afford witnesses."

Sophy dropped to the ground, clutching the pistol. Crawling, she found, was impossible in her long skirts, so she gathered them up above her knees with the hand that held the gun, and made her way awkwardly towards the welcoming cover of the hedgerow. Long before she got there her stockings were in holes and she was scratched and filthy with mud and dead leaves, but in her haste she hardly noticed. All that mattered was to reach the intruder before he discovered who they were. Breathless, a stitch cramping her side, she stumbled along at the edge of the ditch, and as she did so she heard Philip challenging the stranger.

"Qui vive? Friend or foe?"

There was a brief silence, as the figure on the track paused. Sophy stopped as well, for fear of his hearing her.

"Foe, by God!"

George! Sophy broke out in a cold sweat. Surely he would not fail to recognise Philip's voice, and once he did, all was lost. Unless . . . suddenly sick, she gathered herself to move at the first opportunity. She had to deal with George before he discovered the truth and before Philip had to use the other pistol.

"Surrender, or I fire!" George was saying.

Sophy crept further along the ditch, placing each foot deliberately.

"So, my brave young bantam cock, you think you can take me as a prize, hey?"

Even Sophy was momentarily startled by the French accent, several tones higher than Philip's natural speaking voice. She felt a small hysterical bubble of laughter form somewhere in the pit of her stomach.

"I know I shall," came George's defiant reply. "Throw down your arms and give in while you have the chance!" He began to pace slowly towards the elm tree. Sophy could just make out the shape of a double-barrelled shotgun at the ready.

"Do not come any nearer," the Shadow

warned. "I have the mouth of my gun against the head of a friend of yours. One step nearer and he is dead. You would not like his blood on your hands, I think?"

"Prove it."

"Speak!" the Shadow hissed.

There was a thud and a strangled groan.

"He is stubborn, your Captain Ellard," the Shadow addressed George, with quiet menace in his voice. "But he is here, certainly, and his fate lies with you."

"Ellard? He can rot in hell!" George spat, and raised the shotgun to his shoulder.

Incensed, Sophy sped across the grass, but she was not fast enough. Even as she ran, the crack of a gunshot ripped through the night, and the bay cob gave a shrill whinny of fear. With revenge in her heart, Sophy swung her arm up and round, and brought the butt of the heavy pistol crashing down on George's head just as he started to turn to see what the noise behind him was. With a grunt, he collapsed at her feet. Fighting back a wave of revulsion, Sophy stooped and searched him. She found a pistol and a knife thrust into his belt, and gathering these and his shotgun into her arms she ran, stumbling, along the edge of the track to the tree.

She found Philip on the ground, doubled up with pain. With a cry of distress, she dropped her store of weapons and knelt at his side.

"What is it? Did he hit you?"

"No . . . fell off the poxy horse . . ." Philip explained, between clenched teeth. "Take off the . . . bandages and . . . go. Quick!"

With numbed, trembling fingers, Sophy fumbled with the knots she had tied so carefully, an age ago it seemed, in the comparative safety of Thyme Cottage. Despairing, she remembered the knife, and soon the task was done. The horse, uneasy at the scent of blood, snorted and backed away, and Sophy was visited with a sudden inspiration. Groping for two of the pistols, she fired them into the air and the horse bolted up the track towards the turnpike.

"Genius," Philip approved.

Sophy gathered her macabre collection

of incriminating evidence into a rough bundle, then paused, loth to leave him. Philip felt for her hand and clasped it.

"Sophy?"

"Yes?"

"I love you."

She kissed him tenderly, the new-grown stubble of his beard prickling her lips.

"I love you too," she whispered. "Be careful."

And as she ran for the cover of the hedgerow once more, the sound of the approaching dragoons could already be heard.

* * *

The first thing George became aware of was a shattering pain right through his skull. And then, gradually, he realised that his mouth was full of dirt and that he was lying on the ground. Slowly he sat up and groaned, holding his head between his hands. What was he doing here? As the mists cleared from his mind, he recalled the long, nerve-straining wait and the glorious, terrifying, exhilarating fight before the smugglers, cowards to a man, had fled. And then the mysterious disappearance of the Shadow, just when Forster was certain he had shot him down, and the fruitless search through the village.

That was when he fell out with Forster over the best course of action. The dragoons were out scouring the countryside, Forster had said. There was no point in his men doing the same. He was sure the Shadow would try to get back to his boat. But George was still convinced that the Shadow was Richard Ellard, and that in a crisis like this he would seek his brother's aid. Alone, therefore, he made his way to Creek End, and began to search methodically every possible approach to the place. And then what? And then — now it was coming back to him — he had been within an ace of achieving his object, when he had been attacked from behind. Confusingly, Sophy's face seemed to be mixed up with it, but that must just be the product of imagination. There was something else, too, something that nagged at the back of his battered brain. Oh yes — it was not Richard, but Philip Ellard. No. Philip Ellard was held hostage, and the Shadow was a Frenchman. His pet theory had been wrong after all.

Then he heard hoofbeats in the distance, and not realising that they were retreating, not approaching, he shouted feebly. Quite near to him, there came an answering croak.

"Over here."

He staggered to his feet and wove his way towards the voice, which seemed to be coming from the elm tree. He nearly tripped over a prone figure.

"Who's that?" he asked.

"Captain Philip Ellard, R.N., retired."

"Oh." George was momentarily non-plussed. His brain did not seem to be functioning correctly. "I thought you were dead."

"Not yet, boy. Haven't spent . . . best part of my life . . . fighting Frogs . . . just to be shot down by you . . . on my doorstep.

"Did *I* shoot you?"

"Yes, you. Bloody idiot. However, good thing you came when you did . . . they were just about . . . to kill me. You stopped them. Just in time. Very brave . . . extremely, taking on four."

"Four? Were there four of them?"

"Aye. Bastards took my horse. Sent the dragoons after them . . . but no use. Won't get the Shadow. Not on Dauntless."

George digested the new information. He had confronted four desperate men and they had fled before him, leaving behind their hostage. He, George Nugent, had done this. And in the light of this revelation, a good deal of his animosity towards Philip Ellard evaporated.

"Are you hurt?" he asked.

"No. Lying here . . . for my own amusement."

George drew out a tinder-box and struck a light, and in its brief flare took in his rival's injuries. He sucked his breath in sharply through his teeth. In the course of his sheltered life he had never come across anything so serious before, but the realisation that here was someone in a worse case than himself invested him with a new sense of responsibility. The hammering pain in his head seemed to fade a little. He was going to take charge of the situation.

"Look here," he said, "you cannot possibly walk home. I'm going to leave you here and fetch some stout fellows to carry you, and I'll send John Jennings for the surgeon. I'll be back as soon as I can."

"Fine," Philip commented. "Capital. Carry on."

And George strode off for Creek End, leaving Philip to worry about whether Sophy was safe yet before slipping into unconsciousness.

13

THE day started like any other. Susannah came in and drew back the curtains.

"Morning, ma'am," she said, handing Sophy her cup of chocolate, "not a very nice day. Raining, it is, something awful."

"Thank you, Susannah."

Sophy sat up, still searching for the answer to one of the many questions that had kept her awake since her return home at four o'clock that morning. Was Susannah to be trusted? The prospect of a hundred and fifty guineas reward must be a great temptation to a girl about to be married. A handsome bribe certainly would not answer. If Susannah refused it, she would be deeply offended, and if she took it, she would have Sophy in her power, as Philip had once pointed out.

"Susannah," she said slowly, "about last night . . . "

"Oh, don't you fret about that,

ma'am," the girl replied. "Forgotten it already, I have. Didn't nothing happen last night, 'cepting for a bit of a mill in the street." And, being constitutionally unable to be brief and effective, she went on to explain, "My pa's helped with the landings on and off for years, ma'am, and the rest of the family too. We've always been friends of the free-traders. And 'sides," she blushed, afraid of being thought forward, "you and the captain's been very good to John and me. We been wondering for some time if you and him were — well — "

"You can put your mind at rest on that point, Susannah," Sophy smiled. "But keep it to yourself for the time being, mind. There will be an official announcement later. Now bustle about, there's a good girl, and lay out the morning frock with the blue ribbons, and the matching cap."

Sophy had already planned her course of action. She must behave normally, however much she wanted to run straight to Creek End. And the obvious thing to do was to pay a call at Tracey Manor and enquire of Sir Harry the reason for the disgraceful disturbance outside her house last night, and demand that Lieutenant Forster be severely reprimanded for his effrontery.

She forced herself to eat a scant breakfast, though food was the last thing she felt like, and set off through the rain, leaving Lucy in Susannah's care to give credence to the tale of her continuing illness. By the time she reached the edge of the woodland, she was overtaken by James Hanson, in a state of indignation, and bent on the same errand as herself. His wife, he told Sophy, was practically in a state of nervous collapse. If she miscarried the baby, he would know who to blame. Sophy thought this highly unlikely. Mary, for all her appearance of frailty, bred with the ease of a peasant. But she refrained from expressing this opinion out loud. Instead, she made sympathetic noises as James gave his account of the night's disturbances, and wondered what his reaction would be if she were to tell him that it was she who had stolen his horse.

When they arrived at Tracey Manor, they found the place humming with news and breathless with admiration. And the hero of the hour was George.

His head bound up with an impressive bandage, and looking interestingly pale, he was sitting in the morning-room, surrounded by his family, drinking coffee and behaving with remarkable calm.

"Oh, Mrs Franklin, do come in. And you, dear Hanson. Such terrifying adventures! You cannot begin to imagine. But sit down, sit down and you shall hear it all . . . "

Sophy had never seen Lady Isobel in such a taking before. Her sons's dangerous illnesses, his unfortunate tendency to want to rule his own life, even his intended disastrous marriage, all these she could take in her stride. But his unparalleled gallantry had quite shattered her habitual calm. And unfortunately for her, she could not even begin her recital straight away, for James wanted to report the theft of his horse before listening to yet another tale about George, and Sophy, though she was desperate to learn what had happened after she left the scene, felt she had to keep up her part and put in a strong complaint about Lieutenant Forster.

443

Sir Harry dealt with both with his usual genial authority, assuring Sophy that he would personally speak to Forster's senior officer, and informing James that his cob was in all probability back in its own stall by now, as it had been caught by one of the dragoons and brought to Tracey Manor, and was now being returned to the parsonage. Both were properly grateful, though James expressed a strong desire to see the culprits brought to justice, a sentiment echoed by Sophy. Sir Harry positively beamed with pride.

"They shall be, they shall be," he assured them. "And they only just escaped capture last night. My boy here nearly achieved single-handed what all those lily-livered blockheads in uniforms have been trying to do these two years past."

"Really, Father — " George protested, frowning into his empty cup.

To his credit, Sophy noticed, he appeared to be genuinely embarrassed at all the praise being heaped upon him.

Lady Isobel jumped in.

"We had no idea of it, not an inkling. He has been collecting information for months, how I do not know, for he will not say. But he did it without rousing the least suspicion, it seems, for the Shadow and his gang walked straight into the trap set for them — "

"Yes," Sophy broke in, "but why did it have to be outside my house, pray?"

"To be sure of surrounding them," George explained, eager to give an unadorned version of at least part of the story. "If we had surprised them at the staithe, some of them would have escaped by boat. So we let them come on through the village, where it is less easy to get away. Even so," he admitted ruefully, "get away they did. The craven rats didn't even try to put up a proper fight. They just cut their way out and ran."

While Sophy burnt with impatience, the Nugents went over the entire story of the evening step by excruciatingly slow step, until she felt she would scream and tear her hair if they did not tell her son what had become of Philip. At last, at long last, they came to the point.

"And he was just searching along that cart-track," Lady Isobel related, "when he saw four desperate smugglers under a tree — "

"I didn't," George contradicted her, "they saw me first, and — "

"And with no thought at all for his personal safety," Sir Harry went on, "he went right at 'em, telling them to surrender while they had the chance. That's the way, by thunder! That's the spirit that kept Britain free when all of Europe was lined up against us!"

"But as if they did not already have the advantage of numbers, they also had a hostage," Lady Isobel said. "Captain Ellard — "

Sophy's faint cry of horror was hardly noticed. Only Anna-Maria, silently observing the gathering, looked at her with new interest. It was James Hanson who caught everyone's attention.

"And what on earth was Ellard doing there?" he asked.

Sophy froze. The one point they had not thought of in all the hastily-conceived plans. What possible explanation could there be? She looked at George, who had assumed a peculiarly wooden expression.

"I believe," he said gruffly, "he had

strong personal reasons — " his eye met Sophy's for the briefest moment and slid away, " — of his own."

Sophy's heart went out to him in gratitude. He had grown up considerably in the course of one night. But there was no time now for meditating on George's character. She had a part to play.

"But what happened next?" she demanded, letting out all the pent-up anxiety she had had to conceal. "What of Captain Ellard?"

This time all eyes turned to her, registering surprise, then speculation.

"I — " George hesitated, and Sophy wondered just how much of the truth would come out.

"He refused to believe them, naturally," Sir Harry continued for him. "Only course. Tall story like that, no-one would believe it. Too dark to recognise anyone, and Ellard wasn't going to plead for his life, it sounded like a trick."

"I'll tell you something, the Shadow is a Frog, I heard him with my own ears," George put in. "How Forster came to think he was Dutch, I don't know. He must have been too drunk at the time to know what was going on."

"But what did you *do*?" Sophy demanded.

"Well I — I took a chance on its being a trick and shot at 'em, and I heard someone go down, but before I could shoot again, I was knocked down from behind."

"A terrible blow!" Lady Isobel exclaimed. "I would not be surprised if he's scarred for life. It rendered him completely unconscious for several minutes. But in spite of that, he looked after Captain Ellard — "

"Least I could do," George muttered. "He was far worse off than me, and besides, I was the one who shot him."

"*What?*" Sophy sprang up. "Is he badly hurt? Where is he now? *Tell* me!"

"At Creek End. He's all right, really," George assured her hastily. "It was only a leg wound, and I got him back home and sent for Doctor Goodhew straight away. He's all patched up now."

Around the room, a series of significant glances were exchanged.

"If it had not been or George's intervention, our friend Ellard would be dead by now. That smuggler would have killed him." Lady Isobel declared, flying to her son's defence.

Sir Harry agreed vigorously.

"Lucky for him that George arrived just then."

George looked distinctly uncomfortable, and stood up, awkwardly, as Sophy approached him. She wished she were able to make some apology for having hit him quite so hard, but perhaps his present acclaim was an adequate compensation.

"I am immeasurably grateful to you," she said softly. And turning to the company at large, went on. "You must excuse me, but I have to leave at once."

Lady Isobel offered the use of the coach, pointing out that it was raining hard, but Sophy refused. By the time the horses had been put to and the muddy lanes negotiated, it would be quicker to walk.

As she started along the footpath to Creek End, she discovered another pressing reason for walking: Bandy Coates was lurking under the dripping trees, waiting to speak to her. Furtively, they exchanged information. Hardly any of the gang had entirely escaped injury, but only two of them had been hurt badly enough to need a surgeon's attention, and they had been spirited off to Pagglesham. More ominous news was that two more had been captured.

"Can they be trusted to keep quiet?" Sophy asked. "They receive a free pardon and a reward for every man taken if they lay information, do they not?"

"They'll keep their mouths shut tight, never you fret, missis," Bandy assured her. "They know what happens to 'em else."

Sophy looked at him suspiciously.

"And just what do you mean by that?" she asked.

Bandy gave his peculiar cracked cackle.

"Same as what we're going to do to him as give us away," he said with relish. "Got him, we have. Going to make him rue the day he ever told squire's lad what we was up to."

Sophy suppressed a shudder. She did not want to know what a small community did to a traitor in its ranks, and even if she had the power to stop it, she could not do so, for the man's silence was essential. Then her hands flew to her face as yet another flaw in her plan occurred to her.

"The horse!" she gasped. "Dauntless. The Captain was supposed to have been riding him home when he was shot. He's not at Creek End at this very minute, is he?"

"Thass orl right, missis," Bandy said. "The Captain left home riding him, see, and got him stabled out by the marshes. Someone'll send a message sometime today saying as he's been found loose and John Jennings'll go and fetch him back."

He looked shrewdly at her. "I s'pose this is the finish for the Shadow?" he asked.

"It most certainly is."

"Ah." Bandy shook his head mournfully. "Pity. We had some rare fun, and some right good runs. Still, Revenue don't know that, do they? Keep 'em busy looking for him, won't it, while the rest of us gets on nice and quiet with the trade."

Sophy agreed that it would, and put

in an order for some best Hyson tea. Slightly mollified, Bandy made off, and Sophy hurried on her way.

At Creek End she informed the astonished butler that it was his master, not Mrs Vye, that she had come to see, and what was more she did not require to be shown the way. Leaving him holding her sodden cloak, she ran up the stairs, covering them with muddy footprints. At the door of Philip's chamber she was confronted with Charlotte Vye.

"I wondered when we should be seeing you," she commented, coming into the passage and closing the door firmly behind her. "Pray do not start making a fuss, he's asleep."

Sophy dropped her voice to an urgent whisper.

"But how is he? Please, I must see for myself.

"No, certainly not. It is not seemly."

Sophy's fingers itched to slap her.

"Not seemly! I've never heard such nonsense. Let me in. I don't think " she added, "that your brother would be very pleased if he found you had kept me away."

Charlotte wavered slightly.

"I suppose," she said, "we have you to thank for his being here at all."

Sophy was taken completely off-balance.

"What . . . How . . . ?" she stuttered, trying to grasp the full implication of this remark. "I had nothing to do with it," she stated, recovering herself with difficulty. "George Nugent is the hero of the day, so I believe."

With a look of barely concealed contempt, Charlotte said, "Come, Mrs Franklin, you need not pretend with me. Men!" she sniffed disapprovingly. "Forever playing their ridiculous games. They have no idea what the real business of life is about."

"You mean to say that you know all about it?"

"I doubt it, Mrs Franklin, but I am well aware of what is going on. To think that a member of my family should be a common felon. I do not know what the world is coming to. My only comfort is, at least our poor father did not live to see it."

"I did not guess at it until just the other day," Sophy confessed. "I thought

453

he was organising a rising of the common people."

Charlotte looked utterly horrified.

"The very idea!"

Taking her chance, Sophy pushed her aside, and grasped the doorhandle.

"Be that as it may," she said, "you might as well reconcile yourself to this match. And you might find that it is in your own interests at least to appear to approve."

The veiled threat had its effect on Charlotte, though she met Sophy's eye steadily.

"I considered you too tolerant to have a salutary effect on him," she replied, "but perhaps you are harder than you appear."

"I am when it suits me to be," Sophy declared, though secretly she was appalled at the streak of ruthlessness she had discovered in herself of late. There was no need to use the same tactics with Charlotte as she had with Lieutenant Forster. "Charlotte — may I use your name now? — we are already allies, in a way, may we not be friends as well?" she coaxed. "If he takes a fever, someone will have to sit up with him tonight. You will be better able to do that if you take a rest this afternoon, but please let me be with him now."

To her relief, Charlotte saw the sense in this, and at last Sophy was able to let herself into the shadowed chamber.

Philip had slept on undisturbed by the battle outside his door, which Sophy chose to take as a hopeful sign, in spite of his frightening pallor. She swept Charlotte's workbasket with its inevitable length of fringe unceremoniously onto the floor, and sat down on the chair by the bed to wait for him to wake up. With nothing to do now but think, she was assailed by a strong sense of anti-climax, and creeping with it came nagging doubts. She had deliberately laid a trail this morning, and by now half the village would be talking of their intended marriage, for she was quite sure that Susannah would be incapable of keeping such a piece of gossip to herself. And she had certainly said enough at Tracey Manor to set tongues wagging there. But had she been rather high-handed, she wondered, for although she had always assumed there was a tacit agreement between them, Philip had never properly proposed to her. He might not take kindly to having his hand forced.

Through the long afternoon, her tired brain worried at the problem, but could produce no sensible answers. She grew stiff from sitting, and at last, to keep herself awake, wandered round the chamber, fingering Philip's possessions. It was a sparsely furnished room, arranged with the precision of a man used to living in a small space, the austerity relieved by a few souvenirs from his travels. There was a watercolour of Port of Spain harbour, a sketch in ink of a ship — H.M. Frigate *Termagant* Sophy discovered from the inscription — a brass-bound sea chest, rather the worse for wear, some animals carved out of a heavy tropical wood, and, incongruously exotic, a pair of Turkish slippers embroidered with gold thread and turned up at the toes. Sophy picked one up, and traced the intricate design with a forefinger.

"Sophy?"

She looked up, feeling rather foolish at

having been discovered engaged in such a pointless occupation. Philip was wide awake, he might well have been watching her prying into his territory for several minutes.

"How long have you been here?" he asked.

"Since just before noon."

She was wearing that detached, defensive air that had so baffled him during the early part of their relationship. Not that he was altogether surprised, after the way he had tried to deceive her.

"And how did you get past Cerberus?" he asked, infusing a conspiratorial tone into his voice.

"Cer . . . ? Oh, Charlotte. I suggested that it might be better for her if she relaxed her guard. She seems to think I'm not virtuous enough to undertake the task of reforming you."

"I need to be reformed, do I?"

A smile lit her face, bringing back the glow to her eyes, reaching out to him with its warmth.

"Hardly at all. I have an unfortunate weakness for reprobates."

"Then what are you standing over

there for?" Philip asked, holding out a hand towards her. "Come here and let me thank you properly for your part in the drama."

Sophy flew to his side, and kissed him until all her groundless fears dissolved into oblivion.

"That's better," Philip said at length. "You were so distant, I thought I was not going to be forgiven."

"Forgiven? What for? There's nothing to forgive. You're alive, and free, that's all that matters. But — " Sophy hesitated, then went on, "next time you might not be so lucky. I told Bandy Coates that the Shadow was finished." She ended in a rush, hovering between apology and defiance, and to her relief, Philip did not appear to be put out by her interference. Quite the contrary.

"Credit me with some sense," he pleaded, smiling. "That was the last run, the opposition was getting far too close for comfort. And in any case, I've achieved what I set out to do, which was to get Creek End out of the clutches of the moneylenders. With the proceeds of this run, I'll be able to pay off the last of

458

the outstanding mortgages and properly call the place my own."

"But Forster seized last night's cargo," Sophy objected.

"Oh no he didn't, he just got a few things we were taking ashore for local delivery. The bulk of it is still on board the cutter, in Pennyhole Fleet. That's why we didn't stay to defend it, the small amount of goods weren't worth getting caught for. It's a pity, though, for I had some presents for you and Lucy, but I'll get a message through to Bandy and he'll sort out something from the cutter."

"Not more lace, I hope."

"So you did find it, then? You certainly deluded me. Even when you wore it at the ball I didn't know whether it was mine or if you really had found the stuff you'd mislaid."

"It was extremely foolhardy, giving me that. Supposing I had surrendered it to Sir Harry? George wasn't the only person who thought your brother was the Shadow," Sophy pointed out severely. "In fact that whole episode was an unnecessary and dangerous joke."

Philip grinned, unrepentant.

"Poor Sir Harry! he nearly burst a blood-vessel over that, didn't he? I wish I could have seen his face when he first read that note. But it wasn't just a joke, sweetheart, more in the nature of a diversion. I wanted to keep Forster busy while we shifted our base from Dead Man's Creek to Pennyhole. Someone had been spotted prying around there, and I thought it was time to make a move."

"George again," Sophy explained. "He's been on your track all summer."

"Yes, I seem to remember his saying something about it last night. Do you know, I think I could grow to quite like that boy. He showed a good deal of courage and initiative. How is he today?"

"Not much the worse for wear, and enjoying the admiration of his adoring family. He thinks it was he who shot you, and he's feeling somewhat guilty about that, I believe."

"That will teach him not to go playing around with dangerous weapons," Philip said. "But what are we discussing him for? I can think of far better ways to spend the time." And to prove it, he pulled her down to kiss her again. "So many times I wanted you here," he said at last, "and now that you are, I'm too weak to take advantage of it. So you still want to marry me?"

"I don't remember," Sophy said, "ever having been asked."

"I'm asking you now. Sophy, my only love, I owe you my freedom and probably my life, but neither will mean anything unless you share them with me. Say that you will!"

Sophy gazed silently at his anxious grey eyes, his haggard face, pale against the pillows, and was choked by a wave of love for him.

"No more free-trading?" she asked, with a half-smile. "Or diversions? Or revolutions? Won't you miss it all?"

"I can live quite happily without a revolution," Philip assured her. "If ever I feel in need of a dangerous occupation, I'll teach you to sail. What do you say to that?"

Sophy curled up beside him and laid her head on his shoulder.

"I say yes," she replied.

Other titles in the
Ulverscroft Large Print Series:

TO FIGHT THE WILD
Rod Ansell and Rachel Percy

Lost in uncharted Australian bush, Rod Ansell survived by hunting and trapping wild animals, improvising shelter and using all the bushman's skills he knew.

COROMANDEL
Pat Barr

India in the 1830s is a hot, uncomfortable place, where the East India Company still rules. Amelia and her new husband find themselves caught up in the animosities which seethe between the old order and the new.

THE SMALL PARTY
Lillian Beckwith

A frightening journey to safety begins for Ruth and her small party as their island is caught up in the dangers of armed insurrection.

THE WILDERNESS WALK
Sheila Bishop

Stifling unpleasant memories of a misbegotten romance in Cleave with Lord Francis Aubrey, Lavinia goes on holiday there with her sister. The two women are thrust into a romantic intrigue involving none other than Lord Francis.

THE RELUCTANT GUEST
Rosalind Brett

Ann Calvert went to spend a month on a South African farm with Theo Borland and his sister. They both proved to be different from her first idea of them, and there was Storr Peterson — the most disturbing man she had ever met.

ONE ENCHANTED SUMMER
Anne Tedlock Brooks

A tale of mystery and romance and a girl who found both during one enchanted summer.

CLOUD OVER MALVERTON
Nancy Buckingham

Dulcie soon realises that something is seriously wrong at Malverton, and when violence strikes she is horrified to find herself under suspicion of murder.

AFTER THOUGHTS
Max Bygraves

The Cockney entertainer tells stories of his East End childhood, of his RAF days, and his post-war showbusiness successes and friendships with fellow comedians.

MOONLIGHT
AND MARCH ROSES
D. Y. Cameron

Lynn's search to trace a missing girl takes her to Spain, where she meets Clive Hendon. While untangling the situation, she untangles her emotions and decides on her own future.

NURSE ALICE IN LOVE
Theresa Charles

Accepting the post of nurse to little Fernie Sherrod, Alice Everton could not guess at the romance, suspense and danger which lay ahead at the Sherrod's isolated estate.

POIROT INVESTIGATES
Agatha Christie

Two things bind these eleven stories together — the brilliance and uncanny skill of the diminutive Belgian detective, and the stupidity of his Watson-like partner, Captain Hastings.

LET LOOSE THE TIGERS
Josephine Cox

Queenie promised to find the long-lost son of the frail, elderly murderess, Hannah Jason. But her enquiries threatened to unlock the cage where crucial secrets had long been held captive.

THE TWILIGHT MAN
Frank Gruber

Jim Rand lives alone in the California desert awaiting death. Into his hermit existence comes a teenage girl who blows both his past and his brief future wide open.

DOG IN THE DARK
Gerald Hammond

Jim Cunningham breeds and trains gun dogs, and his antagonism towards the devotees of show spaniels earns him many enemies. So when one of them is found murdered, the police are on his doorstep within hours.

THE RED KNIGHT
Geoffrey Moxon

When he finds himself a pawn on the chessboard of international espionage with his family in constant danger, Guy Trent becomes embroiled in moves and countermoves which may mean life or death for Western scientists.

TIGER TIGER
Frank Ryan

A young man involved in drugs is found murdered. This is the first event which will draw Detective Inspector Sandy Woodings into a whirlpool of murder and deceit.

CAROLINE MINUSCULE
Andrew Taylor

Caroline Minuscule, a medieval script, is the first clue to the whereabouts of a cache of diamonds. The search becomes a deadly kind of fairy story in which several murders have an other-worldly quality.

LONG CHAIN OF DEATH
Sarah Wolf

During the Second World War four American teenagers from the same town join the Army together. Forty-two years later, the son of one of the soldiers realises that someone is systematically wiping out the families of the four men.

THE LISTERDALE MYSTERY
Agatha Christie

Twelve short stories ranging from the light-hearted to the macabre, diverse mysteries ingeniously and plausibly contrived and convincingly unravelled.

TO BE LOVED
Lynne Collins

Andrew married the woman he had always loved despite the knowledge that Sarah married him for reasons of her own. So much heartache could have been avoided if only he had known how vital it was to be loved.

ACCUSED NURSE
Jane Converse

Paula found herself accused of a crime which could cost her her job, her nurse's reputation, and even the man she loved, unless the truth came to light.

A GREAT DELIVERANCE
Elizabeth George

Into the web of old houses and secrets of Keldale Valley comes Scotland Yard Inspector Thomas Lynley and his assistant to solve a particularly savage murder.

'E' IS FOR EVIDENCE
Sue Grafton

Kinsey Millhone was bogged down on a warehouse fire claim. It came as something of a shock when she was accused of being on the take. She'd been set up. Now she had a new client — herself.

A FAMILY OUTING IN AFRICA
Charles Hampton and Janie Hampton

A tale of a young family's journey through Central Africa by bus, train, river boat, lorry, wooden bicycle and foot.

THE PLEASURES OF AGE
Robert Morley

The author, British stage and screen star, now eighty, is enjoying the pleasures of age. He has drawn on his experiences to write this witty, entertaining and informative book.

THE VINEGAR SEED
Maureen Peters

The first book in a trilogy which follows the exploits of two sisters who leave Ireland in 1861 to seek their fortune in England.

A VERY PAROCHIAL MURDER
John Wainwright

A mugging in the genteel seaside town turned to murder when the victim died. Then the body of a young tearaway is washed ashore and Detective Inspector Lyle is determined that a second killing will not go unpunished.

DEATH ON A HOT SUMMER NIGHT
Anne Infante

Micky Douglas is either accident-prone or someone is trying to kill him. He finds himself caught in a desperate race to save his ex-wife and others from a ruthless gang.

HOLD DOWN A SHADOW
Geoffrey Jenkins

Maluti Rider, with the help of four of the world's most wanted men, is determined to destroy the Katse Dam and release a killer flood.

THAT NICE MISS SMITH
Nigel Morland

A reconstruction and reassessment of the trial in 1857 of Madeleine Smith, who was acquitted by a verdict of Not Proven of poisoning her lover, Emile L'Angelier.

SEASONS OF MY LIFE
Hannah Hauxwell
and Barry Cockcroft

The story of Hannah Hauxwell's struggle to survive on a desolate farm in the Yorkshire Dales with little money, no electricity and no running water.

TAKING OVER
Shirley Lowe and Angela Ince

A witty insight into what happens when women take over in the boardroom and their husbands take over chores, children and chickenpox.

AFTER MIDNIGHT STORIES,
The Fourth Book Of

A collection of sixteen of the best of today's ghost stories, all different in style and approach but all combining to give the reader that special midnight shiver.

DEATH TRAIN
Robert Byrne

The tale of a freight train out of control and leaking a paralytic nerve gas that turns America's West into a scene of chemical catastrophe in which whole towns are rendered helpless.

THE ADVENTURE OF THE CHRISTMAS PUDDING
Agatha Christie

In the introduction to this short story collection the author wrote "This book of Christmas fare may be described as 'The Chef's Selection'. I am the Chef!"

RETURN TO BALANDRA
Grace Driver

Returning to her Caribbean island home, Suzanne looks forward to being with her parents again, but most of all she longs to see Wim van Branden, a coffee planter she has known all her life.

SKINWALKERS
Tony Hillerman

The peace of the land between the sacred mountains is shattered by three murders. Is a 'skinwalker', one who has rejected the harmony of the Navajo way, the murderer?

A PARTICULAR PLACE
Mary Hocking

How is Michael Hoath, newly arrived vicar of St. Hilary's, to meet the demands of his flock and his strained marriage? Further complications follow when he falls hopelessly in love with a married parishioner.

A MATTER OF MISCHIEF
Evelyn Hood

A saga of the weaving folk in 18th century Scotland. Physician Gavin Knox was desperately seeking a cure for the pox that ravaged the slums of Glasgow and Paisley, but his adored wife, Margaret, stood in the way.